the SHAPESHIFTER
Stirring the Storm

Other books in the Shapeshifter series

the SHAPESHIFTER

Stirring *the* Storm

Ali Sparkes

OXFORD
UNIVERSITY PRESS

OXFORD

UNIVERSITY PRESS

Great Clarendon Street, Oxford OX2 6DP

Oxford University Press is a department of the University of Oxford.
It furthers the University's objective of excellence in research,
scholarship, and education by publishing worldwide in

Oxford   New York

Auckland   Cape Town   Dar es Salaam   Hong Kong   Karachi
Kuala Lumpur   Madrid   Melbourne   Mexico City   Nairobi
New Delhi   Shanghai   Taipei   Toronto

With offices in

Argentina   Austria   Brazil   Chile   Czech Republic   France   Greece
Guatemala   Hungary   Italy   Japan   Poland   Portugal   Singapore
South Korea   Switzerland   Thailand   Turkey   Ukraine   Vietnam

Oxford is a registered trade mark of Oxford University Press
in the UK and in certain other countries

British Library Cataloguing in Publication Data

Data available

ISBN: 978-0-19-275469-1

3 5 7 9 10 8 6 4

Printed in Great Britain by Cox & Wyman Ltd, Reading, Berkshire

Paper used in the production of this book is a natural, recyclable
product made from wood grown in sustainable forests. The
manufacturing process conforms to the environmental
regulations of the country of origin.

For my boys

With immeasurable thanks to Liz Cross, for the cleverest of editorial touches, for endless enthusiasm—and for asking for five.

1

The snow glowed in the half-moon light, a glittering white quilt across the valley. It covered hedges, softened walls, delicately mantled the trees, and drifted across the frozen lake in tapering fingers.

Only one set of tracks could be seen marking the whiteness; tracing a path around the handsome stately house, skirting the frozen water, and then heading straight for the frosted woodland.

A fox, sending a flurry of fear through the winter wildlife, was trotting swiftly west.

Dax Jones reached the first few slender young oaks at the edge of the copse and lifted his snout. It was a *fantastic* night to be a fox. As soon as he'd smelt the snow coming, early that afternoon, the hair on the backs of his arms had stood up and he'd said to Gideon, 'It'll be here by four o'clock! You wait! And by midnight it will be thick all over the fells. We have to go out in it! We can be the first ones to walk in it!'

But when it came to rousing Gideon, the boy had hidden his messy blond head under the duvet and groaned. 'Can't . . . too tired . . . you go, Dax. Tell me what it's like when you get back.'

Dax had shoved him and muttered, 'You know your problem, Gid—you've got no sense of adventure!'

Gideon had snorted, 'Yeah right!' and Dax had grinned, shaken his head, and leaped nimbly onto the windowsill, pulling up the sash and surveying the wondrous scene below.

Now he was part of it. He could have been crunching heavy boot-shaped indents into the cold sugary crust over the grass—but the light touch of his paws on the snow was delightful to him. One of the best things about being a shapeshifter was that he could experience the world three different ways—as a boy, as a fox, and, if he felt like it, as a falcon. Tonight though, in this strange white world, nothing could beat being a fox. Dax streaked across the temporary tundra and deep into the woods, where the snow was lighter, blown in sideways by the wind and powdering down softly between the branches to pick out twig and leaf and berry in silvery-blue highlights. The wildlife tensed, but he was not out to hunt tonight. There was no need. And the smaller creatures could smell this too. Voles and mice moved judiciously away into the undergrowth, but soon relaxed. Dax walked on, passing the badger sett and nodding at the snout of the chief badger boar, just emerging to check out the snow for himself. The badger regarded him for a moment, gave a small grunt of recognition and ambled on out into the moonlight, his striped head turning left and right, sniffing the chilled air.

Dax wished, for the hundredth time, that he was able to actually have a conversation with other animals. He *could* communicate with them, but it was mostly about body posture and scent and the occasional telepathic flash. He had worked out a few months ago that the badgers were quite relaxed around him. He had even gone down into their sett once and found them all staring at him in surprise, but without hostility. Rather like polite relatives who had been visited without warning by a distant cousin. They knew the fox was no threat to them; although Dax walked through his little wood as king—there was no predator higher than he—he'd never be idiot enough to take on a badger.

He was drawn back to the edges of the woodland by the promise of deeper, more luxurious snow to bound through. Leaping from a fallen log, he found himself engulfed up to his furry chin. He couldn't help laughing out loud—a light volley of happy barks. He rolled over onto his back, collecting white flakes on his thick winter coat. Then he was suddenly on his feet again, stock still. Scenting. Listening. Watching. Something was coming.

At the perimeter wall, a quarter of a mile away, a shaft of golden light opened up. The electric gate was moving. A black vehicle was coming in. Dax swiftly turned and jumped back on to the log, where he shifted instantly to a peregrine falcon; sharp round eyes glittering black in pools of yellow. In a blink his vision had improved tenfold. With no difficulty at all he made out a soldier at the booth leaning out towards the car, rifle held across his chest, nodding and in conversation with the driver. The driver's hand, gloveless and large, patted the sentry on the shoulder before withdrawing, and the black four-by-four moved on, following the wide gravel driveway up to the lodge, as the electric gate slid shut behind it.

Who was out this late? wondered Dax. It must be getting on for 1 a.m. Even the scientists were normally tucked up in bed by now. He shivered and felt a tickly sensation at the back of his neck. He'd felt that a few times recently and wondered if it was some kind of warning. But nothing in his life at the moment suggested any trouble coming. There'd been plenty of it over the last couple of years, but for nearly eight months he and all the other Children of Limitless Ability here at Fenton Lodge had simply got on with schoolwork and play and arguing and mucking around without interruption—unless you counted a rather heavy cold they'd all managed to get in the last couple of weeks. No—it had all been pretty normal. Well, as normal as it *got* when you were a Cola.

Dax thought about flying after the car to find out who it was, but it was too cold. Peregrines are not night fliers even in the summer, when a few leftover warm thermals from the day might still be creating a bit of uplift. Here in the deeply chilled Cumbrian hills of January, he could manage a swift wing up and down from his bedroom window, but more than that would be folly. He decided to leave the late night driver to his own business, and have a bit more snow play. The glazed lake was calling to him. They'd all been forbidden to go on it by Mrs Sartre, the college principal, even though for days the smooth sheet of ice had looked about a foot thick, and startled geese kept sleighing across it in confusion whenever they tried to land. As a fox, Dax didn't weigh a third as much as he did in boy form, so he was more than happy to take the risk. Grinning to himself, he made his way ungracefully through the snow, lurching this way and that in the drifts. He wished Gideon was out with him to see this, but at least he wouldn't have to feel guilty about not letting his mate follow him out on to the ice.

The glistening sheet sent prickles of shock into the pads of his paws, even though they'd already been numbed by the cold of the snow.

Dax gasped and then he chuckled; a raspy, growly sort of noise, and put all four paws onto the ice, claws digging in to stop himself sliding. There was no crack—no noise at all. And later he was to wonder why he didn't hear the man coming, given that his fox ears were so incredibly sensitive. All he knew was that five seconds later a white shape descended upon him and seized him so fast and so silently that he had no time to even glance around. He heard his sharp teeth clack together as a hand efficiently snapped his shocked muzzle shut; felt himself lifted expertly and pinned to the chest of his assailant, and before he'd even had the chance to growl he was borne with great speed back towards the wood he had just left.

Panic would have had him screaming and snarling if he had not been able to call now—a little late—upon his senses. He knew who this was, and the knowledge stunned him into silence. Deep inside the wood he was at last deposited on the floor.

'Don't move. Don't speak,' instructed the man, quietly, and Dax realized he was panting hyper-fast, the hair rising and tickling again on his neck, his heart rattling in his chest like a runaway train.

He couldn't believe his eyes when the man pulled his hunting knife from inside the thick white hooded jacket he wore, tested it for keenness, knelt down and took hold of the back of his neck.

'Don't shift. You'll handle it better like this,' said Owen Hind, angling the knife. 'Get ready. Don't cry out. This is going to hurt.'

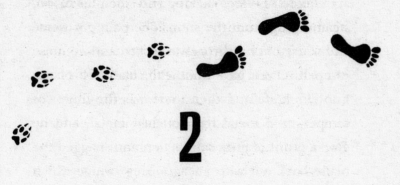

2

When the blade pierced his skin he was so shocked he simply froze. A sudden plume of breath escaped his nostrils and his eyes widened but his head was being firmly held in the crook of his attacker's arm. The blade did not slice or stab. It seemed to corkscrew in—and then—it *foraged*. Dax felt faint. He made no sound. He told himself there *must* be a reason. Owen Hind was right—it did hurt. Hot splinters of pain tore raggedly through his skin as the blade pressed and twisted and a warm river rose up and seeped down through his fur. Dax saw it spatter scarlet stars across the snowy woodland floor.

'God alive,' he heard Owen mutter. 'How much deeper?'

9

Dax felt his legs shaking and smelt his blood, steaming up from the snow. The pain got worse and worse but his throat was locked and no noise escaped. Owen gave another brutal twist of the hunter's knife and then there was the tiniest of scrapes, as if metal had touched metal, and he gave a grunt of grim satisfaction and snagged the blade back out with an agonizing twinge which made Dax shudder. Owen released his hold and the fox fell sideways onto the ground and looked up at him in astonishment. The man was staring intently into his palm. 'OK, Dax. You can shift now,' he said, not taking his eyes from his hand.

Dax found himself back as a boy, shivering violently, hugging his knees. His neck stung painfully and blood dripped down his back. Owen handed him a tissue. 'Mop up as best you can,' he said. 'Sorry, Dax. It couldn't be helped. Here—' He dug into one of his pockets with his free hand and retrieved a sticking plaster. Now he stopped peering at whatever he'd found, curling it into his fist, and looked at Dax properly for the first time in several bloody minutes. His face immediately softened and the coldness left his blue eyes.

He smiled ruefully at his victim. 'It's not good news, Dax. It's really not.' He sighed heavily.

Dax, trying to collect his blood in the rather inadequate tissue, found his tongue. 'No—I should say it's not!' he squawked. 'When you go out to play in the snow and your teacher comes along and without so much as a please or thank you goes and stabs you in the neck! What did you want to do that for?'

Owen reached out, turned him round, and put the sticking plaster across the small, ragged wound high on his neck. Then he turned Dax back round again and opened his palm in front of his face. 'I did it for this. Didn't think the damn thing would be so far in, I have to admit.'

Owen clicked a small torch onto the thing he was holding. In his blood-streaked palm lay a tiny square of metal, no bigger than a lentil. By torch-light, tiny blue squiggles and bumps could *just* about be seen on it. 'What is it?' gasped Dax. 'Was that in my neck?'

'In the base of your skull, to be exact—where I thought it would be. Thank God for that. I wouldn't have fancied working through all the other likely sites. It would've been like a crash course in butchery.' He glanced up and patted Dax's arm. 'Brave lad. Very quiet. Well done.'

'Would you *please* tell me what is going on?' demanded Dax, and his voice was querulous and sounded as if he might cry, so he shut his mouth and gulped and looked hard at Owen, who was now sliding the tiny square into a small plastic tub from one of his many pockets. In the moonlight shafting through the trees and the soft glow of the small torch, Owen, his shaggy hair tucked away inside the fur-lined white hood, looked grave.

'It's not good news,' Owen said, again. Dax stood up, frustrated and angry. Then he swayed, dizzy and a little sick and Owen stood too, and held him by the shoulders until he gathered himself together and looked up again. 'OK, this is what I know . . . or think I know,' said Owen. 'That chip was inserted under the skin at the base of your skull. It's a kind of tracking device. They must have worked really hard to find a frequency you wouldn't detect in any of your forms . . . It was done without your knowledge—obviously— and, just so's you know, without *mine*.'

Dax found his teeth were chattering, the cold creeping into his system now that he was standing out in a winter woodland in just pyjamas and slippers, rather than a thick pelt of fox fur. Or perhaps it was shock. Owen shook his shoulders slightly and leaned in towards him, locking eyes and saying: 'Dax—do you trust me? Do you believe me when I say I *didn't know?*'

Dax heard himself give a soft, ironic laugh as he looked down at the pattern of his blood on the snow. The amused voice that came from his own mouth surprised him. 'Well, let me see now . . . since I've known you you've kidnapped me, drugged me, hit me in the face with a gun, tracked me with armed soldiers and . . . oh yeah . . . shot my best mate's sister.'

He looked up at Owen, who was closing his eyes and rubbing his nose, and then sighed as he added: 'I trust you more than anyone else on this planet.'

Owen laughed softly. 'Good. Good for you, Dax. Now look—you *must not* talk about this. Not to anyone. Not to Gideon. Not to Mia or Lisa. Not even to Mrs Sartre or the other teachers or staff. Promise me.'

'Why? Don't you think they'll want to know? Somebody's stuck something in my skull!'

Owen's head tilted sideways a little as he looked at Dax sadly. 'They already know, Dax,' he said. 'They did it.'

He felt as if he'd been punched in the stomach. The air was sucked out of him and he leaned back against the trunk of a tree, gasping. Owen stood and watched him and then closed his eyes again. 'I don't know what to say to you, Dax. It's bloody awful. I did *not* sanction it. I said no. That it was a violation. I said no . . . '

'You *knew*? You knew they were planning it?'

'Talking about it—not planning it. As far as I knew. Taking advice about it. I said it would be a violation of all your human rights and very possibly dangerous, given that we know so little about how your minds work and how they could react. Bad enough on ordinary kids—but on telekinetics and psychics and telepaths and glamourists . . . and a shapeshifter . . . who knows? I said NO, Dax. And I thought that was the end of it. Clearly I was wrong. I got an inkling tonight, at a meeting with Chambers back at Whitehall, that I had been overruled, and I came back at once, to find out the truth.'

'Wait—wait a minute!' Dax held up his hands

to stop the flow of Owen's awful revelations. 'You're not talking about just me, are you?'

Owen shook his head.

'You mean all of us—Gideon and Lisa and Mia and—and all of us—have had bits of metal put in our heads?'

He nodded. He looked deeply ashamed and reached out to a low branch, leaning his forehead onto it. 'Try to understand, Dax. It's not meant to hurt you—they see it as a way of protecting you. So you can be tracked if you were ever to get . . . well, kidnapped or something. If you went missing.'

'Like cats or dogs?' spat Dax. He felt disgusted, appalled, *furious*. 'You've chipped us like *pets*!'

'I know how you must feel . . . I—'

'You have no right! How dare you?'

'Oh, Dax.' Owen stooped down to collect his knife from the snow, and began cleaning the blood from it carefully with a cloth. Even his trousers and boots were white—perfect snowscape camouflage. Nothing of his assault on Dax showed on him. 'We do have the right. That's what all those forms were about, which the Cola parents all signed. Not the right to damage you, of course, but the right to protect you any way we think best.'

Dax wanted to shout; wanted to hit someone. Owen, most certainly, would do. He'd never land a blow, of course, but he really felt like trying. Instead he stalked away, heading back to the lodge, meaning to shift and fly, regardless of the cold, as soon as he was clear of the trees. Owen silently caught up with him, though, and held him still. 'Dax, you *must* listen to me. You *must*. Do NOT say anything to anyone about this. You could be causing the most terrible trouble if you do. Please—promise me. I have to have your word.'

Dax glowered at him. 'And what will you *do* about it? Are you going to let those chips stay in all their heads? What happens when one of them finds out? What if one of Lisa's spirit mates spills the beans, eh? What if Jacob or Alex read your mind?'

Owen let go of his arms and stood back, looking at him levelly. 'You said you trust me. More than anyone else on this planet. Prove it. Say nothing. I will talk to you again when I've found out more. Your word?'

Dax couldn't protest any more. He was

suddenly exhausted and, more than that, Owen's scent told him clearly how bad the man felt—and how furious *he* was, too. He nodded. 'My word.' He turned to go, but Owen stopped him once more.

'Wait. You need to take this.' He fiddled with something from his pocket and then held out a strip of tape. Stuck to the middle of it was the metal chip. Dax was confused. A memento?

'Look—' Owen took Dax's left wrist and quickly undid the thin leather-weave bracelet on it, which held a curious black and green stone. Turning it over, he taped the chip firmly to the underside of the stone. 'It will stay put—that's very strong tape. You have to keep it on you. If it's not going where you're going, the scientists will find out pretty quickly and there'll be trouble. For now, please, keep it on you. I don't think having it on your wrist instead of by your cranium will make a difference to the tracking.'

Dax strapped the bracelet back on. Then he turned and ran, and was soon flapping bumpily through the sparser branches, desperate to get back to his room and away from the terrible revelations of the last half hour.

Back on his bed, he stared at the bundle of duvet under which his best friend slept, blissfully unaware that he was a pet, chipped and monitored wherever he went.

How could he not tell Gideon?

How could he break his word to Owen?

He had never felt more angry.

3

'Oh dear—a little pustulate are we, Jones? Or perhaps it's mange?'

Spook Williams sniggered behind him as he moved to his place at the breakfast table in Fenton Lodge's large airy dining room. Dax glowered into his cereal. Early that morning he had woken to find himself curled up far down in the bed, deep under the quilt, with a nagging feeling that all was not well.

Not *well*! His hand had flown to the back of his neck and found the plaster and some sticky traces—evidence of last night's horrors. He had sped down to the boy's bathroom to get into the shower and wash away the blood before anyone noticed. In one of the cupboards below the wash-basins he had found a shaving mirror, and, with a towel wrapped around his waist, had angled it carefully, checking the wound through the steam that clung to the glass. It was surprisingly small. It had felt like a ragged crater last night, but it was no bigger than a five pence piece. He had run up to the medical room, thankful to find it empty, and grabbed a handful of fresh plasters. Back in his room, while Gideon still slept on obliviously, Dax tenderly poked at the wound which stung only slightly and positioned a small round plaster over it by touch. He examined his bed and had found just a few spots of blood on the under side of the quilt.

An hour later at breakfast, he was working hard on unclenching his stomach enough to get some cornflakes into it, when Spook's mocking reminder knotted it up again. Spook sat down opposite Dax and Gideon groaned. 'Oi—I want to enjoy my breakfast, not gag on it. Push off, Williams.'

'I expect he's caught something from you,' sneered Spook, lifting a triangle of buttered toast to his mouth. 'Impetigo probably. That's what you get in those dirty little London slums you come from, isn't it? Septic sores. You can't help it, I suppose. Oh look—it's spreading at a frightening rate. Nurse! Nurse!'

Gideon shoved his chair back suddenly, staring at his hands, and Dax touched his shoulder quickly to get an idea of what his friend was grimacing at. Spook was an illusionist and was currently making Gideon see—Dax concentrated hard to get a shadow of it—yes, big sticky scabs all over Gideon's hands, from his wrists to his knuckles, bloody in places, oozing pale yellow pus in others. It was disgusting. He shuddered, relieved that he was resistant to Spook's glamour and could only ever faintly see it if he was in physical contact with someone else who was getting the full effect.

There was a thunk, and a blue milk jug struck Spook hard on the temple, hurling a small white tidal wave across the boy's dark red hair. He cursed and snatched up a napkin to sponge away the dripping mess as it spattered down over his shiny black shirt. Gideon relaxed. Spook had to concentrate to keep an illusion going and his victim's hands would now be normal again. Gideon was looking around the table for something else to seize with his mind and chuck at Spook.

'If I thought, for one moment,' said a cool voice at the door, 'that one of my students was even *thinking* of throwing a glamour or flexing a mind-push outside Development, I think I would *have to* ban all adventure playground and tree house activity for at least a week.' Mrs Dann stood at the end of the table and glared from Gideon to Spook. Tall and dark haired with piercing brown eyes, she was a great teacher but took absolutely no prisoners when it came to runaway Cola power.

Gideon and Spook immediately began mopping up the residue of milk which had hit the table and righting the jug and murmuring 'No—no glamour. No teleing.' It was a rare and brief moment of co-operation, but they knew better than to test Mrs Dann. She smiled tightly, and moved over to the breakfast buffet table for her croissants and coffee.

There was a beat of silence and Darren Tyler, Spook's friend and fellow illusionist, sat down next to him. 'What's with the dairy action?' he asked mildly. Darren was OK, easy going, but pitifully in awe of Spook's superior powers.

'Oh, Gideon here was just lining up a bruising for himself for later,' muttered Spook. 'And his little dog, too!'

Dax snorted. 'Yeah, right. When was the last time *you* got your fists dirty?'

Spook scowled at him. He *loathed* Dax, chiefly because Dax was the only human he knew who could not be affected by his glamour.

'What *is* that?' asked Gideon, tipping his chair back and prodding at the plaster.

Dax winced. 'It's just a spot,' he mumbled, glad that Spook was now talking to Darren and not paying them any attention.

'Whoa! Big one! You must be on *the verge*,' said Gideon, his voice dropping to a dramatic whisper. At nearly fourteen, he was an expert on puberty and got the occasional cluster of pink spots himself, which he would dab at with witch hazel gel, loudly cursing the blight on his fantastically good looks.

Dax sighed and nodded. He didn't point out that his skin had never seen a single spot yet. He took after his late mother and remembered his father saying she had perfect skin, like golden porcelain. He had inherited her dark eyes and thick, glossy dark hair too. He hoped nobody else would start going on about the plaster. He really didn't want to attract attention to the wound. As it happened, he didn't need to worry.

Mia arrived in the room, with Lisa and Jennifer. The sudden draught of warmth and wellbeing alerted them all. Mia, tall and slender, with long brown hair and startling violet-blue eyes, did not need to say hello. An incredibly talented healer, she simply had to *be*. Everyone who first met her was swept away by the good feeling she gave them. You fell in love with Mia at first sight—you couldn't help it. Over time, it diminished a little as you got used to the Mia Effect. She was very glad of it. Poor Mia found the whole thing highly embarrassing. Now she walked past his chair, noticed the plaster on the back of his neck, and simply ran her soft warm palm across it as she passed. She didn't even make any comment, just went on by and along to the buffet table. A tingle of heat spiralled down into Dax's skin and he gasped and then quickly peeled the plaster away. Underneath, his skin was whole and mended and clear again.

'Blimey!' observed Gideon. 'I should get her

to do that for *my* spots. She never has, you know. She only does it for you! It's unfair treatment.'

'Shaddup,' muttered Dax, badly wanting to change the subject. 'Let's go and check the post room.' He couldn't face his breakfast anyway, and Spook's scabby fingers illusion had put Gideon off his sausages. They got up to go, passing Lisa and Jennifer. Jennifer, who wore glasses and had her dark blonde hair in plaits today, looked abashed as Dax moved past her, and faded out just slightly, so Lisa's pretty face appeared to be looking through her ear.

'Told you,' sniggered Gideon, as they got out into the tall, oak-panelled corridor. 'She so fancies you, mate!'

'Get off!' Dax gave him a shove. 'She doesn't.'

'I'm telling you—she does! Every time she looks at you she disappears. She can't help it.'

'Well it must be true then!' snorted Dax. 'She's a glamourist, Gid. The disappearing kind. That's what they *do*.'

'Yeah, but *never* outside Development when Mrs Dann's around. Unless they get all fluttery love bugs inside them and can't help themselves.' Gideon began dancing along the floor making fluttery love bug movements with his hands and gasping in a high-pitched voice. 'Oh, Dax! You make me feel so—so—invisible!'

'Stop it!' said Dax, but he was laughing, in spite of his dark thoughts from last night. With the wound gone now, it was beginning to seem unreal, as if he'd dreamt it. 'Gid, leave it, you're about to—'

'Oh, Dax,' persisted Gideon, still doing the fluttery love bug mime, 'sometimes I think you can look right through me . . . Am I really that transparent? I—doof!' He stopped abruptly and his nose squished upwards apparently of its own accord. Dax cackled as Barry swam into view, looking pink and affronted. Although he was in a vanish, Dax had known he was there, turning the corner from the grand hallway. He could smell him clearly and hear him easily (Barry had adenoid problems and tended to whistle through his nose) and the waviness in the air around him gave it away too.

'You takin' the mick out of glamourists, Gid?' Barry demanded, folding his arms across his stout chest, like a bouncer outside a nightclub. 'And do I *want* your face in my armpit?' Gideon staggered backwards, rubbing his nose with distaste.

'You're not allowed to do that!' he squawked. 'It's not fair! You shouldn't be creeping up on people!'

'*You* shouldn't be takin' the mick out of Jenny,' Barry replied and stomped off to the dining room.

'Oops. Touched a nerve,' whispered Gideon and made exaggerated 'creeping away' movements. 'Follow me.'

Dax fell into step behind him, grinning, but then found himself staring at the back of Gideon's neck. The grin subsided and a surge of apprehension rose in him. And it wasn't just the whole awful business about the metal chips. Something else was coming. He felt it.

In the post room they checked their pigeon-holes. For Gideon it was nearly always worthwhile. His dad sent something two or three times a week, from letters and CDs of his favourite bands to heavy parcels of chocolate. Gideon could eat his bodyweight in chocolate every week, but it never showed on his wiry frame, although Dax often predicted he would billow out in all directions like a Sumo wrestler as soon as he turned twenty.

'Yay!' said Gideon, hauling another weighty paper bundle out of his pigeonhole. 'One for Luke too!' He seized an identical parcel from his twin brother's shelf. 'He'll never get through it. He'll need help. I'll go and give it to him.' Gideon hared away to find Luke. Dax was impressed at how, once again, Gid's dad had thought of Luke too. Both boys were his sons, but he had not even met Luke until the Colas had emerged; had not even known Gideon's twin brother existed. Luke had lived a fairly normal life with adoptive parents and had a non-blood mother who loved him, but Michael Reader loved his newly-found son too, from the moment he met him.

Dax stuck his hand into his own pigeonhole without even looking. It was a formality. He almost never got a letter or anything from anyone. Today, though, was different. A small envelope crackled under his fingers and he glanced down in surprise. It was pale blue and carried an Aberdeen postmark. Dax felt a weird mix of excitement and sour sadness. He knew who this was from. He took the letter out and crossed the imposing lodge hall, with its high ceilings, polished stone floor, and curving staircase, to the library. The book-lined

28

walls and plush red rugs gave the library a pleasant quietness. Nobody else was there. Dax went to the window seat and tore open the envelope.

Dear Dax, wrote his father.

I guess this is starting to sound a bit hollow after so many months, but this time I really am coming to see you. I have had some problems with Gina, and although I really did intend to see you at Christmas, it just wasn't possible to get away. I wish you could have come home, but I do understand why you chose not to. Gina can be hard at times, I know. Try not to blame her, though, Dax. She hasn't had it easy and a lot of that is my fault.

Alice really missed you. She's convinced you're an X Man! She's been very good, though, and told nobody. Well, I guess they wouldn't believe her anyway.

Dax, there's something else. I need to give something to you—something your mum wanted you to have—but I don't think it's a good idea to bring it with me to Fenton Lodge. Do you remember the little friend from the Yemen you had when you were at playschool? Remember his name? And how about the name you used for your little box, with the stars stuck on? Remember? Take the first three letters of your friend's name and then the next four letters of the name you gave your box—

then find that road in Keswick. You'll work it out from there.

I'll see you soon, and we can talk about the thing you'll have found, I hope, by then.

Better eat this letter or something.

Much love

Dad

Dax stared out of the window, screwing the letter up in his fist. His mind worked furiously. What on earth was this about? What *thing* did his dad want him to find? He remembered his little friend at playschool. He was called Firaz. So—the first three letters were F, I, and R. Then the little box with stars on it . . . he shut his eyes and took himself back to the age of three or four. His mum was still alive then. The little trinket box was round and tall, and its sides were grooved like bark. He used to call it his *tree trunk*. So—second word, first four letters. *TREE*. Fir Tree Road. In Keswick. Easy.

Dax sighed. He was in a Cumbrian valley surrounded by fells, and hemmed in by a three metre wall with electric wire and state-of-the-art security cameras, armed soldiers at every exit and entrance point and—hey—he had just remembered: he had a homing chip! He twisted his bracelet and looked under the stone, a glorious mineral of fine green and black lines and bubbles, frozen like a lump of magic, called malachite. A gift from Mia. Every Cola wore a stone of some kind like this, chosen for its qualities to help each of them. Still taped securely beneath his was the tiny metal chip. Dax shuddered. Yes, he of all of them, could most easily get out. He was allowed to shapeshift outside and go for moonlit runs or early morning flights. When they'd tried to stop him shifting outside the house, he had become dangerously ill. So they had to let him out to fly and run as falcon and fox—or risk losing him altogether.

It worked on trust. He had only once broken the boundary, last spring, and that was a matter of life and death. Afterwards he had promised Owen he would never do it again. He shook his head, wryly. He had honestly thought that the bond of trust between himself and his teacher and mentor had been enough for the government agency which ran Cola Club. Now he knew better. If he flew over the boundary they would know instantly. And if he took off his bracelet and its stuck-on chip and left it behind, they would grow suspicious in minutes.

So how was he to get to Fir Tree Road in Keswick, to find this mystery thing? He had absolutely no idea.

He was amazed at the letter. His father, whom he hadn't seen now for a year, never normally got involved with his life in any way. What could it be that his mother had left him? A letter? A video tape? He was so lost in his thoughts that he jumped violently when Clive put his head around the door and said, 'Dax! You'll be late for science! Cub od!'

Clive was wearing a zip-up woolly cardigan, a pair of burgundy trousers with a crease firmly ironed into them, and shiny brown shoes. After all this time at Cola Club, none of the more normal fashion sense had yet rubbed off on him. He shoved his spectacles up his nose and sniffed loudly as Dax got off the window seat and walked across to the door.

'Oh, when will this blasted bug ged *out* of by systeb!' he snuffled, through a flaky looking bundle of tissue. 'You all got rid of it in a beek, and I've had it for ten days! It's nod fair! I can hardly concendrate in class!'

Only Clive would be worried about concentrating in class. He was incredibly bright and a genius at science and engineering. He could make the most amazing things, like working paper models of clocks or candle powered turbine machines. He adored gadgets and hi-tech stuff and his cleverness had saved Dax's skin in the past. Clive was the only boy at Fenton Lodge that Dax had known before he became a Cola. Clive had gone to the same junior school as he had, back in the normal world, and witnessed Dax changing into a fox for only the second time. Later he had used his brilliance with gadgets to track Dax and his Cola friends down and join them when they had been on the run. He was not a Cola, but now he lived with them all the same. The government was happier to have him on the *inside*—and Clive's parents, both scientists, were happy to have him at one of the country's most elite schools.

'You need more tissue,' observed Dax, as they walked to the lab. Clive sighed and pulled another wodge out of his cardigan pocket.

They had all gone down with the cold very rapidly, in the space of about three days, a couple of weeks ago. The entire common room, one night, was filled with sniffling, moaning students and Janey, the college doctor, was regularly dishing out paracetamol and big beakers of water.

'It's what happens when you all live in close contact,' Janey had sighed, as she touched Gideon's forehead and peered down Dax's throat. 'It goes through everyone like a dose of salts. Take the afternoon off and get some sleep.'

Lessons had been weird, with at least a third of the students taking an afternoon nap at some point, but after a week they were mostly through it. Clive was the last to get it—probably because he had had his parents to stay in the luxury holiday cottage up on the fells and was away with them for most of the time. The Cola Project liked to invite families *in* from time to time, rather than have its students go *out* too often. Although most of the parents were aware of what kind of college it was, and had signed the Official Secrets Act about what went on there, the government was still nervous about letting its precious Colas out of its sight. Holidays at home were brief and under surveillance. Phone calls and internet were monitored.

All of this had never seriously bothered Dax

until now. He had understood it, even found it oddly comforting. After seven years of living with Gina, his stepmum, and Alice, his half-sister, it was nice that *someone* cared. Gina cared only for Alice and had never done much to disguise her resentment towards her stepson. Alice was all right, but annoying and obsessed with dolls and pink clothes. Gina hadn't taken to her stepson when she had first met Dax, aged four and shocked silent over the death of his mother. She now had no further use for even pretending. As soon as Dax had shifted in front of her last year, all lacklustre attempts at motherly behaviour were abandoned. She had disliked him before, now she loathed and feared him. It didn't make for a great atmosphere over dinner, which was why Dax had chosen to stay at Fenton Lodge over Christmas.

No doubt the surveillance at his old home continued, to be sure that Gina did not give anything away about the strange goings on at Fenton Lodge. But the government had worked out Gina pretty fast. She was getting money to stay silent, and Dax was certain that was enough.

'So, class—the chemical properties of . . . a potato!' announced Harry Tucker, the science and art teacher. White haired and bearded, he raised an eyebrow and added: 'Now, don't get too excited but I've got a potato for every one of you!'

The class was fun; he was a good teacher and understood them well. As they attached metal clips and wires to their potatoes and measured the natural electricity in them, Dax began to relax after the events of the previous night and the arrival of the startling letter from the father who never came to see him.

He was chuckling with Gideon as they carved gurning faces into their spuds with the spike of a pair of compasses when he happened to glance up at Mia. She was scratching, absently, at the back of her neck. Glancing around, he saw Jennifer do the same a second later. He felt sick.

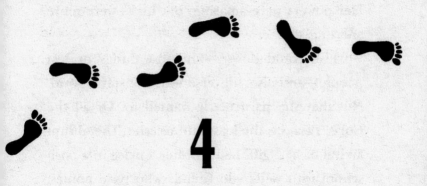

4

Owen wasn't available for Development that afternoon, so Dax went in with Gideon and Luke to have a session with Tyrone. There were several development groups. The glamourists, Spook, Darren, Barry, and Jennifer (Colas who could make you see stuff or stop you seeing *them*), were taken by Harry Tucker. Jacob and Alex Teller, brothers who were telepathic and also incredible mimics, were taken by Mrs Dann. Lisa and Mia worked together with Paulina Sartre, the college principal. She was also a seer and a dowser, like Lisa, able to view things in her mind that were happening elsewhere in the country—even the world. She could sometimes see things before they happened.

Her powers were amazing, but Lisa's were more amazing still.

Lisa could dowse—find lost things or lost people—and also converse with the spirit world. Not that she particularly wanted to. Of all the Colas, Lisa was the least enthusiastic. The abrupt arrival of her 'gift' had cost her a place in a posh school with well-to-do friends who rode ponies. Initially she had hated Cola Club and rebelled against it by refusing to co-operate with anyone, in this world or the next. Now, though, she had mostly accepted her gift, and just got on with it. She had admitted to a spirit guide—Sylv—and spent a good hour every day writing out little pink slips entitled Spirit Communication Notice. This was the best way of getting all the attention seeking dead people out of her head. Once she had passed on their messages to the teachers, who then passed them on to the Cola project scientists for further investigation, the spirits tended to ease up on her for a bit. Sylv also did what she could to hold them at bay.

Lisa held the passed-on in absolutely no awe or reverence at all. Only yesterday she had been overheard telling a deceased mediaeval peasant woman, who'd succumbed to plague, to 'get a life'. Which was a little harsh.

Dax enjoyed his session with Tyrone and Gideon and Luke. Tyrone, just twenty-one, tall and wiry with a friendly smile and spiky dark hair, had a mission to teach Gideon and Luke as much control as possible. Restraint was his favourite word. He was also telekinetic and in D2 the three of them had games to hold and lift and turn all kinds of objects, from shuttlecocks to filing cabinets. The only thing they never did was show off. Tyrone believed that the key to holding on to an almost normal life as a Cola would always be control and restraint.

'There's no reason at all why you should have to show the scientists the full strength of your powers,' he had once said to Dax and Gideon, during a walk on the fells. 'Every reason, in fact, not to. They don't have the right to own everything about you—remember that.'

Although he was one of the staff, Tyrone had no illusions about the scientists. The scientists wanted to study and measure and catalogue all Cola power; work out how much there was; where it ended; what they might do with it. Luke and

Gideon had already shown some scary ability. Gideon had fought with a molten metal monster and Luke had held back the sea. It made people nervous.

'But they *are* the devil you know,' Tyrone had said. 'Better to be here, in your own country, with your own government shadowing you, than getting chased all over the planet by everyone else who wants a piece of you. It's a trade-off.' Tyrone knew what he was talking about. His own powers had arrived suddenly, at thirteen, but he was not classed as a Cola. The Colas had emerged all at the same time when they were all eleven or twelve and had certain things in common—like the fact that not one of them had a mother still living. All Cola mums had died before their children reached the age of four. Tyrone still had a mother and told them his own powers had arrived after he'd come into contact with something strange. That's all he would say. Official Secrets Act. And restraint.

Today Gideon and Luke had a go at lifting Dax. It was rarely very successful, lifting a living creature, but they thought it would be funny to try. Gideon had done it once, in an emergency, and probably saved a life—but hadn't been very effective at it since.

'It's because you're wiggling about so much!' protested Gideon as Dax slumped sideways, after three seconds, six inches off the carpet in D2. His amused face was reflected back at him in the long glass wall to one end of the underground chamber, behind which sat at least two scientists, making notes.

'I'm *not* wiggling about!' laughed Dax. 'You just can't handle it, mate! Admit it!'

Luke and Gideon linked arms, identical expressions on their identical freckled faces, screwed up their pale green eyes, and concentrated hard as Dax sat up, cross-legged, and folded his arms. He rose up again, but began to giggle and then bumped back down onto his backside. 'Ow! My coccyx!' he complained.

'Better leave him be,' advised Tyrone, going to the water cooler and filling a plastic cup. 'I think it has to do with the electrical make-up. It's much more stable in things that aren't alive and sentient. You'd probably be able to lift somebody in a coma or drugged or something quite easily.'

'Let's drug Dax!' said Gideon, rubbing his hands with glee. 'He won't mind.'

'Yeah, no problem,' snorted Dax. 'Or why not just smack a chair over my head?'

Luke grinned and took off his spectacles—the main clue that reminded people which brother was which—and said nothing. He never did say anything. Luke was mute.

Tyrone sneezed. 'Ah, great! I'm getting the Cola Cold! I thought I'd got away with it! It didn't seem to have made it into the staffroom.' He rubbed his throat and nodded. 'Yup. Tonsils are up. Go on, you three—I've had enough for today. I need a doctor!'

'Oh yeah?' Gideon raised an eyebrow at him. He reckoned Tyrone fancied Janey, who was pretty with shiny dark hair and silvery eyes.

'For some *medicine*!' stressed Tyrone, but he did look a little pink as he headed out of the room.

Dax climbed the stone steps from the development basement with Gideon and Luke and the three of them set off for the tree house. Three metres off the wood floor, it was a wide collar of smooth planks around the trunk of an old oak tree, with a guard rail and a canopy thatched with woven twigs and leaves and moss. Gideon and Dax had done a lot of work on it, under Owen's guidance, and most of the Colas had got involved and done something to help. Mia and Jennifer had made woven panels of young hazel twigs which were fixed to the structure between the wooden guard rail and the edge of the platform, creating a low wall around the house. Straight, thick branches rose up in six places, supporting the roof and creating 'windows' between them. Jacob and Alex had made several small, low seats in woodwork, which were positioned against the tree trunk and allowed Colas to settle back comfortably and take in the view of the woodland. Mia had bought candles with her Cola allowance money and hung them in jam jars, on wire loops, at intervals around the underside of the canopy. Once lit, the candles smelt of spicy lemon and in the summer and autumn months they kept the midges away. She had also hung a chain of glinting black stones all around the edge of the canopy. Paulina Sartre had provided these. The stones were black tourmaline, and were, said Mia, a powerful protection against psychic attack. Not one Cola made fun of her.

Dax, Gideon, and Luke scrambled up the icy ladder and into the tree house, knocking snow off the handrails, and settled on the little seats, bashing their gloved hands together to build up some warmth. Something crackled in Dax's coat pocket and he remembered the letter from his father. He hadn't yet eaten it, as his dad had suggested. He intended to burn it on the common room fire this evening. Gideon was watching him. 'What's up with you?' he asked. Dax took off one glove and dug the crumpled bit of paper out.

'Something weird. A letter from Dad.'

'Let me guess,' said Gideon. 'He's coming to see you—*soon*.' Gideon had long since learned that Robert Jones never offered an actual date. Luke smiled sympathetically.

'Well, yeah—obviously,' said Dax, with a humourless chuckle which sent a cloud of warm breath out into the freezing air. 'But something else . . . he gave me a sort of code, to find a place in Keswick. Says that my—my mum left something for me, and it was time for me to have it. He's hidden it or something, in this road in Keswick. Says he doesn't dare bring it here.'

Gideon and Luke stared at him, wide-eyed with interest. Then Gideon grabbed the letter and spread it out on his knee to read it. 'What's all this about a kid at your nursery? And a box?'

'It's clues. It means Fir Tree,' explained Dax. 'Fir Tree Road. That's where I have to go. But I don't know how. I've promised Owen I won't go off on my own again. *Really* promised. After last time . . . '

Luke dropped his eyes to his feet but Gideon glanced up at Dax. 'You had to go last time. We both did. Luke wouldn't *be* here if you hadn't.' Dax nodded. Last spring he had flown across the country, over the English Channel and to France, to rescue Luke who was being imprisoned by a thirteen-year-old girl intent on draining all his Cola power for her own use. That it was also draining his life, she cared not a jot. She was a parasite and had used up and killed a number of people in her life.

Her name was Catherine. She was Luke and Gideon's sister.

'I wonder where she is now,' murmured Gideon, lost in unpleasant memory.

'Still with the French, I guess,' said Dax. 'In

45

a perspex cage in an underground bunker if they've got any sense. I bet she's got to someone by now, though. She always does.'

Catherine knew how to manipulate people to a terrifying degree. She easily convinced normal people that she was sweet, innocent, and harmless. If they only knew that she had coldly planned to drown more than a hundred children in order to steal all their talent, they might be less captivated. If they knew that Dax, Gideon, and Owen, with Tyrone and Mia, had chased through a French woodland to find Catherine cheerfully burying Luke alive, her charm might tarnish a little. If they met Luke, and learned that he was mute because his triplet sister had short-circuited the part of his mind that handled speech and then nearly wrenched out his tongue for good measure, they would probably go off her.

Owen had killed her. Or thought he had. But Catherine was still alive, and had claimed protection from the French government and none of them had seen her since that terrible day in Brittany. None of them had felt her presence since, so perhaps it was true. She no longer had access to Cola powers to steal, so she couldn't get to them as a malevolent astral projection either.

Dax and Gideon shivered at the same moment and Luke just gazed out across the glittering silver-white woodland, his face impassive. The fringe of black tourmaline stones swayed gently from the canopy and all three boys were glad of them.

'So—what am I going to do about Fir Tree Road?' asked Dax, deliberately shifting their thoughts away from Catherine. 'How am I going to get to Keswick?'

Gideon wrinkled his brow and then said: 'Ask Owen.'

'What—just like that?'

'Yep. Why not? We haven't had a trip out for ages. We deserve a bit of a break. And Keswick's only about half an hour away, I reckon. It's got brilliant chocolate shops! Dad took Laura up there last summer, after they'd been in to see me. That's why I got that brilliant parcel from him with all the chocolate hedgehogs and stuff.'

Dax smiled. 'How are things going with him and Laura?' Gideon looked a bit pink. His dad, after more than nine years alone since losing his wife, had found a girlfriend. Laura was slight and pretty, with blonde hair and wide hazel eyes. She and Michael Reader had both come to see Gideon and stay with him at the luxury holiday cottage on the fells above Fenton Lodge. Gideon had been nervous and 'totally weirded out' about the idea of his dad snogging someone. But in the event he had instantly taken to Laura and was now rather proud of his father. 'Can't believe it!' he said at the time. 'He's pulled a babe! Never thought he had it in him!' Laura and his dad must be 'serious'. Laura would have been vetted and then required to sign the Official Secrets Act before she was allowed anywhere near Fenton Lodge. Dax wondered if she knew what she was getting into.

'They're cool,' said Gideon. 'I reckon she's going to be my stepmum. Just as long as she doesn't turn into a Gina.' Dax winced. 'Anyway, Keswick has brilliant chocolate shops. Loads of them. I want to go! I *really* want to go now, even if there is no Fir Tree Road and strange mystic gifty thing from your mum. You've got me thinking about those hedgehogs . . . We've got to ask Owen. Then, I can distract him and you can nip off and—'

'No,' cut in Dax. A sudden, stinging memory made him put his gloved hand to his neck.

'No, I'm not doing anything like that. We'll have to find out where Fir Tree Road is and make up some kind of reason for going there. I won't run off.' There would be no point, he thought, unless he took the tracker chip off the underside of his malachite. And once again, he had promised Owen he wouldn't. There seemed to be a tangled thicket of promises all around him. He had to clamber and duck and twist to get through his life without breaking them.

'My bum's numb,' complained Gideon, getting up and handing the letter back to Dax. 'Let's go and see if Mrs P's got any hot chocolate going.'

They half-climbed, half-slid down the ladder and stomped heavily through the woodland floor, between the trees, trying to warm up. As they reached the lodge, Luke tapped Gideon's arm, and made a few swift movements with his hands. 'Yeah, OK, mate,' said Gideon and made a couple of signs back to him. Luke grinned at his brother, nodded at Dax and then hared off up the steps.

'He's off to get his book—says can we get him some cocoa if there's any going, and see him in the common room,' translated Gideon, as they wandered into the elegant entrance hall and wiped their snowy feet on the bristly mat at the door.

'How come you sign back to him, then?' asked Dax. 'He can hear you perfectly well.'

'Well, you just have to do it to understand it,' shrugged Gideon.

Dax felt extremely proud of him. Since last summer, as soon as Luke was well enough, he and Gideon had been taking lessons in British Sign Language. Tyrone, as Luke's tutor, had also joined in. They were still a long way from being fluent, but getting better every day. Luke also scribbled out messages in the notebook he kept in his pocket at all times. He answered questions in class with a small wipe-clean whiteboard and dry-wipe marker. It seemed to work pretty well, but now even Mrs Dann had been tempted to learn a few basic signs, and the rest of the Colas, even if they barely realized it, were starting to recognize the hand shapes for things like 'drink' and 'Can I go to the toilet?' and 'Sorry, can you repeat that?'

'Do you think he'll ever talk again?' asked Dax. It was a question that someone in Cola Club asked at least once a week. Everyone had hoped that it was just the trauma of what had happened

to him which had silenced Luke, and that gradually his power of speech would return. But Luke
made no sound at all. Ever. Even when he cried—
which he had a few times in the early days after
his rescue from France—it was completely sound-
less, and all the more awful for it. His adoptive
mother had been up to stay with him in the cottage
several times, coaxing and hugging and warming
him with love, but even she had not been able to
bring back his voice.

'Sometimes I find it hard to remember him
when he *did* talk,' said Gideon, shaking his head
sadly. 'Remember, I only ever knew him for a few
weeks before the end of Tregarren.'

Luke and Catherine had been found and
brought to the first Cola Club college in Cornwall
several months after Dax had arrived and met
Gideon. Luke came from the Isle of Wight and
Catherine from a children's home in America. They
were very different. Luke was quiet and bookish,
and demonstrated no Cola power at all, while
Catherine was a bundle of high energy charm,
always excited and friendly and forever hugging
and squeezing everyone. They hadn't known, back
then, that she was stealing talent from everyone

51

she laid her hands on. It was how she was able to display a baffling array of ability, from telekinesis and glamour to healing and dowsing. When Dax discovered what she was doing and put a stop to it, she channelled her fury into an appalling plan, grouping everyone together for one incredible parasitic theft—before trying to drown them under a tidal wave.

That was when Luke's *real* power revealed itself. He had stopped the wave and saved them all, only to be swept away with Catherine. For many months the brother and sister, rescued at sea by a lone yachtswoman, were hidden away in Brittany, until Dax and Gideon went to get them back. Only Dax and Luke knew exactly how close to death they had both come in *that* adventure, although they had both recovered well except for some scars on Dax's arms and, of course, the fact that Luke could not speak.

Mrs P wasn't in the kitchen but Ellie, her assistant, happily made three mugs of hot chocolate for them. She was Mrs P's niece, jolly and plump and permanently flushed from the heat of the stove. She and Mrs P had been brought from Cornwall after the devastation of Tregarren following Catherine's tidal wave. They could be trusted and were, after nearly three years with Colas, unflappable in the face of glamour. Mrs P had even caught Barry out once as he crept invisibly through the kitchen in search of the cake tin, by throwing a handful of flour in his direction. Barry's shocked face had immediately been outlined in drifts of white powder and his sneezes were unstoppable for five minutes.

'Here you go then,' said Ellie, loading their tray and adding some digestive biscuits on a plate. 'And you tell the others to come in to me if they want some too. It's perishing cold today!'

Most of the other Colas had gathered in the common room by the time they got there with their tray. Luke was there, leafing through *Great Expectations*, and beamed happily as they set down the tray on the old wooden trunk that served as a coffee table between the leather couches nearest the fire. Jacob and Alex Teller suddenly skidded up next to them and reached for the biscuits, but Gideon immediately zoomed all six high into the air, shaking his head and waggling his finger. 'Oh no you don't, you gutbuckets! Go and get your own. Ellie's got more cocoa on too.'

'But we want *those*!' sighed Alex, and stuck out his lower lip. 'Why can't we have those? We *deserve* only the best!' Dax and Gideon collapsed into fits of laughter, because Alex was using his Lisa voice, perfect in every detail, and pulling an exact replica of Lisa's pout when she was in a mood. The biscuits dropped back down and stacked up neatly, like coasters, as Jacob joined in, also eerily perfect in his mimicry.

'Quick! Somebody call my maid, so she can place a biscuit in my mouth with silver tongs and dust the crumbs off my perfect chin with a silk napkin! Do it now or I'll set the butler on you! *Doof!*'

The last comment was in his own voice as Lisa suddenly appeared behind him, dressed in a lemon cashmere sweater and beautifully cut cream trousers with knee-high golden suede boots. Her gleaming blonde hair was in a ponytail which now swung furiously as she launched herself over the back of the couch and grabbed both brothers by the ears, knocking their heads together. 'READ MY MIND, you rude little pipsqueaks!' The telepaths stifled their giggles and then both, at the same moment, gulped and looked a little worried, as Lisa sent them a no doubt violent message. 'The next time you mimic me I'll rip your ears *off*,' she promised, glowering at them, her dark blue eyes sparkling with indignation. She let them go and they slunk away fast, rubbing the side of their heads and muttering.

Lisa sank down on the sofa next to Gideon and narrowed her eyes at Dax as he cupped his cocoa and tried hard to stop smirking. The Teller brothers were always spot-on with their impressions, and although he liked Lisa hugely and would trust her with his life (probably), she *did* have spoilt brat tendencies. And a butler (at her family mansion).

'Biscuit?' said Gideon, sweetly, holding out the plate to her. He bit his lips together and sniffed hard.

Lisa narrowed her eyes at him and declined. She looked back at Dax. Lost in chocolatey steam, at first he wondered why, and then he felt a surge of nervousness as he realized she was curious about something and prodding gently at his mind. She was also telepathic, but could only send to, and get messages from, other 'receptives' as she called them. Usually people who were close to her. Dax, being part-time fox and falcon, possessed a basic ability to pick up telepathy when it was sent, and once the communication was open, the telepath could pick up thoughts from him—unless he chose to blank them out. He chose this now, as he felt Lisa foraging about in his head, slamming a cold grey steel shutter down, in his mind's eye. *Cut it out!* he sent to Lisa and she blinked and looked a little sheepish.

'Did you want something?' he asked, out loud.

'Oh, I was just wondering,' she said, airily, 'why you keep rubbing the back of your neck. Caught fleas off a rabbit?'

Dax's hand slapped down onto his knee abruptly. He'd had no idea he was absent-mindedly rubbing his neck, although the shocking incident in the night was still very fresh in his mind and he'd been trying not to think about it all day. Obviously not very successfully.

'It's a nervous twitch whenever *you* come anywhere near him,' said Gideon, through a mouthful of digestive crumbs. 'We all do it.' And he started rubbing his own neck, grinning at Lisa, winding her up.

The sight of his friend prodding the site of

the stowaway chip made Dax feel sick again. He shivered and Lisa, of course, noticed. She ignored Gideon and went back to looking at Dax. Then she lifted her eyes to the air behind him and they fluttered oddly. Gideon immediately shut up, gulping the remains of his biscuit down quickly. Lisa continued to do the strange fluttery thing with her eyes. Then she spoke and the room grew cold.

'A terrible choice. Oh, a terrible choice,' she said, and her voice was like a dark fog descending. The other Colas, Barry, Jennifer, and Darren, stopped talking and looked around. Luke let his book drop into his lap.

'Flame in water and such an ending,' went on Lisa. 'The choice won't be yours, Dax Jones. Death is not the end.'

Then Lisa began to cry.

5

'Well, wouldn't you just know it?' sighed Gideon. 'You settle down with some hot chocolate and biscuits, bag the best seat by the fire and start to relax—then some blonde comes along and says you're gonna die.'

Dax elbowed him in the ribs. 'Keep your voice down! She's upset!'

Mia had arrived seconds after Lisa's strange outburst and now she and Jennifer were huddled with Lisa at the far end of the common room, talking in low voices.

'She's *not* upset!' scoffed Gideon. 'She *loves* it. You were annoying her so she just decided to go all whoo-ee and whaa-eee and freak you out. *Don't worry—death is not the end, Dax!* Honestly!'

'She didn't actually say that,' muttered Dax. 'And she didn't say it was anything to do with me.'

'She said your name!'

They were both silent for a bit and then Gideon laughed, not very convincingly, and said again, 'She *loves* it. Don't give her the satisfaction.'

'Of what?'

'Being freaked out,' said Gideon, so clearly freaked out that Dax wanted to laugh. They both knew Lisa wasn't messing around. She *did* wind them up sometimes, offering up personal and usually embarrassing titbits of information fed to her by their dead ancestors, when the mood took her—but she had never faked an episode like that before. And besides, Dax would know if she was. He would be able to smell it.

'Come on, let's go and see if Owen's back yet. Ask about the trip to Keswick,' said Dax, to get Gideon's mind off it. They left Luke reading. He'd settled back to his book quickly, apparently unbothered by Lisa's latest episode. Luke never did seem very bothered by most things. He was the calmest person Dax knew. He wasn't pretending either. Again, Dax would smell it if he was. He also knew something about Luke that nobody else did. Although it was common knowledge that Luke had already been in the land of the dead, after a fashion, because of the barely alive state his sister had kept him in, what none of the rest of them knew was how it *felt*.

But Dax had been there too. With Luke. Last year he too had been so close to death that he had spent a little time in that realm with Gideon's twin—just a minute perhaps—but it was enough to understand something about Luke. Going there changed you: only a bit in Dax's case, but, with all the time he had spent there, a *lot* for Luke. Dax had never told anyone about that minute out of life. He didn't know how to describe it.

They went up the wide curving staircase, past the first storey where their dorms were and on up to the second storey, where Owen's study could be found, next to the medical room. The staff lounges and bedrooms were up on the third storey. Tyrone was emerging from the medical room as they reached Owen's door, looking puffy and watery in the eyes. Janey came out into the corridor with him, handing him a glass with a pale green liquid in it.

'There you go,' she said. 'Take it back to your room and chase it down with another glass of water,' she said. 'It'll help knock this on the head really fast, but it'll probably make you sleepy, so just go with it, and go to bed.'

Tyrone smiled weakly. 'Thanks, Janey,' he said, peering at the drink uneasily.

She laughed and patted his wiry hair. 'Don't be a wuss,' she teased and he flushed a little— which made him look positively fluey.

'Probably won't be doing Development with you tomorrow, Gideon,' said Tyrone as he trudged past them with his medicine. 'Not if I feel this rotten.'

'Don't worry—get some sleep,' said Gideon, cheerily. 'Poor bloke,' he said to Dax. 'That was a nasty bug. I conked out for a whole day with it. We both did. We made a mountain of snotty tissues, didn't we?'

'A volcano,' said Dax.

They knocked on Owen's study door and heard him call, 'Yeah? Who is it?'

'Dax and Gideon. Can we come in?'

There was a pause and then the door was flung open. Owen had obviously not been back long. He was holding some screwed-up newspaper and a couple of sticks of kindling. 'Good,' he said. 'You can help me get a fire going. It's sub zero in here!'

They worked quickly, building flames from the paper and small sticks of kindling, and then gently adding bigger chunks of split log and small pieces of coal. After ten minutes the fire had taken nicely in Owen's small cast-iron grate and they settled back onto his leather sofa to appreciate it. Owen flicked a glance across at Dax and he could tell that the man was anxious about what he might have come for. Perhaps he feared that Dax had already broken his promise and told Gideon about the tracking chip under his skin.

'What did you come up for?' asked Owen, at length.

Gideon sat up and looked at him earnestly. 'Well, since you ask, you know we haven't been out of here for ages and ages and ages . . . ?'

'Go on,' said Owen, guardedly.

'Well, we're just about going mad now; you know, running up and down the corridors and licking the walls and stuff—trying to bite off our own elbows—and we think we should have a trip out and we want to go to Keswick where all the good chocolate shops are!' Gideon beamed winningly at Owen. He was so utterly convincing that Dax wondered if he had actually forgotten about the *real* purpose of going to the town and was just swept away with excitement about chocolate. Knowing Gid, that was entirely possible.

Owen laughed and shook his head at Gideon. 'Keswick is it? Confectionery capital of Cumbria?'

'Yeah! That's right. My dad sent me some stuff he got there and now I've eaten it all and I'm pining for more. I'm a growing boy, you know!'

'Well, Gideon, although the sugar and cocoa levels in your blood must already be dangerously high, I must admit it has been a while since there was a trip out. I reckon I can get passes for half of you, if I can get two other teachers and an SG along too. The other half will have to wait for the next weekend. To be honest, I'm sure we'll get the staff. They could do with a day out too.'

Dax was thrilled. He'd had no idea it would be this easy. And then he saw something in Owen's face, when the man glanced over, which made him understand, with a sudden hard beat inside his chest, what was happening. Owen was trading with him. His eyes were now resting steadily on Dax and he was telling him that this was a transaction of trust. That Dax had to keep his side of the bargain struck on the bloody snow last night. He looked away from the cool blue stare which Gideon, excitedly listing the goodies he was going to get, had not noticed. He felt angry again. As if he was being played. Soon he would have another conversation with Owen, alone, and find out what else he knew about the tracker chips—and how long it would be before they were all taken out. His thoughts of sharing the Fir Tree Road information with Owen evaporated. If they were bargaining, he'd be better off keeping a few things close to his chest.

The sleek black vehicle cruised along winding roads between the snow-dusted fells and six Colas stared out of the windows at the breathtaking scenery. Alex and Jacob Teller were plastered to the windows and at first Dax thought they were so moved by the view they couldn't peel themselves off. Then he realized they were writing rude messages on the glass with their tongues. Alex put a full stop on his with all the suction power he could manage. Mrs Dann pursed her lips, leaned over and yanked his shoulder. He came away with a loud squelch.

'Honestly, you two!' Mrs Dann wrinkled her nose, as Jacob and Alex collapsed in gales of laughter. 'It's like travelling with chimps!' The brothers' laughter immediately became the wild cackle and whoop of chimps—so exact that even the driver, behind his thick safety screen, glanced back in astonishment. Mrs Dann leaned over between the seats, locked eyes with Jacob and echoed Lisa, the day before: 'Read my mind!' Jacob gulped and shut up immediately, nudging his younger brother and sending him a swift telepathic message to pack it in. Even the silent SG (Owen's shortening for Security Guard), seated behind them at the back, was having difficulty keeping a straight face.

Whenever Colas had a trip out it was in something which could never be described as a minibus. It was like a small touring coach—the kind you see famous bands travelling in. Its windows were reflective on the outside, allowing no view of the passengers. But the main way it differed from the many multi-person vehicles travelling the tourist trails around the Cumbrian fells, was in its armour-plating. It also stocked some impressive on-board weaponry in case of attack. The government wasn't about to be caught out twice.

There had been great excitement among the Colas when they heard that some of them could go out for a Saturday visit to Keswick. As it was their request, Dax and Gideon were definitely going, but for the remaining students there was a lucky dip in a hat and the names that came up were Jacob and Alex, Mia and Spook. The other disappointed Colas were promised the same trip the following Saturday. Now that they were on their way, Dax and Gideon were racking their brains to come up with a way of finding Fir Tree Road. Getting a trip to Keswick had been un-expectedly easy but now they were on the way they realized that their problems were only just starting.

'We don't even know where it is,' muttered Gideon, quietly, under the rumble of the engine. 'We need to get a map book or something.'

'We should be able to get one in a newsagent's,' said Dax. 'I just hope it's not too far away. If it's right over the far side of the town, I don't see how we can get there.'

'We could just ask Owen,' shrugged Gideon. 'Do you think?'

Dax looked down the aisle to where Owen sat with his back to them. There had been no further mention of the tracker chips and he was still angry about it. Tremors of anxiety and resentment ran through him every time he thought about his friends and the chips under their skin. So he did not feel like confiding in Owen and, besides, this was personal—something his mum had left for him. There was no reason why he should have to tell anyone at all.

'We'll ask Owen as a last resort,' he said and Gideon glanced at him in surprise. 'But let's just keep it to ourselves if we can. As soon as we find out where it is, we can try to work out a plan.'

Gideon was still looking at him oddly. Dax felt pushed to explain. Gideon knew he looked up to Owen—more than looked up to him.

'It's personal,' said Dax. 'I don't want to have

to share *everything* in my life. Except with you, obviously.'

Gideon nodded, satisfied. A billow of material wafted past. Spook was on the move, his favourite midnight blue long-coat rippling around him. He had got up from his seat near the soldier (since he'd been used once in a military tracking maneouvre he rather fancied himself as a hero to the guards) and headed for Mia, who was gazing dreamily out of the window, a seat ahead of Dax and Gideon.

'Room for me?' he asked Mia and she sighed, broken out of her reverie, and moved over. Spook loved Mia, like they all did. His vanity added a touch of melodrama to it, though, and he was convinced she must feel the same way about him.

Gideon shoved his face between their head rests. 'When are you going to stitch all the sequins on that coat, Spook, love? It looks almost normal. If you're not careful the humble people of Keswick might not know that you're a world-famous magician.'

Spook flipped his fist backwards and caught Gideon on the nose. A warning growl from Mrs Dann stopped it escalating. Gideon sat back, rubbing his nose but grinning. He *loved* winding Spook up.

They reached Keswick by 11a.m. and spilled out onto a small coach and car park behind the high street. The town was pretty, nestling onto the lower fells beside a large and beautiful lake, which shone steely blue in the bright winter sun. With snow coating its roofs and shop awnings, the high street had an almost Swiss look about it. And Gideon was not wrong: chocolate parlours abounded. Catering for fell walkers and climbers all year round, the town made a lot of its income through providing chocolate and mint cake for visiting adventurers to stuff into their backpacks. They wandered along the high street in a group, Mrs Dann, Owen, and Mr Tucker responsible for two Colas each, and the quiet, watchful soldier, muffled in a thick winter jacket which hid his gun, bringing up the rear, responsible for them all. Owen was also armed. Dax could smell the oil on his gun. It mixed oddly with the scent of happy excitement pulsing through the little party.

At the first opportunity Dax and Gideon dived into a newsagent's and bought a map book. While Gideon made a show of looking at magazines, and Owen leaned in the doorway, surveying the postcard rack, Dax quietly paid for the book and flicked nervously to the gazetteer at the back, his finger running down the Fs until, with a sigh of relief, he found Fir Tree Road. His relief was even greater when he discovered that the road was a spur off the upper end of the high street. Easily within walking distance. He muttered this to Gideon, as he tucked the book into a deep pocket in his coat and put his gloves back on.

'I'll just make out that Dad said there was a great chocolate shop up there,' said Gideon, as they rejoined the others and began rambling further up the high street. 'At least we can have a good look at it and try to work out what it is you're meant to find. You just be all not-carey and we'll make out it's only me having a bit of an obsess, all right?'

'Yeah. Good plan,' whispered Dax. He was beginning to feel quite excited—as if they might pull this off.

Spook and Mia were drawn into a crystals and minerals shop and the others followed them in. The softly lit boutique smelt of incense and glittered with crystal stars and pendants suspended from its low ceiling on invisible cords. Rocks and polished stones from all over the world were on display on glass shelves and the Colas each instinctively searched for a stone which matched the one on their wrist, given to them by Mia a few months ago. Each wore leather strap bracelets, like the one which hid Dax's tracker chip, with a polished crystal or stone on it. Dax's malachite was known as the stone of transformation. Gideon's was serpentine, a comforting stone which warded off parasites. It was grey with flecks of green and red in it and gleamed gently in the light. Spook wore a sparkling yellow-green stone—a peridot. It was Mia's attempt to make him a nicer person. Peridot, according to Mia's Crystal Directory, was meant to make him less jealous and mean. Dax wasn't sure it was working. Jacob and Alex were riffling through a tub of little blue gems which matched their own. The blue stones had little drifts and stars of gold and white across their surface—lapis lazuli, great for assisting in telepathy according to Mia. Not that they needed much help, although they rarely bothered to communicate telepathically with anyone other than each other. Mia did not search for a match to her stone. She often kept it turned under, with the strap side showing. It was black obsidian and Dax wasn't at all sure it was good for her. It made her tougher and for Mia, healer and bringer of calm, this seemed wrong somehow.

The assistant noticed them comparing the stones to the ones on their wrists. 'These are nice,' she said to Gideon. 'Have you all got them?'

'Yeah,' grinned Gideon. 'We're in a sort of club. They're cool, aren't they?' She smiled at him and took hold of his wrist.

'Really nice! What's yours?' she asked Dax and then Gideon, obviously trying to chat her up (she was young and quite pretty), seized Dax's wrist and offered it to her. 'Malachite,' he said. 'Transformation stone!'

'Ooh, you know your stuff!' she giggled.

And then Gideon started trying to undo Dax's bracelet in an attempt to show it to her. Dax snatched back his wrist and said 'No!' It came out much louder and harsher than he'd intended it to. There was a pause in the shop and all the others looked round.

Spook raised his eyebrow. 'Lover's tiff?' he sneered.

Gideon ignored Spook. 'All right, all right, mate! Keep your hair on!' He went back to showing the girl his own bracelet. Dax stepped back towards the door. He noticed Owen looking at him. He stared back and Owen shook his head, very slightly, his face impassive. Beneath the malachite, Dax's personal tracker chip nestled securely. It was all he could do not to rip his bracelet off and stamp on it.

Alex and Spook both bought some more stones. Alex chose an amethyst geode—a tiny cave of glittering purple crystals, revealed by a clean cut through a stone—and Spook bought a heavy chunk of gleaming iron pyrites.

'Fool's gold,' muttered Gideon. 'Good choice!'

The next stop was one of the sumptuous chocolate parlours and Gideon lost himself for ten minutes, stocking up on goodies. Dax nudged him as he gazed lovingly at chocolate coated raspberry fondants. 'Don't spend everything!' he urged, quietly. 'Remember you've got to buy more at the place in Fir Tree Road!'

When they were all back outside again, Gideon started on the next stage of the plan. 'This is brilliant!' he announced. 'Only one more place to go and stock up!'

'You have to be joking,' said Mrs Dann, digging

deep into a paper packet of hot caramelized nuts she'd just bought from a street stall. 'You can't possibly want any more chocolate!'

'You would think that, wouldn't you?' agreed Gideon, giving her one of his most winning smiles. 'But there's this thing my dad told me about. It's chocolate *hair*!'

'Chocolate *hair*?' echoed Mrs Dann, looking disgusted while Alex and Jacob immediately made noises exactly like cats coughing up fur balls.

'It's not like it sounds! It's a sort of caramel thing—they make it go all wispy and stretchy in millions of little strands and then it dries all brittle and they spray it lightly in chocolate. It's amazing! My dad sent me a little bit to try. It's in this shop, called . . . um . . . ' Gideon paused to spin the next bit of his story and Dax marvelled at his imagination. 'I know—the Confectionery Cave! It's in Fir Tree Road—just up there!'

'How do you know it's just up there?' asked Mrs Dann. 'You've never been here before.'

'Looked on the tourist map thingy,' said Gideon, pointing vaguely back down the high street without even blinking. 'C'mon! We can get there before lunch if we go now!'

The others weren't keen. They had already bought a tonne of sweets and now didn't feel like carrying them much further. They wanted to stop and have some hot food at one of the many cafés which were sending out enticing scents of baked potato or cottage pie. Gideon tried again valiantly.

'Come *on*, you lot! I mean—chocolate *hair*! You can't miss that!'

Owen sighed. 'I'll come along with you both. The rest of you, stay together. Go and get lunch in the courtyard place over there. We'll be back in fifteen minutes.'

Gideon whooped but Dax was suddenly assailed by worry. It might have been easy to play dumb about Gideon's pretend chocolate shop with everyone around him, but with only Owen observing it was going to be a lot harder. He still had absolutely no idea what his father meant him to find. How obvious was it going to be? Maybe he'd painted great big fluorescent messages on the pavement instructing: Dax, look under the bench! Possibly not. Whatever it was, clearly Robert Jones had intended only Dax to find it, or he would just have sent it to him and risked the parcel being opened and checked by security. Although there had never been any evidence of the Cola's letters or parcels being checked, Dax was quite certain they always were. With all the gadgets the Cola Project had at its disposal, there was certainly no need to open anything.

They turned the corner into Fir Tree Road just five minutes later. Gideon had rattled on endlessly about chocolate hair and other mad sweets to Owen while they walked, leaving Dax to his worries, but as they reached the road he faltered and Owen said, 'Are you sure this is it, Gideon? It doesn't look likely, does it?'

Fir Tree Road was just a row of ordinary grey-stone Cumbrian houses, curving away up the fell. Dax scanned it, desperate for some kind of clue, but there was absolutely nothing unusual anywhere to be seen.

'I think it might be a sort of factory—with a shop outlet. It's probably further up, around that corner,' he said, flicking a worried glance at Dax as Owen peered up the road.

Owen cupped his gloved hands together and tried to huff some heat into them.

'All right, we'll walk up a little way and see

what's round the bend, but I'm not going any further. I'm so cold my fingers are going to drop off.'

'OK, just a quick look then!' chirped Gideon, and hared ahead. 'C'mon, Dax—race you to the corner!' With no hesitation, Dax charged after him, relieved to get away from Owen before the man could notice how anxious he was. He so badly wanted to fly and scan the area that he was quite sure he'd done the 'alien thing' about three times already.

'You were doing the alien thing like a mad monster from Mars!' confirmed Gideon as Dax caught up with him. 'Owen was going to see it any minute! Get a grip.' When Dax badly wanted to shift to the falcon but couldn't, sometimes just his eyes seemed to go. They would flicker black and yellow and birdlike, for half a second. It was the most eerie thing to watch, making him look like an alien, and had been quite useful in the past—but it was a dead giveaway to someone like Owen that something was stressing Dax. He reckoned he did the same thing when he wanted to shift to a fox too, but as his human eyes were wide and brown, much like a fox's, it didn't really show.

'Oi—not too far!' yelled Owen, walking fast to catch them up.

They slowed down and Gideon squinted at Dax's eyes. 'Nope—you're all right now. Now just *chill*, will you? Doesn't look like we're going to find it anyway, whatever it is.'

Dax slowed his pulse with even breaths and great concentration as they walked on. Gideon was right. There was nothing here to find. No signs on lamp-posts or arrows on the pavement. Nothing that spoke to him at all. His dad had promised but not delivered. No change there then. As they reached the corner he saw that more houses stretched away on both sides of the road—but one of these was a corner shop. Just a small shop, serving the local people, not remotely like the tourist shops in the high street. Dax felt a flicker of excitement.

'This could be it!' sang Gideon, as Owen reached them. He gave Gideon an old-fashioned look. 'Well, it might be at the back!' insisted Gideon. 'Let's just look.'

Owen sighed and followed them across the road. 'It's just a corner shop, you cocoa-freak!' he said, but Gideon was already through the door. Owen followed him in, saying he might as well pick up a daily paper. Dax moved to go in after him but as he reached the step his eyes flicked sideways to the window, which was filled with postcards from local people offering things for sale or looking for work. Dax read through them: Gardener Wanted, Mini Trampoline For Sale, Babysitter Available, Accountant Will Sort Your Tax . . . Down low, only just above the grimy sill, was a small green card. Dax caught his breath as he recognized the slanting writing on it.

It read: *DRJ—collector wanted. Apply within. Name in full and first school on application.*

He read it three times before he could get it into his head. It would make no sense to anyone else. DRJ—that was him. Daxesh Robert Jones, in full. He obviously needed to somehow say that to the shopkeeper, along with the name of his old school. And then what? Get shown into a secret underground grotto? A big shiny parcel? A clip round the ear? Dax had no idea what to expect, but if he didn't go in now, he would never find out.

A bell jingled brightly as he stepped into the shop. An Asian man was behind the till, stout, with dark hair greying at the temples, counting through the local papers which had just been delivered. He glanced up and nodded at Dax and then went back to his counting. Owen was flicking through a motoring magazine and Gideon was poking at some biscuits on a display stand. He gestured at Dax to hurry over. 'What now?' he hissed. 'It's a dead end.'

'No, it's not,' said Dax. And then louder, he added in a casual, conversational voice, 'What's your full name, Gid? Have you got a middle name?' He backed away, in the direction of the shop-keeper, pulling a face at Gideon to humour him. Happily, Owen's view was blocked by the maga-zine stand.

'Yeah, it's Michael, like my dad. What's yours?' Gideon played along.

'My whole name is a bit of a mouthful,' said Dax, now leaning against the counter and glancing back at the shopkeeper. 'It's Daxesh Robert Jones.'

'Dax*esh*?' said Gideon, genuinely quite surprised. 'Well, I never knew that. Great name though. Cool!'

The shopkeeper stopped counting and Dax immediately scented the man's quickening of interest.

'Yeah—but when I was in my infants' school—
you know, Bark's End Infants—none of the kids
could ever say it properly, so it just stuck as Dax.
Which is fine by me. What do you think?' He
turned and addressed this last to the shopkeeper,
who stared at him for a second and then glanced
over at Owen and at Gideon. He rummaged under
his desk as he answered.

'Daxesh is a fine name, young man,' he
answered. 'I have a cousin who shares it with you.
He is a good boy—like you. His father speaks
highly of him as I'm sure . . . ' he stood now, and
shook Dax's hand, and to his immense surprise
Dax realized he was pressing something into it,
'your father speaks of you.' The man smiled at
him broadly.

'My father would thank you,' said Dax, 'for
your kindness.' He felt the small paper package
in his palm, and a strange pull of family towards
the Asian man. He was an eighth Asian himself,
after all—and the gift now in his hand was from
his mother, also of that bloodline. He badly wanted
to ask the man if he had known his mother—or
if he knew his father.

'You are like him,' said the man, quietly, as if

he'd read Dax's mind. 'When I first met him on Cormorant A.' Dax nodded, understanding. This man was a former roughneck; had worked on an oil rig with his dad. There was no family connection after all.

'I'll have this, please—and some Polos,' said Owen, reaching over Dax's shoulder with the motoring magazine. Dax and Gideon moved down the shop to wait by the door, Gideon pulling faces at Dax, agog to know what was happening. 'Come on, time to go back for lunch now,' said Owen, tucking the magazine under one arm and hustling them outside. 'Your chocolate hair is a myth, I reckon, Gideon.'

Gideon sighed and admitted defeat and they all headed back to the high street and the courtyard café where the others were already eating cottage pie or baked potatoes with cheese and downing cups of hot tea or cocoa. Dax didn't even look at what he held. He thrust it into his pocket, his heart racing and full of unfamiliar emotion—feelings that hadn't risen in him since he was four.

A message from his mother. No other Cola could say the same . . .

6

It wasn't until they were back in their bedroom, late that afternoon, that Dax got the package out of his pocket. Gideon had been nudging at him and hissing for a look at it several times on the way back, but Dax had just shaken his head. Now that he had it—whatever it was—he was filled with strange emotions and felt that he might cry as he unwrapped it, and there was no way he was going to risk that with Spook only a few feet away.

During the rest of the trip—there had been a bit more shop wandering, checking out the mountaineering emporiums, after lunch—Dax had felt calm and serene on the surface, while excitement bubbled through him below, along

83

with wave after wave of strangeness. Something from his mother. *Something from his mother.* He could hardly believe it.

Now, with the door firmly shut, the bedside lamps lit as the afternoon turned to dusk outside, and Gideon eagerly gesturing for him to hurry up and show him what he'd got, Dax feared disappointment. What if it was just a trinket? A St Christopher or something? A pair of her favourite earrings? Happy though he would be to have anything that had been hers, his father's strange letter had led him to expect something much more important; something which might explain how he had come to be a shapeshifter; something which would make him proud and strong and happy and sure about himself.

'Oh, will you get a *move on*!' wailed Gideon, snapping him out of his thoughts.

Dax scooped the package out of the pocket of his coat, which lay on the bed beside him. It was roughly oblong—just plain grey-white tissue paper, the type used to wrap up glass in shops. It wasn't even sealed, just rolled and folded around whatever lay inside. His fingers shook as he teased it apart and unravelled it. He and Gideon stared in silence at what was uncovered. It was a piece of something which might have been metal or rock or wax; it was hard to tell. It was somewhere between grey and lilac in colour and about six centimetres long. It was a sort of hexagonal barrel, each plane precisely cut, as if it had been machine worked, tapering to a point on one end, with a flat base at the other. It had little weight, which is what made it hard to think of it as metal or rock. It was more like a kind of resin. In fact it made Dax think of Edinburgh Castle Rock—the sugar stick which was smooth and solid looking on the outside, but light and crumbly inside.

He dug his fingernail into the thing but it made no mark. The surface felt as hard as diamond. He couldn't know if it was honeycombed inside, but it felt as if it should be. As he turned it in his palm and Gideon murmured with fascination, he saw some markings down one side of it. Writing. He snatched it up towards the light, hoping to read a message—but the markings were not any alphabet that he recognized.

'What does it say?' whispered Gideon.

'I don't know . . . it could say anything. It's

85

like—you know—hieroglyphics. Like you see in Egypt.'

'What—birds and eyes and stuff?'

'Yeah—but without the birds and the eyes!'

Dax showed it to him and Gideon peered at it. 'Nope—doesn't mean anything to me either.'

The thing felt warm in his palm and he found himself putting it to his upper lip, smoothing it across the sensitive skin. It smelt faintly of newly cut grass. Dax didn't know what he felt. He was not disappointed but intrigued. What *was* it?

'Can I?' asked Gideon, holding out his cupped hand.

Dax rolled the barrel thing down his fingers into Gideon's hand. He sat back, his hands turned up in his lap, feeling oddly bereft.

'Whoa—it's much lighter than it looks,' Gideon said. And then he gasped in astonishment. The barrel was rolling, not downwards across his palm, but upwards to the tips of his fingers. For a second it stopped there, teetering, and then flipped a few inches through the air and back into Dax's hands. They stared at each other, open mouthed.

'Did you do that?' whispered Dax, although he knew the answer.

'No. Not me . . . Try it again!' breathed Gideon, his eyes wide with excitement. Dax put it back into his friend's hand and again, within seconds, it rolled to the edge of his fingers and pinged itself straight back to its owner.

'It wants you!' Gideon gaped and blinked at Dax. 'It wants you! What *is* it?'

Dax had absolutely no idea, but a deep thrill ran through him as he closed his fingers over the strange gift.

'What shall we call it?' said Gideon. 'It needs a name!'

'It's not a pet!' Dax found himself giggling, elated and fizzy with excitement, as if someone had, indeed, given him a new puppy.

'It *is*!' said Gideon. 'It's *bonding* with you! It needs a name. We can't just call it The Thing.'

Dax grinned and thought for a moment. 'Neetanite,' he said.

Gideon raised his eyebrows thoughtfully and then nodded. 'Sounds good. Where did you get that from?'

Dax shrugged. 'Mum was called Anita. It's

from her. So . . . Neetanite. It'll do until we find out what it is.'

'Neetanite,' mulled Gideon. 'I like it. We need to show it to Clive. If anyone here will recognize the markings on it, he will.'

They found Clive with Barry in the lab. Barry was holding a test-tube steady while Clive poured an evil smelling blue liquid into it.

'Oh, do hold still, Barry!' he was huffing as they arrived. 'It's like working through an earthquake!'

Barry flickered rapidly in and out of view, as if he was in strobe lighting. It was something he tended to do when he got cross.

'Oh, do stop that!' snapped Clive. 'You'll give me a migraine!'

Barry snapped fully back into visibility, his lips pursed. 'Look, Spock, if you want my help you can just show a bit more respect,' he muttered. 'Or else find yourself a retort stand—and then shove it—'

'Up until now I could have managed without you just fine,' said Clive, 'but you know I need the exact body temperature of the human hand for this experiment! Or else I *would* be using a retort stand!'

'Well you can use *Dax's* human hand then!' said Barry. 'I'm taking my exact body temperature off to the games room to do something *fun*. It's the last time I offer to help *you*, geek-face!'

He thrust the test-tube back at Clive, who tutted loudly. 'You'll never get to be a scientist!'

'You'll never get to be *fourteen*,' muttered Barry, stalking off. It was the kind of conversation Clive and Barry had every day. In spite of the fact that they couldn't be more different, they were great mates. They seemed to thrive on their differences. One of their favourite party tricks was for Clive, small and skinny, to ride on Barry's shoulders while he was in a vanish. It looked as if Clive was floating through the air and had caused great hilarity at least once. Since then, it tended to cause great hilarity largely to Barry and Clive.

Dax was relieved that Barry had gone. He didn't want all the other Colas knowing about the Neetanite. Clive could be trusted to keep it to himself.

'We need your genius, Clive,' said Dax, closing the lab door. Clive looked a little pink. He loved being called a genius, especially after Barry had just called him geek-face.

Dax rolled his mother's gift onto the polished wood work surface and Clive squinted at it. 'What's this?' He picked it up and they waited, watching. Held between his finger and thumb, the Neetanite could not roll away from him, but it began to pivot, pulling at one end towards Dax.

'It's not me,' said Gideon quickly, as Clive glanced up at him, one eyebrow raised.

'OK . . . so what is it?' pondered Clive. 'Ooh! It's pulling really hard!'

'Let it go,' said Gideon. 'Just let it rest in your palm.'

Clive shrugged and did so. Three seconds later the Neetanite was back in Dax's palm. Clive blinked in surprise. 'Gosh! That's a bit odd! It must be some kind of light iron and polymer alloy. Have you got a strong magnet hidden on you?'

Dax laughed and shook his head. 'No! It just keeps doing that. We don't know why.' He explained, rapidly, how he had come to have the Neetanite.

'Gosh!' said Clive, again. 'How exciting! I've never seen anything like it.'

'What about the writing on the side?' urged Gideon and Clive turned the object around in

Dax's palm, pushing his spectacles up his nose and examining it closely.

'Yes . . . definitely some form to it. It's a language all right. Not one I've ever seen, I have to say. I'll have to research it. Let me copy it down.' He took a pen and some paper and swiftly copied down the marks and symbols, taking care to position them exactly. 'In some languages a symbol can mean several things, and it's the positioning of it along the line which tells you which,' he explained, 'so you can't be sloppy.'

'What do you think it might be for?' asked Dax.

Clive regarded him solemnly. 'I couldn't guess. The writing is probably the clue. I'll see what I can find out. But what does your fox instinct tell you?'

Dax pushed the Neetanite back into his pocket, closed his eyes and shifted into a fox, sitting still on the cold tiles with its eyes shut. When he shifted back he rubbed his face with both hands, looking perplexed. 'Doesn't make sense,' he said. 'Just one word popped in. Probably rubbish.'

'What word?' asked Clive and Gideon in unison.

'Corridor.'

7

Dax awoke early the next morning and instinctively shoved his hand under his pillow. It closed on the Neetanite. It was still there. It seemed to be content to stay under his head, and throughout the previous evening it had been happy enough in his pocket. Dax sat up and moved himself down to the far end of the bed, pulling the quilt across with him. In the dim light of the winter dawn he waited a few seconds before there was a small movement under the pillow and then the Neetanite rolled silently across his rumpled white sheet and stopped only when it nudged against his knee. Dax put his hand down and it immediately rolled into his palm and lay still.

Gideon slept on, snoring slightly across the room, and then Dax heard the quiet pressing of tyre on gravel. He moved quickly to the window and saw Owen's black jeep pulling up outside. Where had he been this time? Finding out more unsettling news about what the Cola Project was doing to its students? Dax gritted his teeth and made a quick decision. Thrusting the Neetanite into his pyjama pocket, he shifted to the falcon and flew to the window sill. Below him, Owen was getting out of the car, shivering and hauling his black jacket out after him. Dax shot up to the level of the steeply pitched lodge roof, flipped over in the air, inverted his vicious beak to the earth, and then plummeted back down towards Owen. In the cold winter air he reached great speed even in that short distance and Owen yelped as Dax landed hard on his shoulder, not sparing him from his ruthless talons.

Owen cursed and gasped and then transferred the peregrine to the ball of his fist, where the skin was more leathery. He caught his breath for a moment, staring at the fantastic bird folding its gunmetal wings, before rubbing his shoulder with his spare hand. He pulled his fingers away and they were bloody on the tips. Owen gave a dry laugh and then muttered: 'All right. Are we even now, Dax?'

Dax stared at him, unblinkingly, making no effort to fly to the ground and shift. Owen had had enough time to make his investigations. He owed him an explanation about the tracker chips.

'I've run out of time, haven't I?' said Owen, as if he could read the falcon's mind. 'You want answers.' Black eyes glittered in pools of yellow and fixed on him hard. It was easier to be a falcon when you wanted to be hard, Dax had found. Even the fox had some tender feelings. The falcon had none.

'Hang on,' said Owen. He put his fist towards the luggage rack on the roof of the jeep and Dax stepped onto it. Owen put his jacket on, zipping it up, and then found his thick suede gloves in the pockets and put those on too. 'Come on then,' he said, holding out his fist again, better protected this time. Dax stepped back onto it, his talons easily gripping the soft hide. Owen walked towards the lake and traced the path around it. The snow was thawing now and patches of silvery-green grass were showing through. As they moved far from

94

the lodge Owen sighed and said, 'Will you *stop* looking at me as if I'm a pigeon you're about to have for breakfast!'

Dax looked away from him and preened an unruly feather in his left wing.

'I've been talking to the scientists,' said Owen, still moving through the cold dawn. 'They *have* chipped all the Colas, I'm afraid. And as I thought, it's a simple matter of what they see as security. If I had been consulted I would have argued very strongly against this, you need to know that, Dax. I hate it. It's appalling. I would have suggested that chips go into everyone's shoes instead—maybe clothing too. I know—' He waved his free hand at Dax as the falcon flapped its wings indignantly. 'I know you think that's out of order too, but after all the stuff that's happened, to *you* in particular, I have to say, you can understand their point of view.

'And *you* wouldn't need to be wearing anything to go AWOL again, would you? I mean— you really could do a clean getaway if you fancied it. Of course, getting back to a boy again could be embarrassing unless you *like* streaking, but we both know that you can stay in fox form now, maybe even in falcon form, for as long as you want to. You, of all of the Colas, are the hardest to argue for.'

Dax folded his wings again and surveyed the banks of the semi-frozen lake, where tiny water voles scurried in terror, their predator radar warning of his presence. He understood what Owen was saying. He didn't like it one bit, but he understood it. He flew from Owen's hand down to a tussock of grass and then shifted to a boy, once more shivering in his pyjamas. His feet ached instantly as he hadn't thought to pull his moccasin slippers on before going after Owen.

'How did they do it?'

Owen dropped his eyes to his gloves and focused on rubbing them together for warmth. The scent of his discomfort pulsed through the air towards Dax.

'How?'

'It was the colds.'

'The colds?' For a second Dax didn't know what he meant—and then it clicked. 'You mean—we got those colds deliberately?'

'Yes. You were all given a virus in your food. Nothing dangerous—just something that would make you feel ropy enough to have a few extra hours in bed, during class time. Then Janey gave you medicine—all at different times of course. It was effective against the virus, but more importantly it was a drug to put you under.'

Dax saw his breath puff out of him in the air again—a visible cloud of his shock—as his insides clenched.

'Once you were fully unconscious, the chips were inserted under your skin with a needle and the puncture wound coated in a strong antibiotic spray, so there would be no visible sign of infection afterwards. They had to work hard on yours, making sure the tracker frequency was beyond the pick-up of fox hearing. The others were easier. They didn't bother with Clive. No need. Still gave him the cold though, for good measure, in case his clever little mind caught on to anything. They had to work beyond the scope of all his gadgets too, to make sure he didn't pick up any tracker signals.'

Dax seemed to have too much saliva in his mouth. He gulped, several times, and then spat into the grass. He was shaking with horror. Even Janey was in on it. It was just—just—typical!

As soon as someone in his life appeared to be trustworthy, something bitter and dark came along to remind him not to be so stupid. Nobody could be trusted. *Nobody.*

Dax felt his mouth puckering around his furious words. 'Get them out.' It came out as a fox-like growl.

'I can't, Dax,' said Owen.

'You can! You got *mine* out! Get them all out!'

'I shouldn't have done that,' said Owen. 'I apologize. When I came back from seeing Chambers that night I was furious about it. They got me out of the way, deliberately, you see. Sent me off on some errand to Whitehall to see him and some other officials while they got on with their plan, because they knew I would be difficult about it. Chambers let something slip, and then I realized they'd gone ahead with it.

'I was furious and I wanted to do something, and when I saw you moving on the edge of the woods I took action; got into my whites, so the guards wouldn't spot me, and came after you to dig that bloody thing out of you. But I should not have done it. It was a ridiculous, emotional response and I won't let that happen again. I've put you in a very difficult position—because I *can't* take out everyone's chips. For a start most of them would freak out if I even tried, and then the Cola families would get to hear about it—they'd be up in arms and everyone's security would be compromised. And it would be down to me and the stupid actions of Thursday night. I'm not invincible, Dax. And I'm not irreplaceable.'

Dax put his face in his hands. Owen was clever. He knew to save his most convincing argument until last. Dax could not imagine life without Owen. Did not want to. He could rail against him, shout at him, sulk at him, bite him, rip him with his talons, accuse him of anything—and still know that they were OK. There was no other adult in his life like Owen.

'Sorry, Dax. You can't tell them. It's the right thing to do—for now at least. Please. Do it for me.'

'I hate you.' said Dax.

'I know,' said Owen.

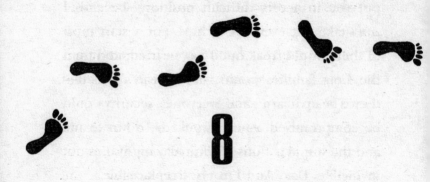

8

'Tree house—four o'clock,' muttered Gideon, as he edged past Lisa's desk. 'Tell Mia. Urgent meeting.'

He reached his desk and nodded across at Dax. 'Done.' Dax nodded back. He and Gideon had been looking at the Neetanite again that morning and had decided that Lisa and Mia should know about it. The four of them had been through so much together that it seemed wrong *not* to tell them about something so amazing. And Dax hoped that maybe Lisa could pick up something by touching the thing.

Lisa was looking at him now. She arched her eyebrows and sent: *Urgent meeting? What's going on?*

He grinned back at her and sent back: *Wait and see!*

She huffed and tossed her head, sending her blonde hair back over her shoulder as she leaned across to speak to Mia.

The door opened but, instead of Mrs Dann, in came Mr Eades, the grey man who usually sat in on Dax's development sessions, either in the room with him and Owen or behind the mirrored viewing glass at one end. It was hard to imagine Mr Eades ever laughing out loud. The man had witnessed the most amazing scenes, but he always behaved as if he were taking notes at the annual general meeting of the Society of Accountants. Even there a normal person might smile once in a while.

'Mrs Dann is required elsewhere today,' said Mr Eades in a voice like dry leaves rasping together in a light autumn wind. He regarded them coldly through his metal-rimmed spectacles. 'I will take history this afternoon. However, before I start, I would like to give you some *good* news.' Oddly, his emphasis on the word 'good' suggested a sense of humour, freeze-dried, as if he knew what a let down his arrival was. 'On account of several weeks of good behaviour, and the success of a recent expedition to Keswick, the Cola Project has decided you deserve some time to . . . er . . . let down your hair.'

They all looked at each other, eyes wide with wonder at what was coming next.

'There is a school not far from here—mixed—which is due to have a half term *discotheque*,' intoned Mr Eades, as if a half term discotheque was some kind of unpleasant but necessary medical procedure. 'Mrs Sartre has been to meet the head teacher and arranged for all of you to go along and . . . er . . . *enjoy* yourselves.' He sounded as if he severely doubted this possibility. 'With, of course, all the necessary security procedures in place.'

There was a collective gasp. A *disco*? With other kids of their own age? Barry gave a small whoop and Alex and Jacob did a high five. Jennifer, Mia, and Lisa began to whisper earnestly about what they would wear.

'The event is at the end of this week, on Thursday evening from seven p.m., and you will be taken from here at six-thirty p.m.,' announced Mr Eades. 'There will be no displays of any kind, or you will face severe penalties—all of you. Is that clear?'

Everyone simmered down and nodded gravely, but grins re-emerged fast. A night out being normal! It was incredibly exciting.

'Now. The economic state of Germany between the wars and how it led to the rise of Hitler,' warned Mr Eades and the lesson, like a bulldog clip on the soul, began to pinch.

'OK, what's the drama?' said Lisa, as she hauled herself up into the tree house. 'And couldn't you have found a warmer place to tell us?'

Mia followed her up and the two girls perched on the little stools, bashing their gloved hands together. After a few seconds Lisa took off her left glove and said, 'Oh, Mia, would you? I'm going to get frostbite!'

Mia smiled and took her hand. 'Come on, all of you, then,' she said, and Dax and Gideon quickly ungloved a hand and put it on top of Mia's and Lisa's. Mia closed her eyes and an incredible pulse of warmth passed through them all, chasing the icy chill right off the edges of the wooden platform.

'Oooh, that's good!' beamed Lisa.

'Doesn't make *you* get colder, does it?' asked Dax.

Mia shook her head. 'No, I've harnessed all your own energy to do it. It doesn't sap mine.' And she did look fine. A year ago she might well have ended up blue with cold, unable to stop giving away too much of herself, but these days she was excellent at containing her powers so that she did not overstretch. She had nearly killed herself that way in the first few weeks that Dax had known her.

'So—what's going on?' demanded Lisa, and Dax dug the Neetanite out of his pocket.

'What is it?' Lisa took it in her hands and turned it over, fascinated. 'It weighs much less than it looks like it would,' she said. 'Oh! *Gideon!*' The Neetanite, after a few seconds tolerating Lisa's scrutiny, had once again begun to roll back to Dax.

'Not me!' said Gideon, holding up his hands and shaking his head. 'Dax!'

'Dax?' echoed Lisa. 'You telling me he's turning tele?'

'No,' laughed Dax. 'It's just what this thing

104

does. We've called it Neetanite, after my mum, Anita. It's from her.' Lisa and Mia looked at him, wide-eyed. Something from a Cola mother! Dax and Gideon told them about the letter from Robert Jones and their trip to Keswick.

'So this bloke who you've never met before just gave it to you?' asked Lisa, as Mia held the Neetanite, which allowed her a few seconds before starting on its journey back to Dax. 'Who was he? Why did your dad give it to him?'

'I think he's someone my dad knew on the oil rigs,' said Dax. 'Must have left the North Sea and set up a shop instead . . . my dad must have realized his mate's shop was close to where we are. He said he didn't want to risk bringing it in himself. All the security stuff and that.'

'How would he know? He's never been.' Lisa didn't mean to be unkind, but her bluntness still made him wince.

'We've been trying to work out what the markings on the side mean,' Dax went on, the Neetanite now back in his palm. He showed them and they squinted at the curious symbols. 'Clive has made a copy and he's going see what he can find out. He reckons there are books in the library with all kinds of writing in them. Luke is helping him go through them. Can you pick up anything from it, Lees?'

Lisa pulled a face and prodded a varnished finger at the lilac-grey barrel. She closed her eyes and for a few seconds everyone held their breath.

She opened her eyes. 'Nope.'

'What—nothing?' squawked Gideon. 'Nothing at all?'

'I'm not a psychic vending machine!' snapped Lisa. 'If I say there's nothing, there's nothing!'

Dax felt a stab of disappointment. He had really been hoping that this strange talisman might have led to something more. In his wildest dreams he thought it might possibly open—finally—some communication between the Colas and one Cola mum. This had never happened yet. None of the mediums, even the others he'd spoken to before their power was wiped out by Catherine, had ever made contact with any Cola mums. Dax felt abandoned.

'So what is it *for* then?' he said and his voice was bitter. 'Just a nice little keepsake? There's not even a letter from her. A few words. She could have left me a few words!'

106

The others looked at him and said nothing. He knew that every one of them had thought something similar over the years.

'They died suddenly,' offered Mia. 'They just didn't get the chance.'

'Yeah!' grunted Dax. 'Like they knew nothing about it!'

Lisa wrapped her arms around her knees and looked at him thoughtfully. 'You think they all knew—our mums? You think they knew what was coming?'

'Yeah, I do,' said Dax. 'And they obviously thought they were better off out of it.'

Again, nobody spoke.

After tea Dax sought out Clive. He found him, again, in the lab and again Barry was with him. Clive was charring a cake over a Bunsen burner and writing down his findings while Barry looked as if he might be about to cry. A smell of burning sugar and butter filled the room pleasantly but to Barry it was torture.

'I can't believe you really did that,' he murmured miserably as he kept a vigil beside the blackening, shrinking, flaming bun.

'Well, I make it a staggering four hundred and thirty-two calories,' noted Clive. 'That's one calorific cake! I have saved you from thirty grams of fat!'

Barry looked very much as if he did not want to be saved.

'I will organize an eating plan for you, based on the average calorie content of school meals, and then we can work in an exercise regime.'

Barry groaned. His grey eyes rested mournfully on the crunchy black remains of his cake and he shook his head. 'I only said my belt wouldn't do up,' he whimpered.

'And that's where it all starts!' chirruped Clive.

Dax patted Barry on the shoulder. 'Never mind, mate. You can always do a vanish and creep back to the kitchen in the night.'

'That's exactly what he *can't* do!' Clive stuffed his hands into his brown nylon trouser pockets and looked at Dax triumphantly over the top of his glasses. 'I've set up a laser trip and an alarm will go off if he sneaks off down the corridor beyond the toilets.'

'But what if someone else goes through it?'

'Won't go off. It's keyed in to Barry's specific mass, bodyweight, and heat signature.'

Barry sighed. 'Give it up, mate. He's got me clobbered. It's probably for the best.' He surveyed his podgy middle and plump chest. 'I'm getting man boobs!'

Clive looked at his watch. 'You've got time to get to the gym before bed,' he pointed out. 'Don't forget to work through the exercises we wrote down—to the letter! No shirking. I'll be down to check on you shortly. You'll be an Adonis six weeks from now.'

'A dough*nut* more like . . . ' muttered Barry and wandered off.

Dax peered after him and then back at Clive. 'What's an Adonis?'

'The epitome of fit and handsome,' said Clive, taking off his glasses and wiping the lenses with the hem of his stripy yellow shirt. 'Of course, he'll never look as good as *me* . . . ' he grinned, well aware of his own odd looks, 'but I don't want to crush his hopes.'

'Have you had a chance to look up the writing?' asked Dax.

'Hmmm. I have. Luke and I spent some time on it. Very curious.'

'What did you find out?' Dax pictured the two

bespectacled boys poring through page after page of reference books—Gideon had told Luke about the Neetanite the previous evening.

'Luke found out nothing, got bored and went off to read more Dickens,' said Clive. 'I found out that it's not any alphabet I can find.'

'What—none of them?'

Clive put his glasses back on and his eyes loomed large and grey at Dax.

'Nope. Sorry. I've been through everything in the library and although it's quite similar to one or two ancient texts, it's not the same. Of course, if I was allowed onto the internet I could search further, but as you know, I can't. The books here are pretty thorough though. I think you may just have a random set of squiggles.'

'No! Not possible. It has to mean something.'

Clive smiled and rubbed his nose. He was over his cold at last, but seemed to have picked up a nose rubbing habit. 'Not everything means something, Dax. No matter how much you want it to.'

Dax flopped onto a high stool next to the lab work surface. He rested his forehead on his arms and sighed.

'Why don't you ask Owen? See if he can get the scientists to look it up? Erm . . . perhaps not then,' added Clive as Dax looked up at him with a jaded expression. Clive nodded and said, 'No, I wouldn't either. It would help if we ever *met* them, of course.'

The scientists who studied them never had contact with them. To stay objective, they remained unseen behind the mirror glass of the development rooms, watching and note-taking but never building up a relationship with the Colas. Mr Eades was the link between the school and the scientists. They had heard that underground passages led into the basement from another complex behind Fenton Lodge—a low building a quarter of a mile away, built of the same pale golden rock as the lodge, with a matching slate roof. Occasionally Colas did see people getting into military escort vehicles and driving in and out of the estate, but always at a distance. Dax had seen them better than anyone else, of course, scanning high overhead, his astonishing peregrine sight picking out the detail, but they were all fairly unremarkable to look at. Around six or seven men and women who took shifts. He had not been able to see inside the scientists' building. The windows were covered with blinds at all times.

'But I certainly wouldn't trust people I couldn't even talk to,' continued Clive. 'I mean, I understand the need for professional detachment, but it's still sinister, don't you think? What are they planning, eh? That's what I'd like to know.'

Dax didn't look at him. 'I try not to think about it,' he said, studying his hands. 'Anyway, don't worry about it. And thanks for looking through all those alphabets. You'd better check on Barry.'

'Heavens, yes—he's probably eating the paper towels by now!' Clive hurried towards the door.

'Is it the disco that's got him all worried?' asked Dax.

'Oh yes,' said Clive, pausing in the doorway. 'He can't fit into his dancing trousers. I don't even *possess* dancing trousers. I don't possess dancing *legs*,' he added. 'I move like a damp cardboard box in a strong wind . . . It's going to be torment.'

9

Operation Normal School Disco took over everyone's lives that week. Thursday night was the main topic of conversation at every meal and in every corner of the common room. Lisa, Mia, and Jennifer were in a clothes swapping frenzy and Lisa was desperately hoping that her father could get some outfit delivered to her in time.

'It's black jeans, really soft, hand-stitched denim, with these little silver chains sewn in down the legs,' she was explaining to Mia and Jennifer. 'And a black and silver T-shirt—Dolce and Gabbana—limited edition. And some amazing boots—Jimmy Choos.'

'Bless you,' said Gideon as he wandered past.

'Ah—ah—aaah—*Jimmy Choos! Jimmy Choos! Jimmy Choos!* Oh, by doze! I deed a dissue—and can someone mix me up some Dolce and Gabbana for this rash . . . ?'

Lisa flung a book at his head. It struck him on the temple because he'd been too busy with his high fashion cold routine to see it coming and stop it. 'So what are *you* going to wear?' she sneered, folding her cashmere clad arms. 'Woolworth's Ladybird range? It probably still fits.'

'You're a snob, you know that?'

'And you're a slob, so we're equal.'

'What, me? Equal to the honourable Lisa Hardman? Oh, thank you, m'lady. Thank you, but I cannot be worthy.' Gideon made bowing and scraping and tugging of forelock movements.

Lisa sat down on one of the sofas and wiped her hand over her brow. 'Oh all *right*!' she muttered, but she wasn't talking to Gideon. 'Get *on* with it then,' she invited, reluctantly. Obviously some spirit wasn't willing to wait until her next Development session to start putting a message across. Lisa carried on holding her head, her eyes closed and an expression of distaste on her pretty face. She clicked the fingers of one hand imperiously, and Mia opened a drawer in a nearby desk and pulled out some pink slips, with Spirit Communication Notice printed on them, and a pen. Lisa began to scribble at amazing speed as soon as she had the pen and paper. For the next ten minutes she was absorbed in nodding and sighing and occasionally yelping as she made her notes. 'Oh, stop it!' she said at one point. 'That's really not necessary. I don't want to see that. And *you*—' she turned and looked right at Dax but he soon realized she was looking at some invisible heckler in front of him, rather unnervingly, 'can watch your language!'

Lisa slapped another pink slip onto the low table. 'Oh, now they're *all* coming!' she wailed. 'That's what you get for being soft and helping one of them out after hours. Yes, yes, all right. Just—get into a queue! I'm not a rugby club barmaid! *Oh!*'

This last exclamation was filled with genuine shock. Lisa's eyes sprang open and she looked around her in great surprise and then up at Mia with confusion. 'They've gone,' she said, in a whisper. She began to look all around her, eyes darting from corner to corner, from the floor to the ceiling. 'They really have! They've gone!'

Mia sat next to her and touched her head lightly. 'You feeling OK?'

'OK? I feel *great*! My head has never been so quiet! Wow!' Lisa's eyes glittered. 'I can't believe it. So quiet . . . I . . . it hasn't been this quiet since . . . well, since I wasn't a Cola.'

'Do you think Sylv has done it for you?' asked Mia. Lisa was always going on at her spirit guide about getting better protection from the more enthusiastic members of the great beyond, whose nagging drove her to distraction. Sometimes Sylv tamped them down for a while—seemed to be able to hold the heaving, clamouring crowd of spirits behind a stout wooden door for an hour or two, so Lisa could pretend she was almost normal.

'I think she must have! Wow! What a star! I'll never call you a mouthy trollop again, Sylv, I promise!' Lisa leaped to her feet, pink and delighted. 'Come on—I don't know how long it'll last. Let's go and practise make-up, like real girls!' She and Mia and Jennifer rushed from the room, giggling and shrieking.

116

'They're real girls, all right,' said Gideon, darkly. 'Who else could get that excited about *shoes*?' Luke, sitting on the couch by the fire with his book (he had finished his last Dickens and was now on to the next), prodded Gideon in the back and signed something at him with a wry smile.

'What's he say?' asked Dax, resolving, for the hundredth time, to learn signing himself.

'He wants to know what *we're* going to wear,' said Gideon. 'Don't worry, mate. It doesn't matter. The girls are going to fall at our feet anyway. What girl can resist the Reader boys, eh? Especially you. When they find out you can't talk they'll be in a complete frenzy.' Luke laughed—a few out-breaths and a flinging back of his head. He was a nice-looking boy, as was Gideon, but without a hint of Gideon's conceit.

'You'll do all right too,' Gideon assured Dax. 'Even if you are a bit weedy. You need to eat more beef. Or pigeon.' Dax elbowed him. He hadn't eaten a pigeon for months. He really tried not to hunt when he was shapeshifted, even though the urge was sometimes incredibly strong. He loved wild birds and animals—even insects—and really didn't think it was right to snack on them between meals.

But they went up to look at their own wardrobes anyway, picking half-heartedly through the clothes hanging there. Luke came into their bedroom with an armful of garments and dumped them on Dax's bed. He shrugged and lifted his palms. He clearly wasn't impressed with what he'd got. Cola Club provided them with clothes, along with their own stuff from home. The college clothes were practical and hardwearing—jeans and sweatshirts, army-style canvas trousers, and T-shirts. At the first college, back in Cornwall, they had had a proper uniform, but that was when there had been more than a hundred Colas—and groups of them had regularly been allowed out unaccompanied to the local village at weekends. The uniform had been necessary.

Here, though, nobody ever went out unaccompanied, and when they did get taken out, the last thing anyone wanted was for them to be identified and connected with the mysterious, remote lodge deep in the Lake District with state-of-the-art security and no visible link with the national grid or telephone network.

Dax put a much smaller pile of stuff on his own bed. It was fortunate that Cola Club did provide clothes because he'd had nothing at all given to him from home since he left it, apart from one incredibly hideous blue and yellow woolly jumper which Gina had claimed to have knitted for him. Dax had been able to tell from the smell that it had not come from his old home, but a jumble sale or charity shop. It lay screwed up at the bottom of his wardrobe.

'It's not great, is it?' muttered Gideon. 'Unless we want to go over there looking like a boy scouts' expedition. Is the scouting look *in,* by any chance?'

Dax laughed and shook his head. 'I haven't a clue. I didn't pick up *Mutant Teen Fashion Weekly* while we were in Keswick. Did you?'

'Oh yeah, I did!' grinned Gideon. 'It said skinny dark-haired blokes who eat spiders are all the rage and mute blond boys with glasses and classic books spot-welded to their armpits are causing a stir on the Paris catwalks!' Luke booted his brother in the backside.

'Oi! Come and see this!' Barry suddenly barged in, waving excitedly with stumps. In his excitement his hands had faded from view. 'They've got stuff for us! Stuff we can wear!'

Dax, Gideon, and Luke joined Barry and Clive as they thundered downstairs to see what was happening. In the wide reception hall, Owen and Mrs Dann were dumping carrier bags—dozens of them—on the polished stone floor. Darren and Spook were already pawing through them and Jennifer was running upstairs to get Lisa and Mia.

'We thought it was probably about time you had some new stuff,' said Owen, smiling broadly. 'You'll find your names pinned to your bags. You can swap stuff around if you want to, but these are sorted out according to size. Barry, I reckon you're stuck with whatever we've chosen for you. I don't think anyone else can swap with you!'

Barry wasn't in the least bit offended. He seized his bags with a whoop and pulled out a dark blue shirt with zip pockets. Dax had no idea what the latest fashions were, but it looked pretty good to him. Soon all the Colas had arrived, amid shouts of excitement.

'Oh, great,' muttered Lisa, gingerly picking up her bags as if they were filled with rotten eggs. 'Party clothes chosen by Enid Blyton and Action

Man!' Dax nudged her hard in the ribs and she glared at him, but then her look softened as she peered into one of the bags and had to admit that what the teachers had bought was quite good. 'Anyway, my own stuff will be here tomorrow,' she said. Dax marvelled at how spoilt she was, even after nearly three years in Cola Club.

'Will it do then?' Owen was watching him as he looked in his own bags. New black jeans, a green soft sweatshirt and lace-up black suede boots had emerged so far. Dax nodded, thrilled at the new clothes, but as he looked up at Owen he felt his grin change to a tight smile. The Secret hung between them, messing everything up. Owen's smile faded too and he nodded at Dax and moved away.

At lunchtime on the Thursday there was a Disco Meeting in the library, which all the Colas had to attend. They were all there early, edgy and full of happy anticipation. Lisa's clothes had arrived that morning, by special delivery at the security gate. She was delighted. Everyone else had been through all their new gear like fashion-hungry locusts. There had been frenzied trying-on sessions, lots of swapping and bargaining, and at least one top ripped in half—but everyone now seemed to be very happy with what they were wearing that night. Even though, as Jennifer pointed out, they would probably look as if they'd walked straight out of a catalogue!

'This stuff is all shiny and new. How uncool is that?' she sighed, but she was smiling happily. Nobody really minded. After all, in disco lights, who was going to notice? 'Just make sure you take the price tags and the shoe labels off!' added Jennifer.

The babble quietened as the library door opened and the dampening presence of Mr Eades arrived. He walked in and nodded to them all to sit down. They did so, finding perches on the leather library chairs, the windowsill, and the low reading table. Mrs Dann and Mr Tucker followed Mr Eades in, and leaned against the bookshelves as the grey man stood motionless, holding a sheaf of folders and a ruler and waiting for complete silence.

'Tonight,' he began, in the voice of an exam invigilator, 'is an important night for you all. Not only is it a recreational opportunity for you, it also provides you with a chance to mix with normal children—and most importantly, to prove your-selves worthy of the trust of the Cola Project.'

Everyone shuffled and looked around the room.

'I need hardly remind you of the gravity of the situation *if* only *one* of you exhibits even the *tiniest amount* of Cola power. The effect will be instant. A six month ban—for *every student*—on any outside expeditions of any kind. Do I make myself clear?'

There was a rumble of 'Yes, sirs' and Mr Eades swept the room with his cold, bespectacled gaze. He nodded. 'Good. I see that you do. Now, here are the rules. No Cola powers, as previously stated. You must also take care not to speak in any detail about Fenton Lodge and the nature of the grounds, the interior, your teachers, the secu-rity aspects, your home addresses, your personal histories or anything pertaining to the secretive nature of your school life.

'You will not talk about telepathy, about glamour, about healing, about psychic ability. You will refrain from discussing telekinesis, shapeshifting, mimicry, and world famous magi-cians.' Spook folded his arms and huffed quietly next to Darren. 'You will not talk about the internet or lack of access to it, you will not talk about Cornwall or Tregarren College or tidal waves. You may discuss pop music. You may talk about people in the popular press. A selection of highly unedifying teen magazines are available for your perusal, in the common room, so you may acquaint yourselves with these unsavoury characters. You may discuss broad-ranging politics, but no particular issues—obviously nothing regarding any aspects of the Ministry of Defence.'

'Can we talk about fish?' Gideon blurted out, suddenly. 'Is fish safe? I mean . . . if I really *can't* talk about the Ministry of Defence at a disco, at *least* I should be able to talk fish!'

Mr Eades's stare was like a laser beam of disdain. Gideon snorted once and then bit his lip.

'You seem to think that the security of your fellow Colas is something to laugh about, Mr Reader,' said Mr Eades, sounding his s's like an angry snake. 'Need I remind you that you and several of your friends have come very close to being drowned, electrocuted, shot, buried alive, and, indeed, crucified in the past two or three years?'

Dax felt himself flush and he instinctively crossed his hands over his upper arms, where ragged pink scars could still be seen if he wore short sleeves. A vision sliced through his mind, of a dizzying blur of colours, along with the desperate sensation of spinning and rising and falling. He grasped the corner of the leather wing chair he was perched on, next to Clive, and steadied his breathing. He hadn't had nightmares for quite a while now, but the flashbacks still happened from time to time. Mia had offered to work on his scars—to reduce them to nothing—but Dax wouldn't let her. They were a visible reminder of something he needed to remember. That the girl who had so horrifically injured him was still out there. That this must never be forgotten.

'Sorry, sir,' Gideon was muttering. The last horror in Mr Eades's list had affected him too, Dax realized. *Catherine—the gift that kept on giving.*

'So—having refreshed your memory—I need hardly add that tonight's outing, while intended to be an evening of fun and relaxation for you all, is a manoeuvre of the most stringent security. No Cola will leave the school gymnasium complex unescorted. No Cola will enter the school grounds

125

after safe delivery to the gymnasium. Every Cola will check in with a teacher once every thirty minutes. There will be no misbehaviour and no untoward physical contact with any pupil from Derwent Secondary.

'Dancing, however, *will* be allowed. I do hope,' he eyed them all with a face like cold leather, 'that you enjoy yourselves.'

Mr Eades left the room and everybody— including Mr Tucker and Mrs Dann—let out a sigh of relief.

'Right,' said Mrs Dann, rubbing her hands together briskly and smiling. 'To important matters. Your new gear. You like it? Does everyone feel suitably cool and trendy?' There was a gale of laughter from the Colas and happy excitement bounced back out once more from beneath the chairs and behind the curtains.

'Good!' said Mrs Dann. 'Because I'm not going in for the Teen Fashion Retail Olympics again in a hurry!'

Mr Tucker was also smiling. 'Have a great time tonight. You deserve it. And don't worry—I don't *think* the youth of Derwent is about to grill you about national security over a Panda Pop.

The coach will be ready at six thirty—don't be late. You want to wring as much fun out of this as you can. And don't forget those unedifying pop magazines in the common room,' he called out, as they began to leave. 'The Celebrity *Who's Snogged Who?* column in *Tat Magazine* is particularly illuminating . . . '

10

Operation Normal School Disco Phase Two was everyone getting into their new clothes and all the girls in a hair and make-up frenzy. Phase Three was getting on to the coach and chattering non-stop about what was happening, where they were going, what the other kids would be like, whether the music would be any good.

Clive, looking unusually cool in a metallic grey sweatshirt, jeans, and fashionable trainers, stood up in the aisle as the coach wound along the gritted roads between the Cumbrian hills.

'OK—here is your test. Pay attention, every-body, or you'll fail in your mission to be normal for one evening.'

The babble quietened down a bit. Clive held a clipboard with notes attached to it.

'Question one: which popular music act is currently at number one in the UK charts?'

There was some earnest discussion.

'Warm Game!' shouted Darren.

'Nope,' said Clive. 'They're at number five.'

'Fuse!' tried Alex.

'Close, they're at number two. Good work!'

'Freezing Primates!' shouted Gideon.

'Oh, don't be so ridiculous,' snapped Lisa, peering at her reflection in the dark coach window and adjusting her hair.

'Freezing Primates—correct!' Clive pencilled a tick next to question one. '*Do* try to remember everyone! The song is called "Catsick".'

Everyone stared at Clive. 'Only kidding,' he chortled. 'It's called "You're a Carpet". No, really—it is!'

Lisa leaned over and snatched Clive's clipboard off him, scanning it impatiently. 'All right, let's get on with it. Latest Bond movie—who's the Bond girl?'

Clive wrenched his notes back off her with a

huff as various guesses—all wrong—were hurled around the bus.

'OK,' he sighed. 'Gadgets. Anyone know what a B-Nut is? A Game-Slider Two? A Ninsobo Prism? Trading cards . . . Yootoogo? Fateweavers? KickSquad?'

Some of the boys got one or two right and the girls were quite good on the celebrity gossip. Mia knew that Fay Chandler, the supermodel, had had her nose done; Lisa was aware of the 'Hat Pin Dress' worn by actress Jennifer Polez—a sensation at the Oscars apparently.

Dax knew nothing about any of it. He had meant to look at the magazines, but hadn't found time. He wasn't sure he could have retained any of this stuff if he had. It seemed like notes from another world—not a world where your mates had a tendency to vanish or spin the hands of the school clock with a hard stare, where a small lump of unidentifiable stuff followed you about and clung to you like a pet, where children had microchips inserted into their heads in their sleep. His world was strange, but the normal world seemed stranger.

Clive, who had an almost photographic

memory, was listing the answers now, and making everyone repeat them back to him. Even Spook was joining in, although he was trying to look sarcastic.

'Well,' said Clive, when they'd repeated everything on his list. 'If you can all remember *that* for the next three hours, you might pass for something approaching normal. Good luck everyone.'

Owen, Mrs Dann, Mr Tucker, Mr Eades, and Paulina Sartre were all travelling with them and most of them seemed hugely amused at Clive's checklist. Tyrone was staying at the lodge, still recovering from his cold. As if five teachers weren't enough, there were also three soldiers on the coach, on guard duty. Dax knew two of them by name, having seen and heard them in discussion with Owen and Mr Eades in the past. The heavy-set one with light brown hair and hard grey eyes was Weston. The taller, darker one was Armitage. The third man—well-built and West Indian—he recognized as one of the duty patrol at the security gate. All three were dressed normally, in casual clothes, but again, Dax could smell the oil on their guns. He wondered if the headteacher of

Derwent Secondary had any idea that the SAS was popping in for a disco that evening.

The school was very ordinary looking—much like the secondary school which Dax would have gone to back in Bark's End, if he hadn't started turning into a fox. It was a low-level, 1970s building, painted white and grey-blue, with a large tarmac playground and a muddy sports field beyond. Coloured lights flickered at the high windows of the school gymnasium and groups of teenagers were heading in through the double doors, handing over tickets and laughing together. Dax felt the hairs stand up on the back of his neck. He was quite nervous. It had been such a long time since he'd been with normal people. 'B-Nut, Ninsobo Prism,' he found himself muttering. 'You're a Carpet.'

'No need to get personal,' said Owen, as he stepped off the coach behind Dax and patted his shoulder. 'Don't worry about any of that. Just have a good time.' He smiled at him and Dax smiled back. It didn't work very well. He was still upset with Owen and he knew Owen was still anxious about him. He was trying to make it right. Dax wasn't used to Owen being anything less than totally confident with him. He did not like any of this.

'OK, lads, Operation Impress The Normal Girls,' said Gideon, slapping his arms around Dax's and Luke's shoulders. 'They're not going to know what's hit them!'

The gym was throbbing with chart music—very little of which Dax recognized—and pulsating with disco lights. The smell was intense. It took Dax straight back to his old days at Bark's End Junior—the sugar paper, the disinfectant, the rubbery smell of the PE equipment pushed against the walls. The smell of other—normal—teenagers was also heady. A host of different perfumes, from deodorant to hair gel to washing powder, assaulted his nose. He wondered if all the Colas now smelt exactly the same, the way families do—smelt of Fenton Lodge and each other—and if the others could smell how alien they were, out in the normal world.

Lisa, Mia, and Jennifer stuck together in a little huddle, glancing around at the other girls and checking out what they were wearing. Dax thought, proudly, that the Cola girls all looked great. Lisa's expensive clothes glittered and her long hair was snagged through with strands of silver thread, woven in cleverly. She looked utterly confident as she moved casually to the music. Jennifer was wearing a short red dress, her brown hair up in a spiky bunch and the mascara which Lisa had put on her making her eyes look quite startling behind her glasses. Mia wore a midnight blue dress, which hung wispily to her knees. She looked tall and elegant.

Gideon was already chatting to a couple of girls and introducing them to Luke. The girls looked fascinated as he explained his brother's handicap and then began to teach them ways to sign, so they could communicate with him through the loud music. Barry and Clive stood a little way off, clutching a can of lemonade each. They were trying desperately to look cool and comfortable, but Dax could see the whites of their eyes and noticed that Barry was beginning to jig along to the music self-consciously, with random giggles rattling across the top of his can. Dax went over and clapped them both on the shoulders, trying to be like Gideon. 'How you doing?' he said and they both smiled weakly at him. 'Yeah . . . ' said Dax, looking around him with a fixed grin. 'I know.'

Spook didn't seem to have any self-conscious-ness at all. He strode through the hall with Darren trailing him, and Dax was irritated to notice a couple of girls paying him some attention as he went. In the blue and orange glare from the disco lights console, Spook suddenly turned and smiled at the girls, raising one eyebrow and holding out his hand. They giggled and stared. Dax and Barry and Clive all groaned aloud. 'He's doing tricks!' muttered Barry, unhappily. 'It's not fair! He's not allowed!'

'He's *only* doing tricks though,' said Dax. 'Just the stuff he's learnt out of books and kits and stuff. I suppose that's allowed.'

Gideon and Luke joined the knot of uneasy Colas and peered over at Spook too as the boy picked something out of one giggling girl's ear—a golden egg, it looked like—and the small, fasci-nated group around him became a little bigger.

'Show-offy git,' said Gideon. 'Come on, Luke—we can do better than that!' He yanked his twin down the room and began to engage one of Spook's audience, introducing her to Luke, who looked resigned to being Gideon's prop. The girl's friend turned around too and Spook shot an annoyed glance at the twins as their sideshow stole his limelight. Dax laughed to himself and went to the canteen window, which had been adapted to a soft drinks and snacks bar for the night.

Around the room Dax could sense the quickening of interest in the Colas. Girls were approaching Lisa and Mia and Jennifer now, exchanging a few words and looks, and then wandering off. Boys were watching them more closely and talking amongst themselves, daring each other to talk to the good looking blonde one. Lisa was playing with her hair, pretending not to notice, but she was hugely enjoying the attention.

Before long, one of the boys ventured across the dance floor, which was half filled with groups of girls all doing the same actions to some song they obviously knew well, and started to chat up Lisa. Lisa posed, one hand hooked into the pocket of her black jeans, and started to talk back to him, while Mia and Jennifer exchanged embarrassed smiles. Of course, in a matter of seconds, the boy began to glance across at Mia. Once, twice, three times—and the fourth time for about thirty seconds, while Lisa stood, hands on hips, raising her eyes to the gym ceiling. Mia shrugged and looked apologetic. 'Sorry,' Dax saw her mouth, and she moved away—but the boy, and two of his mates now, just followed, staring dreamily at her.

Lisa looked very put out, but resigned to it. 'It wears *off*!' she shouted after the straggle of heartsick youths. She shook her head and went to get a drink too. 'And you can take *that* look off your face, Dax Jones!' she snapped as she bought a Coke.

'Sorry,' snorted Dax. Mia had gone to stand by Mrs Sartre and the boys had collected in a small, slightly confused cluster nearby. Mrs Sartre was looking very anxious and Dax suspected that the teachers had forgotten about the Mia Effect, having had three years to get used to it. The principal shepherded the reluctant siren out of the gym and a few minutes later it was Lisa who was of interest again. She was gracious about it. She knew Mia was impossible to resist at first, and now that it had apparently worn off, she was happy to be the centre of attention again.

The DJ began to talk into the microphone, over the music, his voice distorted and too loud.

He looked like a teacher pretending to be a DJ. He had on a T-shirt with the words 'Mad For It' across the chest and a severe centre parting in his greying hair. 'Bell then, bell then, boys and birls!' he boomed. 'Bet's see you ball on ba bancefloor! Wababout *bis* one!' A classic disco hit jangled out of the sound system with a thumping bass and about three more girls peeled themselves off a wall and jiggled across the floor. It was exactly the same as every disco Dax could remember going to—a mixture of keen excitement and extreme embarrassment.

Lisa had three boys chatting her up now. This didn't worry Dax. What did worry him were the four or five girls who stood a few feet away, talking earnestly among themselves and shooting Lisa black looks. One of them appeared to be in tears. Dax put down his Coke and lifted his chin, scenting the air. Amid the carnival of smells he picked up something new. Something that made him walk swiftly through the dancers towards the ring of girls. Resentment and anger was threading through the other scents—along with the sharp salt tang of fresh tears. Dax instinctively cocked his head a little to one side, filtering out the thudding of the music and babble of the crowd and seeking the note of the crying girl.

'*Shouldn't! He shouldn't've said it,*' he made out. And then, '*Stuck up cow.*' And '*Really thinks she's it!*'

'Hi, Lees—wanna dance?' said Dax, brightly, grabbing Lisa's arm and yanking her away from her admirers, who looked at each other and then back at him. Belligerence was rising.

'Oh lord,' muttered Dax as Lisa rounded on him with a face like a scalded cat.

'What are you *doing*?' she hissed. 'Did I say *yes*? What makes you think I want to stand around shuffling about to Abba with *you*?'

Dax grasped her by the elbows and turned her round the other way. 'Look—about one o'clock—little crowd of very angry girls. You're chatting up one of their boyfriends. I smell trouble.'

'Well, big deal! It's not like I'm *making* them chat me up. It's their choice. I'm not doing a "Mia", am I?'

'Erm . . . ' Dax grimaced as he looked back at the boys. Mia was heading towards him and Lisa now, and abruptly the angry muttering had ceased and there was a movement a bit like geese getting into formation as all of them wordlessly trooped after her, dazed and filled with unfathomable love.

Lisa glanced around. 'Oh, you have *got* to be kidding me!' Mia reached them, looking horribly embarrassed.

'I can't help it! I can't stop them!' she whispered. Jennifer now joined them, looking about her uneasily. Dax looked for teachers. He could make out Owen and Mrs Dann at the bar, passing drinks across to Mr Tucker and one of the disguised soldiers. In the far corner, behind the speakers, stood Mr Eades. He seemed to be watching them all, but he just foraged in his jacket pocket and made no move. Clearly the trouble Dax was picking up was all through his fox sense, and their chaperones hadn't noticed it at all yet.

'Come on,' said Lisa, pulling her elbows out of Dax's grasp. 'Girls' toilet—now!'

The three moved hurriedly through the dancers and made straight for the toilets. Dax stepped in front of the first boy in the pursuing queue. The boy, thankfully now dopey with Mia Effect, gaped at him, confused. The others cannoned into him, all wearing similar expressions.

Gideon and Luke, who had been deep into an elbow jabbing session with an aggravated Spook and Darren, broke away and came over towards them, looking curious.

'Everyone OK?' asked Dax, holding out both arms and containing the boys as they bumbled about, trying to see where Mia had gone. He clicked his fingers and several pairs of eyes wandered across to him. 'Oi! Over here! That's right. Do not be alarmed. You have been experiencing Mia Effect. It should wear off any time . . . ' he consulted his watch, nodded, and clapped his hands together again, 'now!'

'Hey!' shouted Gideon. 'Wanna skid? Bet you can't get to the ropes!' He and Luke immediately threw themselves, knees first, at the polished gym floor and skidded several feet across it. In two seconds the dopey boys had all woken up and were hurtling after them. Dax sighed with relief—but only once. Almost immediately he was shoved aside by a posse of angry girls, all heading towards the toilets.

He looked anxiously all around the room for Mrs Dann or the principal, but in the gloom and the thickening dance floor crowd, could see

141

neither. Now the posse was almost out of sight. He hurried after them, and tried to flash up a telepathic warning to Lisa, even though it was forbidden. *Very cheesed off girls incoming! Get out quick!* He got nothing back, which didn't surprise him. His telepathy out to Lisa was often patchy—a skill borrowed from his fox and falcon forms which was much more basic than the talent Lisa or Alex or Jacob had.

Dax skidded out of the gym and into the cool lobby where a couple of Derwent parents were greeting latecomers at the door. The scent of violence was strong to the left. He didn't even have to look. He began to run down the corridor, classroom doors and idling kids flashing past him on either side, until he reached the toilet block. A metre from the girls' door he drew up short. He couldn't go in *there*. A loud babble was emanating from it and Dax heard Lisa getting strident with someone. An ugly squabble of words bounced off the wall tiles—insults, sneers, and threats. Dax bashed against the wooden door. 'LISA! MIA!'

But the bickering voices rose and the accusations grew nastier and more spiteful and—oh no—that was *definitely* the sound of someone's hair being yanked off their scalp. He heard Lisa give a shriek of fury and then there was the unmistakable slap of flat palm on face. Someone gave a shout, trying to calm things down—Jennifer, he thought. Another voice said, 'Go and get Miss!' But nobody came out. A couple of boys emerged from the boys' toilet. Alex and Jacob. They stared at Dax and then listened intently.

'Girl fight!' murmured Jacob in appalled fascination.

'Go and get Mrs Dann or Mrs Sartre!' commanded Dax. 'Now! Go!' The brothers ran off back along the corridor to the gym.

There were now furious screams coming from behind the wooden door. Dax pounded on it again. 'LISA! MIA! I'M COMING IN!' He kicked the door open and as he did so there was a sudden thud of heat in his face which nearly knocked him on to his back.

The screams curdled from fury to terror.

11

Dax scrambled to his feet, gasping, and stared into the girls' toilets. A ball of flame was rolling around the ceiling, and its suspended tiles were dripping, molten, to the floor. About eight girls were in there and at least five of them were screaming. One girl was beating at her sleeve, which was charred and smoking. Lisa, Mia, and Jennifer were backed against the far wall of the white-tiled room, staring up, aghast, at the ball of flame.

Even as Dax caught his breath he was shoved aside and one of the disguised soldiers thundered into the room, followed by Owen. Both began hauling the terrified Derwent girls back out into the corridor, spreading their jackets over their heads to protect them from the dripping molten tiles. The ball of flame abruptly blew itself out over in a corner as Owen went back in for Jennifer. The soldier returned for Lisa, who was haring out towards him anyway, pulling a dazed Mia by the wrist. The expression on Lisa's face was terrible and at first Dax, standing back against the opposite wall and watching all this drama in amazement, could not understand why. She wasn't just frightened—she looked absolutely appalled, as if she had seen something she could not believe. And with everything Lisa had been forced to see in the past three years, it was hard to imagine what could have shocked her so.

Owen took Mia's arm and steered her to the wall next to Dax. 'Keep her here—sit her down,' he said. 'If she looks like she might faint make her lie down.' Dax nodded, gulping, and put a shaking hand on Mia's shoulder. Mia did not shake. She was as still as stone and looked as if she were sleepwalking.

More teachers arrived—from Derwent and from Fenton Lodge—and two of the soldiers stood at either end of the corridor, tensely scanning in all directions. Blankets and water and first aid kits were brought, but it turned out that nobody was actually hurt. The girl with the burnt sleeve was very shaken, but her skin was quite unmarked beneath the charred material.

'No, I don't think we need an ambulance,' Dax heard Owen saying. 'They're all a bit shocked but I think they're OK. We just need to find out what happened.'

But nobody seemed to know. The Derwent girls, between sobs, said they didn't know where the fire had come from.

'What was happening, just before the fire?' asked Mrs Dann, looking grey with worry as she glanced across to the Cola girls.

The Derwent girls shuffled. '*She* started it,' one of them muttered.

'They were having a fight,' Dax said, surprised to find his voice. 'I was outside—I heard. One of them—*her*, I think,' he pointed to the girl with the burnt sleeve, 'went for Lisa. Pulled her hair. And Lisa thumped her. It was all about someone's boyfriend, I think.'

The teachers—both sides—sighed and shook their heads.

'But the fire thing!' said one. 'What happened?'

'Hairspray,' said Lisa. She sounded very calm now. 'They were using hairspray while they were waiting for us to come out of the cubicles. They sprayed a load of it under the door at us. I think they thought it was funny. Someone must have— I don't know—made a spark or something.'

A pause greeted this and then some of the teachers nodded. 'That can happen,' said Mrs Dann. 'Especially on very cold, dry days like today has been. And they are wearing a lot of nylon, aren't they?'

'Should we sound the fire alarm?' asked another teacher.

'No need,' said Owen. 'It's all out and under control. Just make sure nobody comes down here and you can have the rest of your disco, I think. I reckon it's probably time *we* all headed back though. Mia—are you OK now?'

Mia, propping her forehead in her hands, nodded and then got to her feet. She no longer had that weird sleepwalking look, Dax was glad to see.

The trip back was very sober. Spook was

147

muttering angrily. He had just got into a slow dance with a good-looking Derwent girl who was impressed by his glitter-spraying sleeves, when he had been hauled away without ceremony. All the boys were agog to know what had happened in the girls' toilets but only Jennifer would talk about it and that was just to say, 'There was a bit of a fire—because of all the hairspray. That's all.'

Dax said nothing. He felt the Neetanite nestling against his chest through the inside pocket of his coat. He was relieved to be back among the world of the weird—away from the normal one and all its dangers. But he was also getting the first prickle of a very bad feeling. Something was out of kilter. Something not good was pressing into their lives. The microchips were awful and the strain between him and Owen was horrible— but now something else was coming. Something worse than all of these things. Dax rested his forehead against the cold bullet-proof glass of the coach window and wished and wished it was just tiredness after all the drama which was making his skin creep with fear.

It was only 9.30 p.m. when they climbed off the coach outside Fenton Lodge. If Operation

Normal School Disco had gone to plan, they'd still be at Derwent Secondary, dancing with ordinary kids and having a great time. Probably. By now everyone was silent. They remembered the warning Mr Eades had given. It hadn't gone to plan and if any of them turned out to be to blame they might not go out on another trip for months.

As Dax jumped down Lisa walked closely behind him, briefly touched his shoulder and sent him a message. *Come to our room at one a.m. I'll leave the window open.*

Dax kept on walking, his head down and his fur-lined hood up. He sent back: *All right. But don't freak when I wake you up.*

Lisa's message came back cold. *There's no way I will be asleep.*

Dax told Gideon everything he knew as they got into bed. There had been no dressing down or lectures from the teachers about what had happened. They genuinely did not *know* what had happened. At least that's the way it seemed. Dax himself did not know what had happened—he had only heard and smelt it.

'So—you're certain—they were really fighting? You know, not just flapping their fingers and squealing but actual punches?' Gideon looked both appalled and fascinated.

'It was real all right. Don't you remember that time when Lisa thumped Owen in the face, right back at Tregarren? She really knows how. I don't think she actually hit the girl hard, though, or there would've been a big bruise. And the girl *was* pulling her hair out.'

'All about boys, eh?' Gideon grinned and rubbed his hands together. 'Who'd've thought it? Lisa's a flirt!'

'Don't be daft,' said Dax. 'She was just trying to be normal, like we all were. Anyway, I don't even know if it was Lisa they were really having a go at or Mia. You saw the way all those boys were around her.'

Gideon nodded. 'It's not going to get any easier for her, is it?' he said. His amused expression dropped. 'I can't see us getting out with normal kids again, can you? Not unless we go AWOL.'

'Well, we can't,' snapped Dax. 'Don't even think about it.' His insides clenched as he thought about Gideon attempting to go absent without leave, just for a little fun, and getting tracked and snared back again by the SAS. He cursed Owen for making him promise; for using Dax's need of him as the perfect way to stop him telling the truth to his best friend.

They switched off their lamps and settled back into their beds.

'Any chance you can shut the window tonight?' mumbled Gideon from beneath his quilt. 'It's got to be ten below!'

Dax pulled the sash window further down but could not bring himself to close it totally. He could never close the thick velvet curtains either. He had to have the air in his face and the sky within sight. He wondered whether to tell Gideon about Lisa's message. Maybe they should both go along to the girls' end of the corridor and find out what she needed to say. But he knew the message was intended only for him.

He'd tell Gideon about it afterwards. In any case, Gideon had just done his amazing 'shot dead on a pillow' act and fallen asleep in three seconds flat.

Dax managed to sleep a little between 11 p.m.

and 1 a.m. He had no need of an alarm clock. His animal instincts were so finely tuned that all he had to do was repeat the time he needed to wake three times in his mind and he always woke on time. At exactly one minute to 1 a.m. his eyes sprang open. He took off his malachite bracelet and hid it under his pillow, and then shifted to DaxFalcon. Easing his pliable feathery body through the gap in the sash, he flew along between the window ledges until he arrived at the girls' room. As soon as his talons clutched the windowsill Lisa was on her feet, dressed in her silk pyjamas and dressing gown—her feet deep in sheepskin slippers. She didn't speak, but held up her hand, which she'd had the sense to clad in a thick, wool-lined leather mitten. Dax flew to her fist and found his balance, driving his talons in deep, and then Lisa sat back down on her bed, resting her gloved hand on her knee and keeping his perch steady.

Don't shift, she sent. *I don't want to risk waking the others. We keep this in our heads, OK?*

OK, Dax sent back. *Lisa, what happened? What's going on?*

Lisa closed her eyes and breathed out. *I'm not*

sure. I'm really not. But I've got such a bad feeling, Dax—to do with Mia.

Dax surveyed her unblinkingly from his falcon eyes. In the moonlight, every nuance of her anxious face was crystal clear under his gaze, from the fine pores in her skin to the tiniest bead of sweat on her upper lip. Her eyes were the colour of dark blue ink, every lash around them defined, and the tiniest twitch of a muscle below her mouth gave away how upset she was.

Go back to the Derwent school, he instructed, knowing he had to keep her focused to get the right images and words from her telepathically. At once he was in the white-tiled girls' toilet, backed up against the cold porcelain of a row of wash basins, seeing the scene replayed through Lisa's eyes. The five Derwent girls were red in the face, some looking scared and some with eyes narrowed, full of unspent anger. The dark-haired girl shoved Lisa in the shoulder and Dax felt the impact, and Lisa's own fury (never too far from the surface) beginning to surge up. Lisa did not strike back, but let out a volley of sharp, well-honed abuse—she was always quick with words when annoyed. It didn't help. The dark-haired girl's face twisted and, pushing aside a friend who was trying to restrain her, she lunged at Lisa and grabbed at her hair. There was primate-like screaming and shouting. Dax felt the sharp pain above Lisa's right temple, scratching nails, hot breath on skin, and then even greater fury surging all around. The fury, though, was not just Lisa's— or even Jennifer's. Jennifer was scared and wanting to run for Mrs Dann and Lisa had thumped her adversary, was getting ready to do it again, up for a fight but in no way out of control. No, the biggest, most white-hot fury of all came right of field. It was from Mia.

Dax heard himself bashing on the other side of the toilet door, his muffled voice shouting 'Lisa! Mia! I'm coming in!' and then a whoosh and a punch of hot air threw everyone in the small room backwards, stumbling against walls and toilet doors, some of which clattered open inwards— and a white and golden cloud of flame funnelled up towards the ceiling. Mia was flattened against the far wall as the ceiling began to melt, her hands pressed to the wall tiles on either side of her, her ribcage rising and falling rapidly and her mouth moving as if she were saying something. Rage was

154

in her eyes—and for just a fraction of a second the faintest smile was on her lips.

Did you get that? Did you see—that? Lisa sent, urgently. Dax nodded and tried to clear his head of Lisa's images. *Let me out now*, he begged, eventually, and Lisa blinked and sent *Sorry!* and suddenly he was seeing again with his own eyes. She was biting her lip. *Oh, Dax. Oh no. I don't know what to do. It was Mia. Mia nearly set fire to her. Like before with Catherine.* Another graphic image of Catherine, on a stretcher, her hair on fire, screaming, sliced into Dax's mind. It wasn't sent by Lisa. It was all his own. He had been there too the last time this had happened.

I'm scared for her, Dax. What if they find out? What if she can't control it?

Dax glanced across at Mia, who was soundly asleep a few feet away from them. The voices ringing between their minds were loud and panicked and it was hard to imagine that in the dormitory, Mia and Jennifer were sleeping on in peace. *Do you think she did it deliberately?* he asked Lisa, although he could scarcely get the thought out. The very *idea* of Mia deliberately hurting anyone was preposterous. Just before Catherine's hair had caught fire last year, Mia had been, as they all had, shocked and terrified and furious beyond words with her. The girl hadn't only tried to kill them—they had witnessed her digging her own brother's grave while he was still alive. Any one or all of them might have burst into flame, so intensely did they feel it—and maybe thrown that flame towards the object of their anger and hurt and betrayal. Even Catherine didn't know what—or *who*—had hit her.

But *this*? Setting fire to someone over a scrap at a disco?

I don't think she could really have meant it, Lisa was sending back, also gazing at Mia as she slept on, oblivious. *I think maybe she couldn't help it—and I think she managed to stop herself directing it at that girl right at the last second—and that's why the fireball went up. It was right above that girl's head. Her sleeve was just caught by the dripping ceiling tiles—she didn't really catch alight.*

Dax thought for a moment and then sent: *So— you think she might not have full control over it? That's really scary. What happens when she gets really angry next time? But then, if she did redirect it, that means she must have* some *control over it . . . and that's . . .*

Even worse, concluded Lisa.

When Dax sent his next message, he heard it clearly inside his own head, in Owen's voice. *We have to know. We have to know soon. I think we're going to have to do something really terrible to find out, but I don't see any other way.*

Lisa's eyes welled up. *What?* she sent back, and it came back as a whisper.

When Dax had outlined his plan he felt as sick as Lisa looked. *Does it have to be me?* she asked, her free hand across her mouth. *And you?*

Yes. We'll need Gideon too. But we can't tell him until afterwards. We'll need his reactions to be real. Lisa—she will understand. Later. Afterwards. We don't have any choice if we're going to protect her . . . and everyone else. We have to know for sure.

Lisa shook, and her hair tumbled across her face. She left it there like a curtain, so Dax wouldn't see her crying. *She'll hate me.*

Yes, said Dax. *She'll have to.*

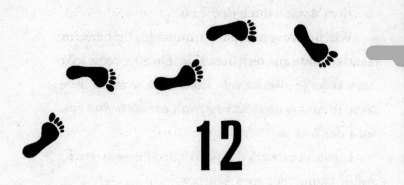

12

Dax knew how to lie. He'd done it before. He wasn't in the least bit proud of this, but it had been necessary at the time. The next morning was to be his best and worst work.

It began with Lisa, before he even saw her at breakfast. That morning Lisa would rise as usual in the dorm with Mia and Jennifer, but although she would talk to Jennifer, she would steer clear of Mia and not say anything to her at all. She would get showered and dressed without a word to her closest friend and then go on down to breakfast without waiting for her.

At breakfast Lisa sat next to Dax at the end of their usual table, leaving no spare seat next to her for Mia, as she usually would, and when Mia arrived, looking uneasily around for her friend, Lisa totally ignored her, sharing a private joke with Dax. They both split their sides with laughter and then stopped abruptly when they saw Mia looking over at them. They changed the subject and talked quietly. Gideon's arrival meant another body to put between them and Mia, and when the girl eventually joined them, sitting as close as she could but still two places away from Lisa, Gideon was caught up in Lisa's next story and didn't pay much attention. He had no idea he was part of their unkind plan—not yet.

As soon as they finished eating—and thankfully nobody noticed that neither he nor Lisa could get down more than one triangle of toast and a little tea that morning—Lisa went out with Dax, saying, loud enough to be overheard, 'I'm going to talk to Mrs Sartre now. There's no point in waiting. I need my own space.' In the corner of his eye, Dax saw Mia look up, confused and hurt. Jennifer had joined her by then, also unaware of the plot—but was busy talking to Barry across from her. Like Barry, she wasn't very perceptive, so she didn't notice anything amiss.

159

In class that morning Lisa did it all with body language. She angled herself on her chair and desk, so that her right shoulder made a wall between her and Mia. She faced away from her friend and opened her textbooks at an angle to make even those a barrier. She did not glance at Mia even once. Dax, who could feel Lisa's absolute wretchedness buffeting at him in telepathic waves, marvelled at her acting ability. She answered several of Mr Tucker's questions smartly and with no sign of the misery she was feeling. She wrote hard in her book and did not share a single word or look with Mia. Mia began to shrink. Her shoulders became more stooped and she continually glanced over at Lisa, trying to make eye contact and work out what was wrong.

It was hard for Dax, keenly sensing what was happening—it got a lot worse when Mia looked over at *him* with a beseeching expression, trying for a clue about Lisa's odd behaviour. With all his heart Dax wanted to smile at her sympathetically and shrug; give her comfort as she had given it to him— to all of them—countless times. But instead he kept his expression stony, looked right through her, and then dropped his attention back to his books.

At break Lisa rushed straight to the library where they had arranged to meet. She slammed the door shut behind her, leaned against it and checked that nobody else was there, before gasping out a series of anguished breaths. 'This is horrible! Horrible! It's destroying her. She's so sensitive it's fifty times worse than it would be for anyone else. Oh hell, Dax—are we doing the right thing? I don't know how much longer I can keep this up.'

Dax felt just as bad, but his resolve wasn't weakening. 'I think we might sort it out by the end of today. I did think it might take two or three days, but she's really distressed already. If we do the next couple of bits, I think she'll be ready for the last stage. I've asked Gideon to take the equipment out to the tree house and hide it there. He doesn't know what it's for and he's gagging to find out, but I've promised him it's a surprise he won't want me to spoil. That's pretty horrible for me, too, in case it helps. Lying to my best mate.' Dax grimaced, rubbing his malachite bracelet subconsciously and thinking about the other little deception he'd been forced into—against them all. What would Lisa think of him if she knew?

'This is *all* horrible.' She wiped her hand over her brow. 'Why are we doing this again?'

'Because it's the only way to know for sure. She won't do it again unless she can't stop it. It's like what happened to me, when Owen first found me. He had to know I was turning into something, but he knew that asking me wouldn't get him an answer. Back then, the only time I shifted was when I got really scared or panicky or angry. That's what he had to make happen. So he got these blokes to throw me in a truck and drive off with me and then he used this drug on me—Triple Eight it was called—to make me go crazy with fear.'

Lisa stared at him in horror. She had never heard about this.

'It was awful,' said Dax. 'Really awful. But it worked. I forgave him. There was no other way. If I knew where they kept Triple Eight, we'd be using that instead. Now, are you ready for the next bit?'

Lisa nodded grimly and then winced and raised her eyes to the ceiling. 'Oh not *now*, Sylv,' she muttered. 'Tell them to wait for Development, *please*. I just can't be doing with it now!'

'They all came back again, then,' said Dax,

remembering Lisa's little holiday from her badg-ering spirits a couple of days back.

'Yeah,' she sighed. 'About an hour later—in a big flood. Selfish see-through little goblins. I'd slap some of them if they were solid enough.'

Dax laughed, in spite of the horrible day they were going through. It was comforting to hear Lisa doing a bit of her regular ghost-bashing.

Lunch was a repeat of breakfast, but this time Mia moved her seat further away and glanced across at them silently, making no attempt to join in their conversation. Again, Dax and Lisa kept their heads together, talking in quiet voices whenever Mia looked their way. They laughed out loud from time to time, but mostly snickered behind their hands. Halfway through pudding, which Dax was desperately trying to eat when his insides were churning with self-loathing, Jacob Teller brought Lisa a sealed yellow envelope.

'Message from Mrs Sartre,' he said, loudly.

Dax smiled, bitterly. Good. He had asked Gideon to give the message to Jacob, saying it was for Lisa and from the principal. Gideon had demanded, this time, to be let into the game—and it was all Dax could do to put him off until teatime. They'd better hope this worked today—he could see there was no way that Gideon would stand it into tomorrow.

'Oh good,' said Lisa and made a show of opening the envelope and reading the paper—which was in fact blank. 'She says I should go and see her—talk it over. See what can be done.'

Dax sighed and said, just loud enough for Mia, who was stirring her soup and not eating any of it, to hear: 'It's probably for the best. I expect she'll understand. Do you think Jennifer will go with you?'

'Probably,' said Lisa, turning her face away from Mia and looking at Dax with pain etched across her face. 'I think she feels the same way.'

Mia stood up. She walked towards them. A pulse of her warmth preceded her and Dax knew she was desperately trying to be included. He felt like the worst kind of git.

'You're very secretive,' said Mia, with a laugh so thin it frayed.

Lisa stared up at her and then gave her a tight smile. 'Hmmmm,' was all she said and then looked at Dax.

'OK, none of my business,' said Mia and

walked away. When she put her bowl and spoon down on the rack of trays it juddered like a percussion instrument.

'What are you two *up* to?' asked Gideon. He had been stuffing down his food fast and having signing chats with Luke, and neither boy had really been paying attention. But he'd seen the last minute of their terrible game with Mia.

'Oh, you know—just girl stuff,' said Dax, lamely. Lisa got up and left without a word. Gideon stared at Dax. He wasn't fooled. 'Do you trust me, Gid?' said Dax, looking at him squarely. Gideon nodded. Luke was staring at them both now. 'Then wait,' said Dax. 'Just until about four o'clock. Can you do that?'

Gideon nodded again, slowly. 'O-K. Four o'clock,' he said. 'Then time's up.'

Before the end of lunch, Lisa ran up to their dormitory, having first checked that Mia was in the common room, and stripped the sheets and duvet and pillow case off her bed. She swiped her table-top clutter into a bag and deposited the whole lot in her wardrobe, under some cases. At a glance, when Dax peered in, it really looked as if she was moving out.

'OK,' he said. 'Now take off the bracelet she gave you. Leave it on the windowsill where she can see it. Now, she needs to come up here before we go back into class.'

They went back down and Dax casually asked Mia if he could see her Crystal Directory, which she kept in her bedside drawer. Mia immediately smiled and went to fetch it. They didn't see her until French class ten minutes later.

'*Dépêche toi*, Mia!' said Mrs Sartre. 'You should have been in your seat five minutes ago. Sit down, please.'

Mia apologized and dropped the Crystal Directory on Dax's desk as she passed. She didn't look at him. Her face was still and shut down, like an empty shop. All life gone from it. Dax knew that it *was* possible to feel worse than this. He knew he would be feeling it at four o'clock.

The light was fading fast when they got there. It was 3.50 p.m. and Lisa was shaking with agitation as much as the cold. Above them in the tree house were the pieces of equipment that Gideon had delivered. He would come along at four—agog to know what the game was about. Mia would be here sooner, they hoped. Lisa had brushed past her in the corridor not five minutes ago, rather roughly, and said, 'I need to have a word with you. Don't say anything to anyone else— if you can manage that—just come out to the tree house. Don't keep me hanging around or I won't bother.'

Mia had been too shocked to say a word as Lisa caught up with Dax. Now they waited, leaning against the ladder, for the snap and crackle of the woodland floor to announce her arrival.

'I hope you're right about this, Dax,' Lisa muttered into her scarf. 'If you're not she might never forgive me. She might not anyway. And another thing—if you're right—this could be really dangerous.'

'You did put on what I told you to?' asked Dax.

'Yesss,' she snapped. 'I'm not an idiot. No nylon or man-made stuff.'

'Good. And remember—if it looks like she's going to go off, drop to the ground and cover your head, OK?'

'She wouldn't though—she wouldn't—' Lisa

cut herself off as there was a snap of twig and Mia arrived through the trees, wrapped in her winter coat, scarf, and gloves. She stood a few feet away from them both, her beautiful violet-blue eyes huge in her pale, anxious face. *Just one day*, grieved Dax. *Look what we did to her in just one day.*

'What's going on?' said Mia. Her voice was not shaky, but controlled and flat. Good. She was angry too. Better.

Lisa folded her arms across her chest and looked her friend in the eye. 'What do you think is going on? I've had enough, that's what.'

'Enough? Of what?'

'Spending twenty-four hours a day with you—and your tendency to set light to people.'

Mia's mouth dropped open and she stared from Lisa to Dax. '*What?*'

'You know what I'm talking about,' said Lisa and the sneer and contempt in her voice chilled Dax, even though he knew she was acting it. 'You make out you're all sweet and lovely and wouldn't hurt a fly, and everyone thinks *I'm* the stroppy cow and you're Little Miss Perfect—but at least I don't go torching people just because I fancy their boyfriends.'

'I don't! I didn't! How can you say that?' gasped Mia. 'Dax! Make her stop! You know this isn't true!'

Dax shrugged and put his hands deep into his pockets. 'I know what I saw last night—what I heard and what I smelt. It was all coming from you.'

Mia stared at him, horror and dismay on her face. Not good enough. Dax had to get her anger too. He went back in. 'And I saw you flirting with all those boys earlier. I think you were really puffed up with it and then you got jealous when they went back to Lisa—because they'd liked her better in the first place anyway. All you've got is the Mia Effect. And that wears off, doesn't it? I mean, it's worn off for *me.*'

Mia's eyes glittered. 'I did *not* flirt with anybody!' she said, her voice lowering with fury. 'How can you say that? You *saw* what really happened. Why are you both being like this? And why are you moving out, Lisa? What did I ever do to deserve this?'

'Admit it!' shouted Lisa. 'You're a pyrokinetic and you *love it*! You don't want to be the Feel-Good Fairy. You want to be Fireball Girl or something. You're jealous of all the stuff I can do and I don't blame you. After all, what are you? You're just a big walking jar of Savlon. Nobody pays you any attention because you're actually pretty boring. I was sorry for you for ages and so I haven't said this but after last night—'

'What the *hell* is going on?' Gideon emerged, blinking, into the small clearing by the tree house. 'Are you all *mad*?'

Here was the final bit, thought Dax. Gideon's shock was palpable. Mia needed to see it, to believe what was happening. 'Sorry, mate,' said Dax. 'But we just had to tell it like it is. Mia's a pyrokinetic. She's dangerous.'

'You're joking!'

'Gideon, I'm *not* joking! I need you to stay back. I'm sorry, Mia, but we just can't trust you any more. Not after last night. We thought—after Catherine—that it might really have been just the once. But last night . . . '

Mia was looking from one to the other of them, breathing hard. 'I can't believe this,' she was gasping. 'I can't believe it—after all we've been through. You don't trust me. Well, you don't *deserve* my trust!' There was a sob in her voice, but also a growl of anger.

'We don't need it,' cut back Lisa. 'We just need you in a safe place—somewhere fireproof.'

Mia shook. Her face seemed to shrink and her eyes became dark and flat like the obsidian stone on her bracelet. The air began to sing in Dax's ears and a hot hot smell filled his nose. He shifted to the falcon, flew up to the tree house, and was back in boy form in an instant. Inside it were two water fire extinguishers. 'Gid! Up here! Now!' he yelled, but Gideon was already clambering up.

'You should have told me! You should have!' he said, as he seized the other extinguisher and snapped its safety latch away.

Down on the wood floor Lisa pushed Mia further, tearing into her with ugly words and shrivelling her hope that this was some kind of cruel joke. Dax, his hands shaking and his heart thundering, fumbled with the heavy canister and pointed its nozzle.

'You're a psycho! A weird, dangerous psycho! I want you out of my life!' bawled Lisa and then there was a flash and a punch through the air and Lisa hit the floor, burying her head in her hands. Flame zipped past Dax's face like lightning, so close he smelt his hair singeing. Then a tree behind Lisa exploded in blazing shards of bark. Lisa screamed and so did Mia. Gideon and Dax turned jets of water down onto the flaming tree and steam hissed high into the air. It was out in ten seconds. Only the outer bark had burned. Flakes of it scattered down like black snow over Lisa, who was on her knees, holding Mia, crying, and begging for forgiveness.

Dax put down the extinguisher and looked at Gideon—who mirrored his grim expression. They had their answer.

13

'How did you know to do that?' said Mia, much later. They were in Dax and Gideon's room and Lisa had wrapped a blanket around Mia's shoulders and kept hugging her and smoothing back her hair. She looked shattered.

Dax wrapped his arms around his knees. He felt as exhausted as Lisa looked. Gideon had pressed chocolate onto them all, but only Mia, strangely, had been able to eat any. She looked— *older*—somehow. And she looked at *him*.

'You knew exactly how to hurt me most,' she said. 'Didn't you? How?'

'It was easy. I just thought about what would mess *me* up most in the shortest space of time.

Losing all your trust and friendship; having you all turn on me. I would have gone nuts.'

'You were very clever,' she said. 'Sometimes you scare me, Dax Jones. Are you more than half animal, do you think?'

Dax looked away and at Gideon, who was still angry with him for not involving him from the outset. He wondered how many more of the people he loved he would hurt that week. 'You do understand, don't you—all of you—why all that had to happen?'

They nodded. He'd explained it twice already.

'Now we have to work out what to do next.'

'Why do we have to do anything?' said Gideon. 'Mia won't let it happen again, will you, Mia? So we just say nothing.'

Dax rubbed his face tiredly and looked back at the healer who had turned so desperately dangerous in the past twenty-four hours. 'Well, what do you think? Have you got it under control?'

Mia dropped her gaze, at last. 'I don't know,' she said, sounding less hard and more like her old self. 'I didn't do it deliberately—not at the school and not today. You do believe that, don't you?'

'I do,' said Dax. 'We all do. But we think you must have some control, because you managed to redirect the blast—both times—with just a moment to spare.'

Mia nodded. 'Yes, as soon as the fire leaves me I sort of re-set. My normality comes back. And I know that I don't really want to hurt anyone. Except Catherine last year. I wanted to kill her. I guess there's no point in lying about that.'

'Yeah, well,' said Gideon. 'We all wanted to kill her. Nothing odd there.'

'Who do we go to?' said Lisa. 'Owen? Mrs Sartre? And what will they do? There's never been a Cola like this before. I'm scared about what they'll do.'

'We say nothing for now,' said Dax. 'Mia, you have to promise—nothing more like this. If you feel anything building up, you'll have to run or scream or—do something, anything, to let the anger out. You've got to be on guard in Development too. In case they find out something. Do you understand?'

She nodded. 'I know. I've been on guard for months. I never wanted this to come back. I don't know why it's happening. I want to cure people, not hurt them.'

Gideon sat back against the radiator beneath their window and broke off another chunk of chocolate. 'What about the investigation over the disco thing? Will they work out that it was Mia? I mean, that hairspray story was a bit far-fetched.'

'I'd like to see you come up with something better,' snapped Lisa. 'Especially when you've just escaped being flash-fried! Anyway, part of it's true. They *were* spraying hairspray at us. Nothing like enough to make something like that happen but *they* wouldn't know that.'

Mia took Lisa's hand—the first Mia-ish thing she had done since they'd brought her back. 'I'm sorry, Lees—I'm sorry to all of you. And I do forgive you, for what you all said and did earlier. I know you didn't mean it. I know you had to. You were brave, as well—you could *all* have been flash-fried.' A familiar wave of Mia's healing warmth stole over them all and Dax had to get up and walk to the window because he felt so bad he couldn't look at them.

'We say nothing,' he said, after a gulp, watching more snow begin to fall through the darkening sky. 'We do nothing. Maybe that's all of it. Mia's had a wake-up call. It won't happen again.'

Later still, Dax lay in his bed and stared out at the cold night sky. The bad feeling he had carried since the disco was still with him. He was very, very worried about Mia. He remembered Owen saying to him, right back when they'd first met, how tough it would have been for Cola Club if they'd ever had to deal with a pyrokinetic. He wondered if Owen knew already about Mia—after all, he had been there in France when Catherine's hair had caught fire. None of the teachers had spoken of it since, so maybe Owen hadn't said anything about his suspicions at the time. But after the disco incident . . . surely he wouldn't be fooled by the hairspray excuse, even if all the other teachers were.

Owen would come for Mia. Soon. And maybe he should. Dax didn't want to be responsible for someone burning alive if Mia's anger got out of control again. But he also didn't want to be responsible for the end of her freedom—well, what freedom any of them *had* these days, with their chips and their soldiers and their watchful scientists.

'You know, you *could* talk to me, about what you're thinking.' Gideon's face, squashed up between his pillow and his quilt, looked hurt. 'You used to do that once.'

Dax sat up and wrapped his quilt around his middle. 'I still do, Gid. The only reason I didn't tell you about the Mia thing was that she needed to see you looking really, genuinely shocked—so that it would all seem real.'

'I know, I know.' Gideon sat up testily. 'I got that bit, and I'll let you off that one. It did work, after all. But you're brooding away about other stuff, aren't you? Why aren't I hearing about it?'

Dax sighed. 'OK, I'm worried about what might happen with Mia; that Owen knows, because he's too smart not to, and that *something* might have to happen. Like when we were worried about you when everyone thought your powers were out of control and they had a concrete bunker lined up for you to live out your days in. Only with you, it turned out you *weren't* losing control. With Mia . . . well, we just don't know, do we?'

'Nope,' said Gideon. 'And what if next time she has a mare she ends up toasting someone? I reckon we'll feel well guilty. Even if it's Mr Eades.'

'So what do we do?'

'I don't know.'

'Me neither.'

'What about the rest of the stuff?'

'What?'

'That's not all you're stressing about, is it?'

Dax worked through the worries in his head. 'I want to know when my dad's coming. That's one thing. I want a date. But I probably won't ever get one. I want to know what the Neetanite is for— and we can't work it out. I want a message from my mother, and I never get one . . . and . . . ' Oh, how he longed to say, *And most of all I'm worried about the microchip which was inserted into the base of your skull while you were drugged a couple of weeks ago.* Instead he concluded, 'I don't know. I've just got a bad feeling. Something . . . incoming. Don't know what.'

Gideon shivered. Dax's bad feelings tended to be justified, if you just waited long enough. His animal instincts gave him an advantage that even Lisa did not have. While Lisa could get all kinds of messages about the future from the spirit world, she didn't necessarily understand them, or have a clear idea of what they meant. Dax's prescience was different. It ran through his veins, night and day, awake or asleep. So far, it had never been wrong. There had been a terrible tsunami in the eastern ocean, which Dax had heard about. Thousands of people had died in it—but all along the devastated coasts, animals of all kinds had moved inland and to higher ground an hour before the disaster struck. Some had even saved their owners. Dax understood this now. He didn't think another tidal wave was coming, but something was. Something not good.

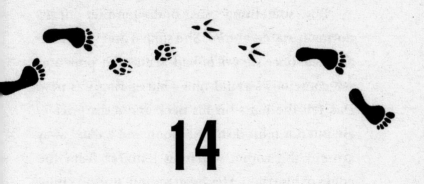

14

'Told you, mate!' Gideon nudged Dax as they ladled porridge into their dishes in the dining room the next morning. Dax huffed as a splodge of oats and milk landed on the serving table. 'See— now tell me she doesn't fancy you!' Gideon grinned and his eyebrows went up and down rapidly.

Dax glanced around and saw Jennifer leaning against the windowsill, her arms folded, regarding him with a soft smile. He looked back again to his food and then up at the mirror hung on the wall above the serving table. He wrinkled his brow, watching Jennifer's reflection. She was still staring fondly at him. He felt himself blush as Gideon sniggered next to him. 'What did I tell you?'

But something was odd. Jennifer never normally stared at him. She smiled and said hello and yes, once or twice, had been a bit pink and self-conscious around him—but staring was new. Dax felt the hairs on his neck and arms prickle. He put down his dish and spoon and walked away around the room, watching Jennifer from the edges of his vision. Her head moved, tracking him. She was quite relaxed, holding one of the pop magazines they'd had delivered before the disco, and just observing him contentedly.

Dax had a sudden realization of what was amiss. Jennifer thought she was invisible.

He walked closer to her and then glanced up at her, smiling. Jennifer's eyes widened in shock. She looked behind her and around her and then back at Dax.

'Hi, Jenny,' he said. 'You OK? In a bit of a dream world, it looked like.'

'I—I thought—' she stammered. Then she peered at him, confused. 'You could see me then?'

'Yes. Clear as day. Everything OK?'

'No . . . um . . . yes. Fine. It's just that, well . . . I thought I was in a vanish.'

'Not concentrating hard enough,' said Dax,

with a grin, and went back to his porridge. Jennifer quickly left the room. She had gone very pink.

'What did she say?' hissed Gideon, as they sat down and began to dollop spoonfuls of golden syrup on the top of their porridge.

'Nothing much. It was weird, though, because she thought she was in a vanish. And she wasn't.'

'Must've lost concentration through being so in *luuurve*,' gurgled Gideon through a full mouth.

Dax nudged him hard. 'Stop it!'

There was a breathy sigh off to Dax's right and then Jennifer simpered: 'But what can I do, Daxyboy? I just can't resist your big brown eyes and your furry tail and the way you cock your leg over the geraniums . . . '

Dax spun round, choking on his porridge, to find Jacob staring at him, doe-eyed and dreamy, his chin resting on his hand.

'That's revolting, Jake!' spluttered Dax.

'But I just can't *help* it . . . ' added Jacob, fluttering his eyelashes, while Alex, sitting across the table with his cooked breakfast, doubled up in fits. 'It's your animal magic!'

Gideon was also in fits now. Dax grabbed a sausage off Jacob's well-loaded plate and poked it straight in the boy's fluttering left eye. Jacob squawked in protest, but couldn't stop laughing, even with ketchup in his eyebrow. Alex recovered himself and got stuck back into his breakfast, but Dax could see him eyeing his brother with a naughty smile on his face. Obviously imparting more jokes about poor Jennifer. He waited for Jacob to start sniggering and snorting, but Jacob didn't. He just mopped his eye, shrugged, and started eating the sausage he'd just been attacked with.

Alex continued to stare at his brother, but after a few seconds his smile faded. He looked around at them all, in some confusion. Dax only noticed because a sudden scent of anxiety pulsed from the small boy. 'Jacob!' he said, and his brother looked up.

'What?'

Alex peered at him and then shook his head. 'Oh never mind! Get back to stuffing yourself.'

Jacob shrugged again, and did.

Dax found it hard to undo the knots in his insides across the next few days. The other Colas relaxed as, in spite of the misadventure at the disco, the promised trip to Keswick for the second half of them went ahead as planned that Saturday. Lisa and Mia's friendship seemed to be completely mended.

But Dax could not shake off his feeling of foreboding. The worry about Mia nagged at him all the time, the sour secret of the tracking chips ate at his insides twenty-four hours a day, the confusion about the Neetanite buffeted what was left of his attention. On Tuesday afternoon, while the rest of the Colas went to the gym for PE, he excused himself for flying time, but instead went off to the woods as a fox. He needed to run. The snow had gone now, but a frost still clung to the hollows, painting the landscape with silver and purple as the sun began to slide down behind the fells. He ran and ran, tail streaked straight out behind him, through the wood, past the tree house where little evidence of Mia's fire could be seen—although its smell was still strong in his fox nose—and on deeper towards the badgers' sett. The animal scents all around him soothed his troubled mind and he heard Mia's cool words: 'Are you more than half animal, Dax?' echo through his head.

What if she was right? Maybe the brutal thing he'd made them all do to Mia was because he *was* more than half animal. But no—an animal could not have cared so much about its friends as he did. The fox liked some company but was quite independent. The falcon needed nobody and nothing but the sky and its prey.

The badgers were at home today. Dax smelt all five of them: father and mother and three cubs. He felt irresistibly drawn in towards them. Ducking his head low, he eased into their earthy hallway and pressed himself down it. There was a time, not so long ago, when being in a confined space like this would have brought on a panic attack. But since he'd spent a minute being dead last year, this didn't seem to trouble him any more.

The badger family, drowsy and warm, looked up at him curiously, five pairs of silver eyes in the comfortable gloom. Dax wondered if he'd be chased off, but after a long stare, the head of the family rested his black and white snout back down on his mate's head and she settled hers back down on her cubs. Dax sent 'need to rest' at them. He knew they wouldn't get it word for word, but the scent he gave out, coupled with a simple telepathy, should work. They relaxed again and one of the cubs even seemed to shuffle up to make space for him in the warm curve of their dormitory. Dax turned once, curled his tail about him, and settled down, his back against the back of a badger cub.

He didn't exactly sleep, but he drowsed wonderfully. His breathing began to match the breathing of the badger family and he felt the tension melt from his sinews as he inhaled their fuggy air. For the first time in days and days he felt something like peace steal across him. In his not quite asleep, not quite awake state, he realized that another animal had crept in to enjoy the badger family's hospitality.

Dax lifted his snout and regarded his old friend. The wolf was back again. He sighed. If that didn't mean trouble ahead, nothing else would. Once a boy—and the only other shapeshifter that Cola Club had found—the wolf had been killed suddenly before he could revert to his human form. The spirit wolf had attached itself to Dax and occasionally gave him clues and warnings— sometimes so obscure that Dax wanted to scream. Always, it turned out, accurate.

It's good to see you again, sent Dax. The wolf

nodded and rested its muzzle on its paws, regarding him calmly. *It's OK,* went on Dax, *I know you're going to warn me about something. I've felt it coming anyway. I know something's . . . incoming.* The wolf continued to gaze at him, rather sorrowfully. *Go on then,* urged Dax. *Give me one of your famous riddles!* The wolf raised its snout and tilted its shaggy head to one side. *OK, I'll ask then. Do you know about the Neetanite?* It nodded. *Is it important?* Now it made a gesture so like a shrug, Dax nearly laughed out loud—but he didn't want to wake the badgers. Typical! Nothing was ever easy with the wolf.

All right. What do I need to know?

For a few seconds the wolf just continued to look at him and then it sent a powerful smell into his head. Dax couldn't work out what it was, but it was strong and dark—it made him think of moving machinery, of oil and fuel. Mixed with it was a salty smell and a sense of heat. He shrugged back at the wolf. *OK. Got that. Doesn't make any sense though. Am I surprised?* The wolf blinked and this time words came from it. *Hear the learned ones in their low place.* Dax gulped and nodded, hoping it would get better. *In the corridor you need an anchor.*

188

One will hold you. Or you do not go. Dax felt his furry brow wrinkling as he tried to memorize the wolf's odd words. If his past experience was anything to go by, they would all mean something. Something he needed to know. The wolf was beginning to fade, the tangle of roots hanging behind its head beginning to show through its haunted eyes. Dax was desperately hoping for more, but the wolf was just repeating, *Hear the learned ones in their low place. Soonest,* it added. *Soonest.* Now it was just a grey shadow, but the last message it gave him made him shiver deeply, because he knew he had heard it before.

Death is not the end, Dax Jones.

A second later there was no sign of the wolf. The badgers slept on but for Dax the relaxation was over. He crept from their sett regretfully. He needed to be sure he didn't forget any of the messages. As soon as he was clear of the trees he shifted to the falcon and shot straight up and around to his bedroom window. Happily, the room was empty. He didn't want to delay in any way by talking to anybody, while the words marched round and round in his head so he wouldn't forget them. He found an envelope and a pen in his bedside drawer and quickly scribbled them down. *Hear the learned ones in their low place. Soonest. In the corridor you need an anchor. One will hold you. Or you do not go.* And, finally, with another shiver, he wrote: *Death is not the end, Dax Jones.* He remembered now—it was Lisa, just a few days ago, after her spat with Gideon, who had spoken exactly those words, in the middle of a trance.

Dax didn't like to think what it meant. He *knew* death was not the end—it was obvious when you hung around someone like Lisa. That didn't mean he wanted to hurry towards it any faster than he had to. *I'm not ready to die—not for a long time,* he heard himself whimper, small and childish in his own head. He shook himself back to feathers and went straight back out of the window before any more such thoughts could enter his mind. He thought he knew what the *soonest* message was about. *Hear the learned ones in their low place.* He knew where the learned ones gathered—and it was a low place. It was time he did a little surveillance on the scientists.

First he flew back to the wood, shifting to fox to run through it, and then to boy to climb up into the tree house. He opened one of the little stools that Jacob and Alex had made. They had put hinged lids on them, so a few supplies, like candles and matches and sweets, could be kept there. Dax undid his Malachite bracelet and dropped it into the stool box. He was glad now that Owen had talked common sense to him on that awful night in the snow. Now the tracker chip would show the scientists that he was holed up in the tree house—when in fact he was going to be much, much closer to them than that.

He climbed back down to the woodland floor and then found a small gap in the trees. He didn't want to risk flying out from the edge of the wood, where he might be seen and recognized. Normally he would never attempt to go straight up from the middle of the wood, but today it was necessary. He had to get up high beyond the cold low cloud as fast as possible. A chimney of light spilled down into the trees a few hundred metres from the tree house and Dax shifted and shot up through it, rather bumpily, with no warm rising air beneath his wings. He had to flap hard but made it up through and high into the sky in seconds. Mercifully the shroud of mist wrapped around him almost instantly. It was highly unlikely anyone could have seen him, even if they had been scanning the skies with binoculars.

Dax navigated instinctively through the cloud, turning north-east towards the far end of Fenton Lodge's grounds where the low, tiled building with the covered windows lay. As he dropped lightly down through the cold air and left the cover of the fine hanging mist, he saw the apex of the tiled roof hurtle towards him. He pulled up silently and found a perch along the ridge of grey slate. Along the roof was a chimney. No smoke rose from it. He flew to the stack of sandstone bricks and then dropped to where the roof met with it at a gentle angle. He hoped the slate was rough enough to give his four paws a good hold, because staying here as a falcon was no good to him. He needed to hear what was happening in the building below, and falcons were only good for speed and eyesight. He steadied himself against the chimney stack, hoping for the best, and shifted. One hind leg slipped as he flexed his sharp claws into the slate, but he soon gained a foothold. The fox hugged the roof and tilted its head—and voices came, funnelling up through the chimney.

At first there wasn't much to make out from it all. A woman and two men were talking, idly, about all kinds of things to do with their day; their findings at the development viewing rooms, what so-and-so should do about his girlfriend troubles, the weather, and then some comparisons of figures and read-outs—none of which meant a thing to Dax, and were not at all helpful. Then he froze and shrank hard against the roof as he heard brisk footsteps on gravel approaching the building. He didn't need to peer over the ridge tiles to see who was coming. He could smell that it was Mr Eades. The man punched in a code at the security panel on the door and then stepped into the building. Dax could hear his progress down the corridor and then nothing. For a long, long while, the boring chatter between the three scientists went on and then a door clicked open and Dax could hear that Mr Eades was on the move again. A few seconds later another door clicked and the three scientists paused in their chatter to greet the man, respectfully. There was a rustling of paper and then Dax heard Mr Eades murmuring, quietly and indistinctly at first, as if to himself—and then quite clearly addressing the scientists.

'This is most encouraging. Really most encouraging,' he said. His voice, so grey and flat in the lodge, seemed actually quite animated. He was excited. Dax could smell the man's keen anticipation wafting up through the chimney stack.

'We think we've ironed out all the glitches,' said the woman. 'We've been tracking them all, and all of the white-out spells are where we would expect them to be. I'm not sure how remote it can be yet, but the early results indicate several miles.'

Dax realized grimly that they were talking about the tracker chips. So, Mr Eades was in on it too. This didn't surprise him. He wondered if Mrs Sartre, Mrs Dann, and Mr Tucker and even Tyrone knew about it. He hoped not. He decided to think not. He liked them all and having to feel bitter and hurt towards Owen and Janey was really bad enough.

'Jones was always going to be tricky, given his unique biology,' a male voice was continuing. 'But so far, so good—although we haven't really calibrated it properly yet. We can do that this

194

afternoon.' Dax felt the fur prickle all over his neck and shoulders. It was eerie and unpleasant to hear himself talked about as if he were nothing more than an experiment. But then he guessed, to these people, this was precisely what he was.

'Well, the disco night was a great success,' went on Mr Eades, much to Dax's surprise. How had it been successful? Didn't they know about the girls' toilets incident?

'Apart from that fire thing, obviously, but Hind assures me this was just a freak situation brought about by too much hairspray and hormone; could have happened to any bunch of adolescent females in a confined space. The control pad was consistent throughout the evening, with every one of them—although we didn't play around too much with it. Don't want to set off the clairvoyant or the shapeshifter—if anyone will pick something up it will be them. Which is why I am so relieved at the way it's gone so far. Almost too good to be true.'

Damn right, thought Dax. He dug his claws harder into the roof, anger burning through him.

'So—speaking of Jones—why don't you show me what it can do? Just a blind run. Where is he?'

'Tree house, sir,' said the woman. 'Probably brooding about his dad, poor love. Worthless roughneck.'

'Cheryl,' cut in the other man. 'Why do you insist on getting yourself involved?'

'I don't,' she protested. 'I'm just saying . . . OK—he's been there a while now. He's got to move soon, I think. It must be freezing. But if he doesn't move when we switch we'll know, at least, that we're not tickling anything in that strange brain of his . . . '

Dax realized that he needed to get back to his bracelet. If it remained still for much longer the scientists were going to get suspicious. Feeling slightly sick at the idea of them 'tickling' inside his brain, he shifted and shot back up into the darkening sky again, returning to the tree house the way he had come in.

He strapped the cold bracelet on, checking as he did so that the chip was still firmly taped to the underside of his malachite. It was. It glinted at him malevolently and he longed to crush it with his heel. But he couldn't. Not without risking all kinds of even worse trouble.

The light was beginning to fade and he was

tired from his flying and the several shifts he'd been through. He was suddenly swamped with hunger too, and decided to wing it straight back from the top of the trees again, to get to the dining room faster. If he went back in fox form some poor rodent was going to get killed. With his remaining strength he found the gap in the canopy and shot back up again, angling straight for the lodge.

He was about ten metres up, above the semi-frozen lake, when he shifted back to a boy.

15

In the two seconds he had before he hit the lake, Dax could only register the astonishing heaviness of his body, flailing clumsily in the air. The crack, when he hit the ice, was like a gunshot, and the explosion of cold water almost stopped his heart.

Instantly his ears and eyes and nose and mouth were filled with inrushing water, so icy it felt like a million needles. His chest jerked once with shock and his throat went into spasm as the lake probed callously down towards his lungs. Dax felt his eyes roll up into his head and his body begin to turn slowly, head down, sinking, hair caressing his face like a grieving mother. His last view was of the rising moon, blurred and bright, through the ballet of fractured glassy shards in the indifferent water which had claimed him.

16

Spook Williams was at it again. The git. He was thumping him in the chest. Really hard this time. They'd had some nasty scraps over the years, but even though Dax was a head shorter than Spook he had won more often than lost. Spook never did land much of a punch.

Until now. Dax was so winded by the force of the fist smashing into his lower chest that he could make no noise. He just rolled onto his side and threw up—mostly cold water. He must be ill again—he was shivering so hard he couldn't even see properly and Spook looked, for all the world, like a strange man in a white coat. Mr Eades was peering over the man's shoulder, looking greyer than ever, and absolutely furious. Dax's eyes blurred and he felt as if he should sleep, in spite of the violent trembling.

'You cretin!' spat Mr Eades, with more passion than Dax had ever heard in him before. 'You ocean-going, jewel-encrusted, fur-lined *excuse* for an imbecile!'

'It's all right! He'll be OK. He can't have been under for more than a minute,' replied the excuse for an imbecile, but his voice was shaky and he was clearly terrified.

'The government says it sends me the cream of the cream and I get a snivelling little test-tube scrubber like *you*!' went on Mr Eades. 'If Jones has so much as a *sniffle* this time tomorrow, you're off the project! In fact there may not be a tomorrow for any of us. We may have to speed everything up now. Damn, damn *idiot*!'

'It was an error,' admitted the scientist. 'We read him as fox, not falcon. We need to recalibrate. It was lucky he was over the lake, really— it cushioned the fall.'

'Shut up!' snapped Mr Eades, as someone else approached. 'Do not say another *word* if you value your job! Ah—' The note of his voice changed abruptly to mild concern. 'Mr Hind, one of your charges played a little close to the edge of the ice, I'm afraid.'

Dax heard Owen swear under his breath and felt a rough thick blanket being wrapped efficiently around him.

'Good job Hinton and I came by when we did. The boy wasn't under for long. Don't think there'll be any long-term damage. Perhaps you'd better get the healer girl.'

Owen carried Dax swiftly back into the lodge and up to the medical room. In a daze, Dax was dimly aware of being deposited, fully clothed, into a warm bath. Then Mia arrived and rested her hands on his head and chest and within a minute he was regaining the use of his senses. Owen and Janey stood back against the white-tiled wall of the medical suite bathroom, looking mightily relieved as he blinked and coughed and shook his head.

'How are you doing now?' smiled Mia, resting back on her heels.

'OK. I think.' Dax pulled himself up into a sitting position, the rippling warm water very odd around his jeans, sweatshirt, socks, and trainers.

'Wet, at any rate.' He laughed shakily and everyone breathed out and grinned.

'What happened?' asked Owen.

'I don't know. I was flying and then . . . then I just shifted back into boy form while I was up in the air.'

They all looked shocked.

'I fell into the lake. It was—it was cold, like death. I thought I was dead.'

'You probably would have been if the water had been a degree or two warmer,' said Owen. 'The freezing cold would have sent your heart into shock. I don't think you seriously inhaled any. You'd be coughing like an old miner by now if you had.'

'But why did it happen?' Dax shivered despite the warm water. 'That's never happened before.'

'I don't know,' said Owen. 'But I don't want you flying again until we find out. Next time you might be seventy metres up over the fells.'

Janey made him stay with her in the medical room, in pyjamas, wrapped up in a blanket on one of the beds. Dax wouldn't get into it. 'I'm fine,' he kept insisting. 'Honestly, I can go now.'

'Not *yet*,' replied Janey, scribbling away at her

notes on her nearby desk. 'Something like you've just been through can have delayed effects. You wait here for one more hour and if you're still feeling fine, you can go gently back to your own room.'

Dax was determined not to go to sleep. He found it really hard to say, even aloud in his own head, but he no longer trusted Janey. It was hard because she was still so likeable, so warm and bright and caring. Yet he knew that she had been the one who drugged him a few weeks back, so that the scientists could implant a chip in the base of his skull. He reasoned, as Owen had, that she probably thought it was all for his own good, but it was still sneaky and he couldn't get over it. Eventually Janey let him go and he shot back to the bedroom to find Gideon waiting anxiously.

'They wouldn't let me come up and see you! What's that about?' complained Gideon. 'Said I might stress you! *Stress* you? I ask you! What happened? What was it like? They said you fell out of the sky! What happened?'

Dax propelled Gideon backwards by his shoulders and got him to sit down on the edge of his bed. 'Just shut up for a second and I'll tell you!'

He related the story, missing out his rooftop spying mission on the scientists, while Gideon stared at him, pale green eyes round with shock.

'Blimey! You should be a goner!' he breathed. 'And who was it then, that got you out?'

'One of the scientists—you know, the ones we're not supposed to see. Mr Eades was really laying into him about it.'

'What—saving your life?!'

'No—no, I think . . . ' Dax tailed off, screwing up his face and trying to remember what Mr Eades had been hissing so angrily about. Ah . . . the chip. They had been playing around with the tracker chip . . . The trouble was, he didn't know how much of what he had heard was real and how much dreamed. He'd thought Spook was there to start with. None of it really made much sense.

'So why do you think it happened? I mean, mate—that's scary. If you're going to start shifting back without warning . . . '

'I know, I know . . . Owen's forbidden me to fly.' Dax sighed, wearily. All the relaxation he had briefly had with the badgers had evaporated and his anxieties and that feeling of incoming threat was still with him. He wished that he could believe it was all about the drop into the lake—that this was what the wolf had been warning him about, but he knew it wasn't.

'Death is not the end.'

'You what?' said Gideon, unravelling a big bar of Cadbury's Dairy Milk and breaking off a row of chunks for his best friend. Dax had not realized he had spoken the words out loud.

'It's what the wolf said, while I was in with the badgers.' He related the wolf's message. '*Hear the learned ones in their low place. Soonest. In the corridor you need an anchor. One will hold you. Or you do not go.* And, finally, *death is not the end, Dax Jones.*'

Gideon gulped down his mouthful of chocolate. 'Isn't that what Lisa said to you that time—when she was all trancey and woo-ey?'

'Yep,' said Dax.

'Well, there you go then. The "learned men in the low place" is the scientists . . . the wolf must have known one of them would come out and save you. And you were nearly dead, weren't you? In the lake? But then you weren't and . . . ' he petered out, as Dax shook his head.

'It's not yet,' sighed Dax. 'I wish that was all, but it's not yet.'

Gideon was quiet for a while. He looked really worried. Then he looked up and said: 'What if it's the Neetanite? Have you thought about that? Maybe it's doing something to you.'

Dax felt the Neetanite stir in the chest pocket of his pyjamas. During his adventure in the lake and the warm bath afterwards, it had stayed lodged in his soaked jeans pocket, and he'd transferred it to his pyjamas as soon as he changed. Now he held it in his palm.

'I suppose it could be . . . but—it doesn't feel bad. It came from my mum. It can't be bad.'

Gideon shrugged. 'Maybe it's not *bad* but it's just sort of messing you up? Maybe you should put it in a box for a while.'

Dax had to agree that Gideon could be right. He might blame his fall on the chip—but if it was just on his wrist could it interfere with his flying? If the tracker pulse was strong enough . . . maybe . . . But it *could* just as easily be the Neetanite. He put it inside the drawer of his bedside table. They heard the strange hexagonal barrel slowly roll across the wooden base of the drawer and knock against the corner closest to Dax. It knocked a few times and then lapsed into stillness.

Mrs P sent some soup and crusty brown bread and butter up from the kitchen, as Dax had missed tea. He and Gideon shared it, sitting on the window seat and watching more light snow beginning to fall. After the food Dax began to feel very sleepy— the effects of the day finally catching up.

'C'mon,' said Gideon. 'Brush teeth and bed.' He sounded as if he was Dax's dad. Dax grinned and did as he was told.

Soon they were both bundled up in their quilts.

'OK, stop thinking about it now,' said Gideon. 'It's all a bit freaky, I know, but all we probably need is a good night's sleep. Tomorrow everything will be back to normal.'

17

He was a fox before he'd even shot up in his bed, ears cocked and fur bristling. Something was happening. Something abnormal. He heard thumps in the building around him and realized that it was very dark—no light spilled out from any windows onto the driveway below.

His heart raced. He could smell fear. Fear and confusion. And now he could hear voices—other Colas and older, male voices. Urgent. Curt. He shifted back to boy form to call to Gideon and as he did so their door crashed open and he was blinded by the halogen flare of a torch.

'Dax Jones, Gideon Reader—this is an

emergency. You need to get out of bed, get dressed and come with me immediately.'

Dax recognized the voice and the smell. It was Weston, one of the soldiers who had accompanied them to the school disco a few nights ago. 'What? What is it?' he demanded as Gideon sat up, staring and scared, dazed in the torchlight.

'No time for questions. This is a Cola directive. There has been a serious breach of security. Get dressed. Now.'

In the rooms around them Dax could hear similar demands being barked at the other Colas. He expected Owen to arrive at any time. He got into jeans and warm jumper, socks and trainers as fast as he could, tying up his laces with shaking fingers. What could be wrong? As the soldier stamped impatiently and swept his torch across to Gideon, Dax instinctively grabbed the Neetanite from his drawer. It had been clinging to the very top, desperate to reach him, and shot straight up his sleeve and into his armpit the second he put out his hand.

They were marched downstairs and told to get their coats from the cloaks cupboard in the hall. The Colas stared at each other in the moving light of half a dozen torches, some whispering urgently to each other, but nobody ready to shout out yet. Six armed soldiers, in black combat clothing, thick black jackets and helmets with visors, held them all in a group as they did up their coats, wide-eyed and nervous. Then Mr Eades arrived, gave them one sharp nod and said 'Go,' and they immediately ordered everyone outside and into the waiting coach.

Dax scanned in all directions and lifted his face to the air, trying to scent Owen. He could not. Fear, until then just tap dancing in his belly, now began to march determinedly for his heart. 'Where's Owen?' he asked the soldier who had come for them but the man just scowled at him.

'Get in—now!' he commanded, and Dax followed Gideon up into the small armoured coach.

Lisa pulled Mia up behind her and the girls grabbed seats just in front of Dax and Gideon's. As the other Colas piled in around them, still shocked and whispering, Lisa peered through the gap in the headrests.

'Didn't you get my message?' she hissed at

Dax. 'What's going on? Is this something to do with you?'

'No, I didn't,' Dax muttered back. 'And why would this be anything to do with me?'

'Well you had Owen all up in arms, didn't you—falling in the lake and all that! I thought maybe he'd freaked out and decided to ship us all off to a giant padded cell somewhere, before something else happens!'

'So,' Dax glanced around him as six soldiers now joined them on board and the engine struck up a sedate rumble, 'you think this is all *my* fault?'

'Wouldn't be the first time,' said Lisa.

'Everybody! Please listen!' Mr Eades was standing up in the aisle at the top end of the coach as it moved across the gravel and away from the darkened lodge.

'We have had a serious security breach at Fenton Lodge. I am empowered by the Ministry of Defence to remove you all to a place of safety. You will remain calm. You will stay seated. You will stay quiet. There will be no questions. There will be no flexing of any kind of Cola power. I will tell you more as and when you need to know it.'

Spook Williams stood up. He looked scared

212

but also affronted. He opened his mouth to speak but before he could utter a word the soldier behind him—who Dax recognized again as Weston who had last been on this coach with them as a chaperone to the disco—grabbed his shoulder and shoved him back down into his seat so hard that all he could do was gasp in shock.

'Yes, that includes you, Williams,' said Mr Eades, coldly. Spook gulped and stayed where he was. Dax and Gideon stared at each other. What on earth was happening? Dax looked through the dark tinted window of the small coach and felt his heart begin to hammer. Behind the blacked-out edifice of Fenton Lodge a deep red glow was building. The scientists' block was on fire.

Dax nudged Gideon and pointed and his friend nodded back at him, his face taut and scared in the dim light of the coach interior. At the security gate was another shock. Nobody was there. The electric gate lay open and the lodge which normally housed two or three armed soldiers was empty and dark. The coach sailed past without stopping and was out on the dark snowy road beyond in seconds.

The Colas sat silent and fearful, six black-clad

soldiers placed at intervals along the coach, while Mr Eades took his seat and seemed to be using a mobile phone to text a message to somebody, judging by the high-pitched signals Dax could hear. He kept waiting to get a message in his head from Lisa, but nothing came. Perhaps she was too upset, like the rest of them. Even the Teller brothers simply sat, staring at the back of the seat in front of them. They might be in conversation in their minds, but there was no outward sign of it.

They had been roughly shepherded from the place they had all come to think of as home at around 2.20 a.m. At around 3.30 a.m. the sky was just as dark, but the lights of a major city lit up the horizon. Staring through the window, Dax nudged Gideon, who raised his eyebrows in amazement. Neither of them had imagined that a safe place would be anywhere near a city. Colas were usually kept in the remotest location possible. Dax glanced up at the soldier nearest to them—it was Armitage, another of the disco chaperones. He badly wanted to ask where they were going, but the man's face looked like granite. Just as Dax had made his mind up to ask anyway, the coach abruptly turned down a narrow road, pulling away from the main carriageway and into a wooded area. Everyone began to stir. They could all sense that they must be arriving somewhere soon. The unlit road was almost like a driveway—perhaps it was a military base somewhere.

After three or four minutes on the unlit road, during which time no other vehicle passed or followed them, the coach finally turned right into a space among the trees and pulled to a stop. Mr Eades stood up and faced them all again.

'Pay attention everybody. You will not speak. You will not shout. You will do precisely as you are told. There will be no Cola power displayed. You are to be transferred to another vehicle. No panic. No talking. No argument. Do I make myself clear?' They nodded, too fearful to say anything. 'Excellent. I think we will get through this together very well.' Mr Eades gave a tight, cold smile and Dax had a horrible rush of misgiving. The smell. It was the *smell* on the man. It was raw excitement with a sour under-scent of bitter determination. The soldiers had the same smell, but this was normal on them—on Mr Eades, the dusty teacher and taker of notes, it was completely alien and quite terrifying. Dax stared across the seats at the man as he and Gideon got into line with the other Colas and began to move down the aisle. Mr Eades looked up and then caught his eye. He stared back, his grey eyes glittering behind his spectacles and his face impassive. He reminded Dax of a shark. Cold. And deadly.

'Wait!' Dax said. 'Wait! I want to know—' his outburst ended in a yelp as the soldier behind him shoved him so hard between the shoulder blades that he cannoned into Lisa in front of him.

'Hey!' shouted Lisa and Gideon in tandem.

'Silence!' barked Mr Eades. 'Don't force me to take drastic measures!' His nostrils flared as he added this last threat and the scent of bitter determination looped up and over the excitement.

Lisa! Dax sent, as he regained his feet and moved on down to the coach steps. *Something really bad is going on here! We shouldn't be here!* But Lisa didn't seem to pick him up. She didn't look back and no response came back into his head. Outside, a ring of soldiers had formed around them. They seemed to have attached their torches to their helmet visors and were slinging their rifles over their backs. Hands free. Dax gulped. The hair on his neck and arms prickled a warning. He looked around for an escape route. He could shift, but flying in this darkness as a peregrine would be folly. With the blazing white torches ringing them in, he couldn't see above him and had no idea what he might hit. Shifting to a fox would not help him. These men were fast and trained and they knew what to expect. He would not get past them, and even if he could, he did not want to leave his friends.

Suddenly, to his left, there was another blaze of light—red—as the tailgate lamps of a lorry suddenly switched on. A flat thin oblong of yellow light now appeared and grew rapidly to a square. The back of the lorry swung down mechanically until it was level, to reveal a lit, empty container—the sort that you see in city docks. Dax had a flash of memory. His first ever run in with Owen had occurred in the back of an empty lorry. That time had had a happy ending, but this time looked bleaker. The soldiers began to roughly guide the Colas towards the lorry.

'Hurry! Get a move on! We're all in danger out in the open!' Mr Eade's strident tones were laced with satisfaction and Dax glanced at the man again, his narrow face revealed by the steady light from the lorry. A ghost of a smile was on his thin lips.

'No!' Dax shouted and began to battle back through the others—and now they all began to resist, fear and panic leeching from them into the cold night air, swirling around Dax's senses and making him furious. 'We're not cattle! You can't put us in there!' A soldier grabbed him expertly, hauling his right arm back behind him and locking it painfully. A second later a rifle barrel rammed across Dax's jaw and throat.

'You will do as your teacher says, sonny,' a voice growled in his ear, which he recognized as belonging to Armitage. 'If you know what's good for you.'

Lisa was screaming and shouting now and Jennifer sobbing. Mia was silent, holding on to them both as two soldiers forced them up the ramp and into the container. Dax saw that it was double-skinned metal, with a thick layer of insulation between the skins. The hard metal floor had a few rugs thrown over it, and there were bottles of water stacked in a box in one corner. The other corner held two covered buckets. It was horribly clear that somebody had planned this carefully. Now he would have shifted. He would have taken any chance to get away and get help, but the soldier still held him in an agonizing half-nelson, with the rifle barrel almost cutting off his airway. They knew all about his abilities and were not taking any chances. Gideon was struggling too now, and Dax expected him to do something to warp the lorry or burst its tyres—maybe haul some of the armoury off their captors with his mind power. Luke, punching out hopelessly just behind him, must surely be about to do the same.

But despite the looks of desperate determination on the telekinetics' faces, nothing happened. They were flung brutally up the ramp and into the lorry, crashing into Alex and Jacob, who had been clinging together for support, looking angry and terrified.

Spook's head was bleeding. He and Darren had also struggled and been given rough treatment and it looked as if Spook's head had hit the wall. Barry and Clive huddled into a corner, white with shock.

Once they were all in, Dax too was flung up the ramp by Armitage. The soldiers fell back, standing three-a-side on either edge of the ramp as Mr Eades walked up it, his polished black leather shoes clipping on the metal. He had his mobile phone to his ear and was now smirking as he listened to someone on the other end of the line.

'Yes,' he said. 'To order. We are on target for the rendezvous. The auction is set for midday tomorrow.'

The Colas gasped and stared around at each other. Some of the soldiers grinned at their shock. Auction? Dax suddenly remembered something Owen had said to him more than a year ago, after his adventures in France with Gideon, Luke, Mia, and Catherine. He'd said that once the French had taken Catherine, it was only a matter of time before France found out about the Cola Club. Only a matter of time before the rest of the world got wind of it. And then the rest of the world would want what Britain had got.

'People all over the planet are going to want you,' Owen had said. 'And you wouldn't like what they'll want you *for.*'

Dax closed his eyes. In this lorry were eleven priceless auction lots—two boys who could move immense weights with their minds, two who could

220

create extraordinary illusions, a boy and a girl who could vanish into thin air, brothers who could mimic anyone and anything perfectly and speak through their thoughts, one girl who could converse with the dead and locate anything or anyone on the planet, one boy who could change into animal form . . . and one . . . and one . . . Dax felt a stab of even sharper fear. What if . . . ?

'Good,' went on Mr Eades, the smile still stretching his tight mouth. 'I foresee no problems. Everything—and everyone—is under control. Don't you love this push-button world we live in?' He smirked again. 'Yes, we have twelve here, but one is not a Cola. We have all the true eleven. Would you like the non-Cola disposed of?'

Clive and Dax exchanged horrified looks across the inside of the container.

'Hmmm. Well, he's quite useful in some ways—might be a handy tool. Leave it to me. I'll think on it. Midday then. We expect to be in position half an hour before the bidding begins. *Salut!*' He snapped the clamshell phone shut and slid it into his pocket. Now he looked around the silent, shocked group of teenagers with an expression they had never before seen on his thin face. Triumph.

'As you will probably have gathered, this is not quite the security mission you might have expected,' he stated. 'You can be very excited. You are about to embark upon the trip of a lifetime. Who knows where, this time next week, you will be? Tunisia? Greece? Saudi Arabia? China? America?'

'You traitorous, conniving, cowardly little—'

'Shhhhh!' Mr Eades wagged a finger at Lisa, who was being restrained by Mia and Gideon now. She was almost purple with rage. 'Oh, Miss Hardman, how I will miss your spoilt little outbursts. I do hope an orthodox Arab power takes *you*. How very apt to have you in a society where you will be forced to walk three steps behind your master!'

'I will get you!' spat Lisa. 'I will dowse you and I will get you!'

'Maybe,' he said. 'If your master lets you. Why don't you read my mind . . . ?'

Lisa stared at him, her eyes flashing with fury and then widening with confusion and horror. She sank back against Mia and Gideon and stopped struggling.

'Having a little difficulty, Miss Hardman?'

sneered Mr Eades. 'Oh dear, oh dear. What, no friendly spirits offering advice, either? So very fickle, the dead . . . ' Lisa was looking at the floor, her hands over her mouth.

'Now, try to share the water nicely, and keep the buckets upright when you've filled them,' said Mr Eades. He was hugely enjoying himself. 'It may get a little bumpy at times. I will probably not see you for several hours—and that,' he put his hand into his jacket pocket and pulled out a small black rectangle with grey buttons on it, much like a TV controller, and held it out, pointed towards them, '—does not worry me . . . remotely.' His tight smile became wider and revealed pointed canine teeth as he pressed a button on the black device. 'Locked,' he said, and the soldiers stepped back, the lorry engine started up, and the flat tailgate of the container swiftly rose up. In four seconds it had clanged shut, sealing off the night air completely and leaving no noise inside except for the rumbling of the engine beneath them and the scared, hitching breathing of the Colas trapped inside.

18

Soon the lorry began to move, bouncing across the uneven patch of woodland it had been parked in and making its way, presumably, back to the narrow service road.

'Sit down, everyone,' said Dax. His voice sounded steadier than he felt. 'Stay calm. We need to think.'

'Think?' spluttered Spook, clinging to the side of the lorry and sliding down onto his haunches. 'What's there to think about? Why the hell aren't you ripping the roof off, Gideon? Luke? What are you waiting for?'

Luke and Gideon looked at each other bleakly, and Dax felt a surge of cold realization.

Of course. The clues had all been there. He'd been extremely dense.

'Come on,' said Gideon, holding out his hand to Luke. 'Let's try together.'

They grasped hands and both looked grimly towards the sealed tailgate. 'Better hang on to something in case it works,' said Gideon. Then he and Luke got down to the lorry floor and sat, cross-legged, trying to keep stable as the lorry lurched unpredictably, and locked their identical green eyes on the catch at the base of the metal door. Everyone else was on the floor by now, and they held on to the metal ridges and struts of the container walls as best they could. Luke and Gideon stared and stared and Dax felt himself stop breathing, willing them to make something happen. But nothing did.

'We can't,' said Gideon at last. 'It doesn't work.'

'Oh hell,' moaned Lisa. 'I thought it was just me.'

'What do you mean?' demanded Dax, although he was increasingly sure that he already knew.

'I've been getting more and more time off,' sighed Lisa, miserably. 'At first I thought it was brilliant—great to get away from all those dead moaning minnies—but sometimes even when I wanted to get in touch, to talk to Sylv or something, I couldn't. I can't now. It's all shut down. No Cola power at all. Maybe it's all used up.'

'No,' said Dax. 'It's not. OK, all of you, hands up who's had the same thing. Maybe over the last couple of weeks.'

Everyone stared at him and then, one by one, the hands went up. Everyone, except Clive, of course.

'We haven't been able to talk to each other every time, in our heads,' said Jacob, and Alex nodded. 'It's just happened a few times. We thought it was just—I dunno—because we'd had a cold or something.'

'I thought it was that too,' said Jennifer. 'When I thought I was invisible and I wasn't. You remember, Dax? I was still really cloggy in the head. I thought maybe that was why. Like a cold could really make a difference. It's not that, is it?'

Dax put his face in his hands, and found it already burning with shame. He now knew what had happened, should have known it from the moment he was fished out of the frozen lake.

'It *started* with the cold,' he mumbled. 'That's when it all started. I am—I am so sorry. To every one of you. Gideon—Luke—Mia—Lisa—you most of all but even . . . even Spook. I am so sorry.'

'What the hell are you talking about, Jones?' demanded Spook, anchoring himself more firmly to the metal struts as the lorry turned a tight curve and they all began to slide to the left.

'When you got that cold . . . ' Dax gulped. 'Well, it wasn't just by chance. You were given it. Deliberately. By the scientists.' Everybody stared at him. Nobody said a word. He closed his eyes briefly and then had to plunge on. 'Janey gave you something for the cold and when you'd taken it you fell asleep. While you were asleep the scientists did something to you. They did it to me too.'

'What,' Spook's voice dripped ice, and the expressions on his friends' faces were not much warmer, 'did they do to me?'

Dax undid his bracelet and turned over the malachite stone. He peeled off the tape and held it up in the flat yellow light of the container. The chip was barely big enough to see. Everyone screwed up their eyes and peered at it.

'This,' said Dax, 'is a tracker chip. At least, I *thought* it was a tracker chip. Like the things they use for cats and dogs, in case they stray. While you were drugged, the scientists made an incision in the skin at the top of your spine—at the base of your skull—and put one of these inside you. So they could track you—track all of us—wherever we went.'

Everyone was now touching their neck, looking sick and disbelieving.

'I can't help noticing—*mate*—' Gideon's voice was also horribly cold. 'That *your* chip is somehow *not* in your neck. And ours still are.' His look was colder still. Dax felt his insides shrink away in horror. How could he ever justify keeping his best friend in the dark?

'It's—it's not how it looks,' he began, desperately. 'I—I mean—look, Owen cut it out of me. A while ago. He found out about it and was really angry and just—cut it out of my neck before I even knew what was happening. I thought he was going to kill me!'

Realization was dawning on Gideon's face. 'Oh—the spot on your neck! The thing that Mia healed. It was that. And that was *ages* ago!

228

So—let me work this out—you let me walk around like a microchipped cat for how long?'

'I wanted to tell you! I did! Owen made me promise not to.'

'Ah yes. The Great God Owen.' Gideon curled his lip. 'Well, now we all know who's most important to you, don't we? Handy for him, eh? Having a monitor. An obedient little mole. Did you give him reports on how we were all coping with our little trackers—never guessing? Never working it out?'

'No! Of course not!' Dax was assailed with wave after wave of disbelief and horror and he realized, darkly and bitterly, deep inside himself, that the agonies he had put Mia through earlier that week must have felt exactly like this. Only she hadn't done anything to deserve it. He had.

'He told me that . . . that . . . ' The words ran around his head like scared mice and he knew there was no way they wouldn't squeak when they came out. And there was no point in trying to explain now. There were more important things to be said.

'Look, you can hate me all you like!' he said, trying to keep the grief out of his voice. 'You need to know that it's worse than that. The reason I fell out of the sky yesterday was because I had my tracker on me when the scientists were playing with it—and it's not just a tracker. It's some kind of blocker. It blocks something in our heads when Mr Eades presses the buttons on that remote. *That's* why your powers have been cutting in and out. It's nothing to do with a cold or anything else. Whenever he pushes the button the thing in your neck routes straight into your brain and shorts out your Cola power—whenever he wants it to. Go on—all of you—try something now. You won't be able to. He's switched you off. It was the only way they dared to do this to us.'

Everyone stared at him for a second and then they gathered themselves together and began to focus. A few seconds passed before they could all accept it. Then Lisa crawled across to Dax and rested her hand on his shoulder, for support as the lorry rolled on, rather than to offer him any comfort. Her dark blue eyes were filled with contempt as she spoke. 'Get this thing out of me now. Take your bracelet off, shift to the falcon, and do what you have to do. I want it out *now*.'

Dax had stuck his own chip back under his

malachite and now he dropped the bracelet and sent it skidding to the far end of the truck. 'No,' he said to Lisa. 'It needs to be Mia first.'

'I don't really think you're in a position to be telling us *anything* we should do!' said Lisa and again his insides crawled and flinched as nobody spoke up in his defence.

'It's just that . . . Mia will need to heal you all. It hurts. And there's blood.'

'Fine. Mia first. Now get on with it.'

Dax closed his eyes, tried to steady his heart, which was skittering about inside him like a pea in a rolling barrel, and shifted. His talons scratched into the thin paint on the metal floor as Mia turned her back to him and pulled her hair up off her neck. Lisa steadied her friend and looked at the peregrine. She bunched up her fist and held it against the top of Mia's spine, for Dax to use as a perch. She didn't yelp when he landed on it, even though he had to dig his talons into her bare skin to steady himself. Dax had thought he could feel much less when he was in falcon form. Now he discovered he was wrong. The boy within the bird wanted to cry and run away, but the bird without the boy fixed its eyes on the spot just below Mia's hairline, and then, without hesitation, drove its vicious beak into her warm skin.

Mia jerked and gasped but did not cry out. Jennifer gave a little moan of horror as the blood began to trickle down Mia's neck. Dax found the chip quickly and retrieved it in his beak as Lisa pulled a hanky from her coat pocket to mop the blood.

'Is it out?' said Mia, and she sounded very young.

'Yes,' said Lisa as Dax deposited the sticky black speck of plastic on her knuckle. 'Can you heal yourself?'

'No,' said Mia. 'You know I can't. But it's nothing. Don't worry.'

'Me next,' said Lisa.

'Why you?' cut in Spook. 'We all need to get those things out of us.'

'I need to get through to Sylv,' explained Lisa, with more calmness than Dax would have expected. 'She might be able to reach Mrs Sartre.'

'Well, how do you know they're not in on this?' said Spook. 'They all knew about the tracker chips! What makes you think they haven't organized the whole thing with that git Eades?'

'I don't believe that,' said Lisa. 'Mrs Sartre would never do it. Nor would Owen.'

Dax shifted back to boy, so he could speak.

'Owen knew about the tracker chips—he told me about them, about the drugging and everything. But he didn't know about the blocker switch. I *know* he didn't. And he would never sell us out. Never. He would die for us!'

Spook looked at Dax as if he were vermin. Not for the first time, but it was the first time Dax had *felt* like vermin. 'Or maybe he's just got you nicely brainwashed. He's your hero, isn't he, dingo? Replacement for your no-show dad. Can't blame you, I suppose.'

'Enough!' It was Mia. The one who had the least reason to defend him. 'Stop turning on him. Can't you see he's trying to help us? He's right too—Owen, Mrs Sartre, Mrs Dann, Mr Tucker, Tyrone . . . they're all in it for us. I know it. You must know it too, or you're incredibly dense, Spook. Stop whining and start helping. Give me your glove.'

Spook looked mutinously at Dax, but he handed Mia his thick suede glove and she put it on as Lisa now turned around and pulled her

233

hair up off her neck. Mia put her gloved fist in the same position against Lisa's spine and Dax shifted again and flew to it. Already he could feel Mia's waves of warmth, buffeting across Lisa's skin, ready to offset the pain. Lisa flinched and gave a short cry as the falcon tore into her neck, but Mia soothed the pain instantly. As soon as the chip was out, she touched her fingers to Lisa's bloody neck and the wound repaired itself within seconds.

Lisa put both of their chips into one of the buckets in the corner of the container. 'Next,' she said and Spook turned around and Dax prepared to attack yet another Cola. But then the lorry lurched to a halt and the engine cut out. Instantly the light inside the container went off, plunging them all into inky darkness. Spook cursed and Lisa shushed him.

'Listen—Dax—go to the fox. Where are we?'

Dax had already shifted, his ears cocked and picking up a myriad noises around the truck. A rhythmic push and pull, a swell of noise that came and went, mechanical notes, thrumming engines, shouts from men in the distance, metallic clangs and one low, low note which sounded for a few seconds and then stopped. If the noises didn't convince him the smell certainly did. Oil and salt and tar and weed.

He shifted back, gulping. 'I think we're at a port. This container's going on a ship.'

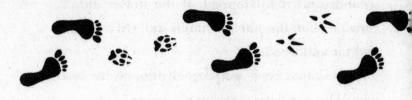

19

There was a shocked silence for a few seconds and then Jennifer began crying again and there were murmurs and groans. The perfume of panic pulsed around Dax and he knew that he was adding to it.

'We have to do something!' said Lisa. 'Bang on the sides—make a lot of noise!' Immediately everyone, as if relieved to have a way to let their panic out, began to shout and scream and bash against the sides of the container. Dax remained still, cross-legged on the floor. He knew it was hopeless. The container had been insulated and the only reason he had been able to hear beyond it was because his fox senses were so much more

236

powerful than human senses. Even the outside smells came through from air ducted in from the engine. There was no source of fresh air directly into the container—and therefore no way in which the noise could escape. The seals around the door were tight. If someone walked very close to the lorry they might just make out the vibration of their desperate thuds, but as it was almost certainly passing through with high level Ministry of Defence clearance (even if Eades was faking it), it was highly unlikely any ordinary dock worker would be interfering.

Eventually the cacophony subsided. Dax shifted back to fox so he could see them all, slumped defeated on the floor. He sent a message to Lisa, knowing that now it could get through. *Lisa, I don't want to take away everyone's hope, but this is insulated. We won't be heard. The only chance we have is if they open the door.*

Lisa's frustration and fear carried back into his head with her message. *How do we make them open the door? How do we?*

Dax looked up at the ceiling of their prison. Yes. He was certain of it. *We have to make a fire,* he sent back.

Are you insane? We'll be roasted alive before they find out! There are no gaps, are there, for the smoke to get out?

Dax tried to sound very calm as he sent back to her. *No, there is no fresh ventilation—just some air pumped through from the engine. But that doesn't matter. There's a smoke alarm on the ceiling.*

After a pause, in which Spook and the Teller brothers began banging and shouting again, Lisa sent back: *OK. But what if it's not working? Then we all roast.*

We've got the rugs, offered Dax. *If the worst comes to the worst, we can put out the flames with those. And the water.*

Lisa stared up at the ceiling, although she couldn't see anything in the dark. *And our oxygen supply? How do we replace that?*

Dax clicked his foxy teeth with frustration. *Well, would you rather just wait for a nice sultan to buy you?*

'All right,' said Lisa, out loud now. 'Everyone, listen to me. Shut up you lot. It's no good. We can't be heard. We need to make a fire and set the alarm off, so they'll open the door. Then we can storm them.'

'You're nuts!' shouted Gideon. 'We'll all fry!'

'No we won't. Trust me. We've got blankets and water in case it gets out of hand. Now—has anyone got a match?'

There was silence. Dax shifted back to boy so he could speak again. 'We know how it's going to be done. Mia. Please.'

'I told you—I can't just do it to order.'

'Yes you can,' said Dax. 'When you're stressed enough. Aren't you stressed enough now?'

Mia's answer was a sudden bloom of flame in the pile of blankets beside her. 'Apparently yes,' she said as the Colas who had not seen this before all gasped and murmured in astonishment.

'Wait,' said Spook. 'Take out our chips first!'

'Can't,' said Dax. 'Not enough time. We're moving again.'

The lorry had begun to edge forward and Dax could pick up other sounds—crane type sounds. Any time they might be grasped with giant iron claws and swung up onto a ship's deck. 'Come on, Mia!' urged Lisa. 'Make it smoke!'

The small funnel of flame got redder and wider and the smell of burning blanket became thicker in the air. Dax desperately hoped he hadn't just prompted Mia to incinerate them all before they got auctioned.

'Get by the door,' he said. 'But keep low—the smoke will rise.' Already they were coughing. 'We've got to get out and run and make a lot of noise—so anyone working nearby will know about it.'

The smoke thickened and for a few long, awful seconds, Dax thought they would have to put the flame out and then die of lack of oxygen anyway—but then a beeping noise cut through the coughing and wheezing. For twenty seconds nothing happened and Mia choked out, 'It's no good! I'll have to put it out.'

'No!' Dax could hear footfalls outside. 'Get ready to blast it up big behind us as we go out!'

A second later the tailgate knocked and thudded metallically and then the night air was flooding in, along with orange glare from the docks. Dax wasted no time. He shifted to falcon and flew straight at the face of the man he saw first, who, thankfully, had his visor lifted. Dax went for the eyes and had the grim satisfaction of hearing the man scream as his talons struck. He couldn't wait to blind him properly though, as one beat of a fist would almost certainly break his neck. He was away a moment before he would have been clouted senseless and as Mia's fire flared up behind them and the Colas spilled out into the dock and scattered, Dax shot high into the air.

It was only as he reached the thirteen metre high arc of one of the docks' myriad sodium lamps that Dax realized how hopeless it was. The lorry was parked far from the main dock traffic on a deserted quayside, against which a long low container-ship lay, with a rusting hulk of an ancient barge berthed behind it. The only other vehicle was a giant trolley-type crane on tracks, which, he knew from his father, was known as a straddle carrier. Surrounding the back of the flaming lorry were all six soldiers, one clutching at his face, three training rifles on the Colas as they tried to escape and two making a grab for whoever they could get. The Colas were fit—they did lots of sport and gym and swimming—but they could not outrun trained soldiers. He saw Lisa punch out at one of them and he caught her fist and turned her arm around, snagging her down. To his horror Dax saw one of the soldiers pull a short, thick-barrelled gun from his hip. He levelled it at Mia who was trying to drag Lisa out of the other soldier's grip.

There was a dull crack and Mia dropped to the ground and lay still. Lisa began to scream. Dax felt faint and tightened his talons on the lamp. He could hardly believe his eyes, but the evidence was cruelly sharp under his falcon gaze. Mia lay slumped on her side, her eyes slightly open and her mouth slack.

'Head count!' shouted the commander again. 'Where are they? Shoot at will!' Another crack and Darren was also on the concrete. Dax felt his world begin to spiral away. He was losing his senses. This could not be real. 'One went to a bird. Dark-haired kid—chip must have failed. Where is he? Get him for me now!'

Dax! Don't stay! You have to go! You have to go! Lisa's message sounded like sobs and he could see her trying to reach Mia, but unable to move from the iron grip of her captor. *Go! Go! Go!*

Dax knew she was right. Gideon was down there. So was Clive. And Luke and Lisa and Mia . . . or maybe not Mia any more. His heart wrenched but he knew there was no other choice.

The others could not escape, but he could. And he might be the only chance they had left.

Dax leaped from the top of the light and flapped hard to get high above the revealing orange glare of the docks. He could probably outmanoeuvre a bullet by day, but at night it was hard work to stay airborne. He headed out to sea, towards the dark skies above the water. Grief and horror flew with him. Three miles out he saw a small fishing trawler at anchor. It was dark and hopefully its skipper was asleep below. Dax dropped to the bridge and collapsed onto the rusting, salt-washed roof. He knew he was out of reach of Eades and his men and should have felt relief. But all he wanted to do was cry.

He shifted back to a boy. Birds and animals don't cry. Dax Jones had to.

20

Just before dawn Dax decided to break into the trawler. He had lain in a sort of stupor for two hours, trying to make sense of everything that had happened. He knew he had to get to Owen, but the problem was that he couldn't even lift his head off the roof of the bridge. Eventually he was rested enough to get up to a sitting position. He listened hard and detected no sign of anyone on board the ship and no scent beyond the ever present smell of fish and engine oil. He knew he had to eat, or there was no hope of getting off this boat and getting help.

Dax slid his shaking legs over the edge of the roof and jumped down onto the deck below, collapsing as soon as he hit the wooden planking. After a minute to recover, being gently rocked by the mild sea, he turned his attention to the door which led into the bridge and to the decks below. In fact, he didn't have to break in. The door was open. Inside, steep wooden stairs led below to some basic living quarters and the galley—a tiny kitchen area with a miniature sink and stove and some cupboards beneath. Dax ransacked the cupboards and found biscuits and crisps and tins of fruit and corned beef. In a drawer he found a tin opener. He worked it around a tin of pineapple and then drank out the juice, heedless of the sharp rim. The fruit sugar flowed into him like five star fuel. Sitting on a battered red leather bench with a narrow dark wood table along it, Dax tore into the shortbread biscuits and then the corned beef and the packs of salty crisps. He ate and ate, as if he had been starved for weeks. Eventually the clamouring of his stomach quietened down and he began to feel almost normal.

As his strength returned, the clarity of his memory returned with it. This was less welcome. Mia was shot. So was Darren. Both might be dead. But he had to stop thinking about that. He had to clear his head. Where were they all now? Had the container-ship left with them or without them? Were they still on course for Eades's 'rendezvous' at midday?

Dax went into the tiny toilet and washroom, used the none-too-clean lavatory and washed his face at a grubby little sink with one small tap over it. The boy that gazed back at him from the smeared mirror stuck to the wall was strained and looked much older than he had yesterday.

Dax went back up onto the deck. Now he needed to fly again—to get to Owen. First he would do a recce of the dock—see if there were any traces of the others. He was just about to shift when something thudded into the stern of the boat, juddering it on the calm water. Dax leaned out over the edge and stared down nervously. Perhaps the owner was back, come over from the shore on a dinghy—but he'd heard no engine. There was another small thud, almost a slap, against the hull and Dax's eyes widened with amazement. A long-fingered hand was clutching on to one of the black tyres roped to the side of the trawler. Below it was a soaking wet head of dark red hair. Clinging to the boat with his eyes shut and his dripping face like parchment, was Spook Williams.

His least favourite Cola could not speak for several minutes. Dax dragged him up on to the deck with some difficulty, as he was weighed down by drenched clothes, and almost senseless. As soon as the boy slumped onto the wooden planking Dax went down into the trawler for a blanket and returned to wrap it around the shivering figure. Next he fetched water in a tin mug, along with the biscuits. It was some time before Spook could even grasp the mug.

Eventually though, he drank and some of the colour began to return to his face as the blanket did its work. Dax steered him below where it was warmer, and put the small kettle onto the tiny stove after switching on the gas bottle beneath it. Soon he was able to replace the mug of cold water with a mug of sweet tea and by the time Spook had got halfway through it, and eaten a couple of biscuits, he was able to speak again.

'This is all your fault.'

Dax sighed. 'If you say so.'

'You should have told us. What happened to "Every Cola for every Cola", eh? Didn't you tell me that? Didn't you say we all had to look out for each other? That time on Exmoor?'

'Yes, I did. And I meant it. And I was . . . it was just—complicated.'

'Yeah, right.'

Dax sat down opposite him and touched his forehead to see if he was getting any warmer. Spook swiped his hand away angrily. 'Get off me, dingo!'

'Fine. Get hypothermia. I don't care. But we've got to think what to do next.' Dax felt the uncomfortable stirrings of respect for Spook as he added: 'How on earth did you get away? And how did you get all the way out here?'

Spook stared into his tea. 'Everyone went for the land side,' he muttered. 'But not me. I knew my best bet was the dock side. I went over the edge and into the water—in the gap between that old barge wreck and the dock.' Dax shuddered. He could imagine how frightening that would have been, caught between a rusting metal hull and the slippery, weed-lined side of the dock wall, nothing but cold black water holding you up.

'I heard the noise—heard the shots,' went on Spook. 'Who got shot? You must have seen.'

Dax tried to keep his voice steady, but it still came out high and hurt. 'Darren,' he said, and Spook looked up at him, aghast. 'And Mia.' Now the boy's face crumpled.

'Were—were they dead?' he whispered.

'I don't know. They looked dead, but I don't know.'

There was a long silent pause, while both boys grappled with their emotions.

'They searched for me—and you,' went on Spook, at length. 'But they knew they'd blown it with you, and they couldn't see me because there was a hole in the side of the dock wall and I pushed myself into it. I thought they'd get me with that tracker in my head, but I don't think any of those thugs had the control thing with them. Only Eades. They gave up after about ten minutes and then I couldn't hear much of anything from where I was.'

'So how did you get out here?' asked Dax. 'This has got to be three or four miles off shore!'

'I swam.'

'You swam?'

'Well, I didn't *fly*, did I? Have you forgotten? I'm a champion lane swimmer. I was top in it at my old school.' Now Dax did remember. It was one of the many things Spook regularly crowed about, and he had spent a lot of time in the pool at Fenton Lodge.

'The sea was calm and after a couple of hours, when I couldn't hear anything else from the dock-side, I didn't want to risk climbing back up so I decided to get out to a buoy I could see about a mile away. Only it turned out to be more like three miles, I reckon. I hung on to that for a while, and then when the light came I saw a trawler and reck-oned I could reach it. And I did. Had no idea *you* were on it, of course.'

'Just as well,' said Dax. 'You'd never have got on it by yourself. You were nearly done for. I can't believe you've survived the cold, either! You should be dead of hypothermia.'

Then Spook looked up, and the curl was back on his lip. 'I would have got on. I don't need you.'

Dax said nothing. He poured himself a mug of tea now and tried to live with the creepy feeling of being impressed by Spook.

'So then, what's the big plan *now*?'

'I was going to fly to Owen,' said Dax, 'before I found you.'

'Well, don't let *me* stop you! Fly off now. I don't care.' Spook pulled the blanket tighter around him and winced and Dax finally paid attention to the smell he'd got a few wafts of while they were talking. Blood. Spook's blood. He leaned across and pulled the blanket back from his shoulder and saw the dark red patch down the back of his blue sweatshirt.

'What did you do?' he asked, appalled, although he already knew. The evidence was right in front of him. A ragged star of a wound high on Spook's neck, kept bleeding by the salt water.

Spook reached into his jeans pocket and hauled out a small penknife. 'I got it out, while I was down in the water by the dock. It took ages, but there was a bit of rope to hang on to in the hole—and there was no way I was going anywhere with *that* inside me.'

Dax stared at him, amazed. He'd never have thought Spook would have the nerve. 'Look,' he said. 'I don't care what you think of me. Listen. You have to get dry and I have to get something on that wound. Then we need to get to Owen. Both of us.'

'I told you—go! I don't need you.'

Dax clicked his teeth in frustration. He began to search through the cupboards for a first aid kit. He found nothing in the galley, but in the dark bunk room at the stern of the trawler he discovered a green box containing bandages and plasters. He also found some dry clothes; trousers and jumpers—even underwear, in some drawers under the bunks. Happily Spook did not need much persuading to get into them, although he eyed Dax warily when he waved a plaster at him.

'Look, I'm not going to nursemaid you. I've got better things to do,' said Dax. 'But you need this plaster on or you'll bleed all over the dry clothes and then you might attract attention when we get ashore. Just turn round. Let me sponge it off and put this on.'

Spook scowled, but he turned round and then allowed Dax to mop the blood away with a cold, wet flannel and dry it with tissue. Now that it was out of the water the wound was finally beginning to clot. It looked awful; Spook had sawed into himself with a penknife that was obviously not very sharp. It must have hurt immensely. 'Are you sure you got it out?' Dax asked, before he stuck down the large waterproof plaster.

'Yesss,' hissed Spook. 'I wouldn't have carved myself up like a pork chop for nothing! I got it under my nail. I felt it. Then I threw it in the water. If I hadn't they'd probably be here getting us now, wouldn't they? If they've tracked it they must think I drowned. Anyway, they're not here, are they? They're probably well out in the North Sea by now.'

'Did you see them go?' Dax realized he should have kept watch from the trawler. He might have seen a container-ship go out. But nothing could have kept him sharp and awake in the last couple of hours.

'No, of course I didn't. I was in the water in the dark. But I heard the ship go—and felt it in the water. Backwash nearly drowned me when the engines started up. It went about twenty minutes after I hit the water. They must have hurried it up a bit after our fire stunt. I didn't hear any sirens or helicopters or anything, though. We didn't get anyone's attention.'

Dax looked at his watch, which was on his right wrist, because all Colas wore their stones on the left, and saw that it was 8 a.m. Four hours from now there was a 'rendezvous' somewhere in the North Sea. And then the auction would begin. With somewhat fewer lots. Possibly only seven if Mia and Darren were dead.

'We've got to get to a phone!' he said. 'We've got to get back to land and find a phone and try to get to Owen.'

Spook was now clothed in fisherman's gear— thick weave baggy jeans and a grey knitted jumper. Fortunately he was tall and the adult sizes fitted him quite well. He had found some thick, oiled wool socks too. He looked a lot better.

'Go!' he said. 'Fly to land. I'll come in by boat.'

'You know how to sail this thing?'

Spook shrugged and climbed up to the bridge, where he put his hands on the wheel and peered at the dials. He flicked a switch and the trawler's engine suddenly coughed and burst into noisy life, sending vibrations through the deck. 'Can't be that much different to my dad's motor cruiser,' said Spook. 'I'll take it to the beach area, run it aground and get up on to the shore.' He indicated a beach further north, which looked sandy. 'You can meet me there. Tell me what's happening. If you like. I don't care. I'm doing my own thing now anyway. I'm not in Cola Club any more. Not after this.' He touched his hand to the plaster. Dax couldn't blame him—especially after he'd probably lost the only two Colas he really cared about, too.

'What if you get seen by people, going onto the beach?' asked Dax and Spook smirked.

'They won't see me. They'll be distracted by a wrinkly old sea dog doing cartwheels.' Of course. Spook had got rid of the chip and now he could protect himself with illusion again.

'OK, well—good luck.'

Spook didn't look at Dax. 'Yeah,' he said. 'Try not to fly into any windows.'

Dax went outside as a chain began to clank noisily up into the trawler's underside. Spook was bringing up the anchor. Dax glanced back once at the fourteen-year-old skipper, and then shifted and flew into the sky.

21

Finding a working public telephone wasn't easy. The first two that he tried, in the busy streets of the city, were vandalized. Eventually he found a row of phones under plastic hoods at the railway station. Looking uneasily around him at the crowds of commuters, Dax dialled 100 and asked for a reverse charge call to the Fenton Lodge number. He knew the number by heart, but feared that it would not connect—that it had been knocked out of working order by the troops who had kidnapped them the night before and set light to the scientists' quarters.

As the operator made the connection he held his breath—and was then amazed and relieved to find it ringing. When the call was answered, he did not recognize the male voice which said 'Fenton Lodge'. The operator asked if a reverse charge call would be accepted and the voice said, 'Yes—go ahead.'

Dax gulped. Who was this? Was he safe to talk to?

'Go ahead, caller,' said the operator. 'You're through.'

'Yes—thanks,' said Dax. There was a pause in which the operator's connection clicked off, leaving him alone on the line with the mystery voice.

'Who is this?'

'Who are you?' said Dax. His voice was shaky and he coughed, trying to control it.

'This is Control. Please give your code.'

Dax gasped. His *code*? He had not had to give his code in for months and months. Control had never been set up at Fenton Lodge. He had had to call Control every single day when he spent some time back at home with Gina and Alice eighteen months ago, but not since then.

'B Chase Web Zero Vulpine,' he said, the words pouring instantly from his memory.

'Mr Jones. Where are you?'

'I want to speak to Owen.'

'It's vital that you tell us your location.'

'I want to speak to Owen. Nobody else.'

'Mr Hind is not available at this time. Please give me the number of the payphone you are calling from. Mr Hind will call you back within ten minutes.'

Dax felt desperate. The idea of talking to Owen was the only thing which was keeping him together. If he gave in to his fears about the strange voice and slammed down the phone, there was no telling when he would speak to Owen again. Ten minutes was not long to wait.

'Mr Jones. Your number. Please. We can't help you without it.'

Dax peered at the number on the grubby plastic label over the payphone and read it out.

'Can you tell us what has happened to you?' prompted Control again but Dax just said, 'You've got my number. I will wait ten minutes—no longer. I only speak to Owen Hind.' And he slammed down the phone, his heart racing.

Dax turned and scanned around him from under the scratched plastic hood. He felt incredibly vulnerable. He just couldn't believe that Mr Eades would have let him and Spook go so easily. Even if he was cutting his losses for the auction, he would still fear being traced by the government and he must know that Dax was free of the chip and could fly—back to Fenton Lodge, if need be, and tell them everything he knew. And that's what he would do, Dax decided, if he didn't get a call in ten minutes. He would go back to check on Spook and let him know what was happening, and then fly back to Fenton Lodge.

The phone jangled and he jumped violently, spun round and whipped the receiver to his ear. For a few seconds there was silence.

'Who is this?' said Dax, finally. He heard a familiar sigh on the line.

'Dax—thank God! Are you OK?' He felt a lump in his throat but swallowed it down, determined not to sound pathetic. Hearing Owen's voice made him want to start crying all over again. He had such terrible things to tell him.

'I'm—I'm OK,' he managed. He took a breath. 'But the others aren't. Spook and I got away but the others didn't. It was Mr Eades. Can you believe that? Mr Eades is auctioning them to other countries—at midday today. We think they're on a ship somewhere in the North Sea.'

'OK, Dax. Now, you need to stay calm. I'm coming for you.'

'I'm at—'

'It's OK, I know where you are,' cut in Owen. 'Is Spook with you?'

'No—he's on a fishing trawler. Probably on a beach by now—there's a sandy beach north of the port. I'm going back to meet him in a minute.'

'OK, I'm coming to get you both—but Dax, I want you to stay where you are. Don't go back to Spook. I will be with you in thirty minutes and we will both get Spook. Stay there—can you promise me that?'

'Yes,' said Dax and the strangled sound was back in his voice because he knew what he had to say next. 'Owen . . . I think . . . I think Mia might be dead. And Darren.'

There was a brief silence at the end of the phone but Dax could sense Owen closing his eyes.

'Dax, just stay there. Keep your head down and stay among a crowd of people if you can. I will be with you very soon. Hang in there.'

He stood under the phone hood for another

five minutes, looking warily around the station for signs of Mr Eades's men. He knew he was being ridiculous. They would hardly be skulking about in black with rifles over their shoulders. The intense odour of cigarettes and old chewing gum eventually drove him away from the payphone and across to the busy café area close to the departures board. He reasoned that his best chance of locating an enemy would be through his sense of smell—highly sensitive even when he wasn't in fox form.

He pulled up the hood on his winter coat and sat down at a free table. Someone had left a newspaper there, so he pretended to read it, while concentrating hard on what his nose was picking up. After fifteen minutes he began to think that he really would see Owen soon—that he'd be rescued and so would Spook and somehow everything would turn out OK for all the Colas. In his left armpit the Neetanite suddenly lurched and twisted. Dax reached in under his coat, through his collar, and pulled it out. The strange cylinder trembled in his palm and then spun slowly, like the needle on a compass, and stopped still. Dax moved his hand and the Neetanite immediately adjusted itself, so that its pointed end remained angled in the same direction. It really *was* like a compass needle. Dax edged himself around the table and it adjusted again. Always pointing in the same direction. *Which* direction? And why? Dax glanced along the row of shops and kiosks and spotted travel goods on sale in the store just opposite the café. He had another ten minutes to wait for Owen. He pocketed the Neetanite and stepped quickly across to the shop and looked down the rack of goods until he found a compass, needle pointing steadily north inside its plastic packaging. He pulled the Neetanite out again and let it rest on the flattened heel of his left hand, while holding the compass with his right. As he moved his position, both objects in his palm adjusted. The compass held true north and the Neetanite held north-west.

A deep shiver ran through him. Dax had no idea what this meant and he didn't have time to think about it. As he crouched back down to hang the plastic compass packet back on its display rack he suddenly picked up an unmistakable pulse of a scent. Gun oil. With it came the thick reek of male sweat and high level adrenalin. From more than one direction. Staying crouched by the rack,

Dax edged around so that he was hidden from view from the main floor of the station. Scores of people were passing to and fro—but what Dax saw was the *movement* more than anything else, in the two men walking several feet apart, twenty metres away from where he had been at the café table. They may have looked casual to other people but Dax recognized the swift, economical steps and the discreet scanning of the building around them. Armed professionals. Looking for someone. They were looking for him. It had only taken another inhalation to identify Weston, travelling with one of the other soldiers who had betrayed them in the early hours of that morning.

How had they known to seek him here? The phone, probably. Most likely they were monitoring call boxes all over the city. And now what? Owen was still seven or eight minutes away. Could Dax hide out here until he arrived? No—already the woman at the till was giving him odd looks. Dax thrust the Neetanite back into his coat pocket, ignoring its attempts to spin itself north-west against a glove, and stood up. His pursuers had their backs to him, but he didn't have much time before they would turn around, in their casual way, and scan with assassins' eyes in his direction. He moved quickly deeper into the shop and tried to work out what to do. He could shift, but a falcon flying through the station would almost certainly attract attention—and he would have to stay low until he reached the exits, exposing himself to their bullets.

'OK, everyone—time's up! We've got a train to catch. If you haven't spent your money by now you're too late.' Dax looked up at the owner of the shrill voice. A woman in her thirties, dressed warmly and carrying a bag and a clipboard. She was addressing twenty or so children—probably on a school outing—who were scattered among the books and magazines around the shop or paying at the till. They grumbled and began to group together as the woman checked them off on her list and chivvied them along. Dax saw his chance. As the group huddled together and then began to move away towards the train gates, he hurried along after them and fell into step. A couple of the girls, about his own age, gave him an odd look, but didn't say anything. He kept his head low and his hood down over his brow and moved in pace with them, and for nearly half a minute it seemed to be working, until the woman with the clipboard glanced back and then strode down the moving line of children towards him, leaving a colleague at the top end.

'I'm sorry, are you lost? I don't think you're with us, are you, young man?' Through the cacophony of the station her shrill voice rang out like a bell and Dax felt alarm flare through him. He glanced over his shoulder and saw movement. Professional, armed movement. He kept walking. 'Young man, are you quite all right? Can you hear me?' insisted the woman, so, *so* loudly. He groaned. They were running for him now, heavy army boots striking the stone floor faster and faster. Dax pushed through the crowd of children as the shrill woman shouted out in annoyance and the professionals closed in. A guard was checking tickets on Gate 7, where they had been heading for their train. Dax shoved him aside and ran full pelt along the platform, dodging passengers and suitcases on trolleys. Now there were more shouts.

'Everybody get down!' bellowed Weston. 'This is a security alert! Get down! Known terrorist on platform seven.'

There were screams and the footfalls behind

him grew louder as his pursuers got closer. Dax glanced once over his shoulder and saw the sweat gleaming on Weston's forehead and the man's teeth, clenched. His colleague was close behind him, pulling his gun out from his chest harness.

'Give it up, lad!' called Weston. 'There's no getting away this time.'

Oh no? thought Dax. He had been conditioned against shifting in public for so long now that it hadn't happened instinctively, but after the last twenty-four hours he reckoned all the rules were off anyway. Fifty metres away, the station roof ended in a frill of old wooden boarding. Dax shifted and, to shouts of shock and amazement from British Rail passengers and staff, soared up into the white winter sky. Three bullets followed him but he had corkscrewed around and up and out of sight into cloud before they had been unleashed.

A minute later the earth had fallen so far away beneath him that the station looked like a matchbox—the railway line like black cotton threads. He had been flying north-west for two minutes before he remembered that he was meant to be getting to Owen. But how could he do that

266

now? And what about Spook? Then Dax realized, with a thud of guilty shock, that he had clearly told Owen over the phone where Spook was, even though Owen had not asked. He must have guessed there was a chance someone else was listening in. That's why he'd shut him up before he could say more. With the phone lines tapped, Eades's men would have known where to find Dax anyway, but Spook—he'd given him away! Dax wheeled around in the air, pulling away from the north-west with a deep reluctance that he didn't understand, and descended fast, south-east, eyes scanning the coast for the sandy beach where Spook should have landed by now. He recognized it quickly and blessed nature for his peregrine eyes as he even spotted the trawler, lying at an awkward angle on the beach and Spook striding up the grassy slope away from the sand wearing a black trawlerman's coat.

He also saw something else. Further along the coast road, two black four-by-fours were approaching. Had they been sent by Owen? Or by Eades? He moved above the vehicles and then plummeted down to them, strong wings halting his drop and pulling him into a low coast eight metres above the moving cars. He scanned the interiors and saw men in both driver and passenger seats. He didn't recognize the first two and hope flared in his heart that these were Owen's men. Then he pulled ahead to look into the leading car and his hopes were dashed. The driver was clearly Armitage, looking grim and focused. Dax fervently hoped that Spook was working on his illusion of the cartwheeling salty sea dog as he strode away from the beach. Spook had less than five minutes before Eades's men reached the car park by the beach—and the boy was heading directly for it. Dax shot up into the air again and located the red hair and familiar strut, then he lost no time in hurtling down to Spook's shoulder.

Spook yelped and shot Dax a furious look as he landed on the thick material of his stolen coat. Dax dropped to the ground and shifted back to boy, gasping: 'We have to go—we have to run *now*! Black cars coming. Eades's men.'

Spook stared at him and then tossed his head. 'Forget it, Jones. I'm safe enough. They won't see me. They'll only see some old geezer.'

'Don't you think they *know* what you can do?' insisted Dax, glancing urgently towards the west, knowing the black four-by-fours were only minutes away. 'You think they're not going to round up every single person in this area and check them out! They've probably got DNA matching equipment! And you can't keep an illusion like that up for long anyway, can you? Not for yourself. It doesn't work so well on yourself, does it?'

Spook blinked and Dax knew he'd convinced him. Like every other Cola, Spook suffered with the Loved Ones' Buffer. Especially when it came to himself.

Dax grabbed his arm and began to drag him along, and finally the boy began to look scared and was soon running fast. 'Where to?' he puffed as they hurtled back along the beach. Dax had a falcon mind-map still in his head. The ring road, heading north. He could fly there in a minute, but with Spook, even running full pelt, it would take ten. He expected gunfire to ring out behind them at any moment and kept looking back over his shoulder.

Spook glanced back too, and just as four black figures emerged on the edge of the beach, he stopped and turned round.

'What are you *doing*?' yelled Dax.

'Shut up!'

'Are you insane? They're over there. They'll see us any moment.'

'No they won't.' Spook lowered his chin and looked back down the beach from beneath his brows and Dax saw the coolness fall across his face, the way it fell across Gideon's face when he was about to use his telekinetic power. Half a mile along the sand and shingle, the air shivered.

'What are you doing?' repeated Dax, his voice low.

'I'm doing *you*,' muttered Spook. 'You're running off down the beach looking like you're peeing your pants.'

It was obviously a good illusion. The men in black gave chase.

Dax began to pull Spook along again, backwards. 'Come on! They've probably got binoculars. They might look back this way at any time!'

'All right—*wait*!' snapped Spook. 'There, you've just shifted into a dingo and cringed off behind a stack of deckchairs. Now we can go.' He turned and followed, running harder than Dax had ever seen him run before.

At last they reached a busy dual carriageway

heading out of the city. They collapsed for a while in the shelter of some bushes on the verge and then Dax hauled himself and Spook up again. 'We can't wait,' he gasped. 'We need a lift. You have to hitch for us.'

'Me?' Spook curled his lip in disdain. 'I've never hitch-hiked in my life!'

'Better start now. Do an illusion. Look like a babe or something.'

Spook stared at him, appalled.

'Well, if you don't think you *can* . . . '

'Of course I can! But I'm not doing it for a second longer than it takes for a truck to pull up!'

Spook stood up, shot Dax another withering look and then held out his thumb. Around him the air wavered again, like the air above a hot road in summer, and within thirty seconds a truck was slowing down and pulling towards the verge. As soon as Dax and Spook hoisted themselves up into the cab the driver, a stout man in his fifties, looked disappointed.

'Where's the girl?' he said, in a London accent.

Dax and Spook looked at each other and shrugged.

'Just us,' said Spook. 'How long have you been driving?'

'Too long! Thirty-four years!' sighed the man, pulling away. 'Where're you two off to then?'

'Are you going . . . north-west, by any chance?' asked Dax, as the Neetanite twisted again in his pocket.

'Yep—Fort William. How far do you want to go?'

'All the way,' said Dax.

Spook glared at him. 'What about Owen?'

Dax shook his head. 'Didn't go as planned,' he said, quietly. 'We'll call him again soon. But not now. Not anywhere around here.'

Spook eyed him sceptically. 'I hope you know what you're doing, Jones. And don't think I'm just going to follow you around. I don't need you. I don't need anyone.'

Dax couldn't say any more. Partly because they now had to chat to the driver, who wanted to know their names and where they were off to—but also because it was hard to explain. He *did* know exactly what he was doing, but he had no idea why. In the last thirty minutes, since the Neetanite had begun to spin and insistently point north-west, he had been filled with the conviction that he *must* follow it. He had no idea where *to*. He only knew that the force of his conviction was growing with every minute that passed. It had even overtaken his need to get to Owen and to try to save Gideon and Lisa and the rest of the Colas—and half an hour ago he could not have believed that anything on this planet was more important than *that*.

As Spook talked to the driver, telling him that he was called David and Dax was called Gaylord (the driver hooted with laughter) and that they were looking for work in the ski resorts of the Highlands, Dax stared out of the window in silence, his head tilting true north-west, and made his apologies for what he was going to do.

I'm sorry, Owen. I'm sorry, Gideon. I'm sorry, Lisa, Mia, Clive . . . all of you. Whatever happens now, I go north-west . . . Please forgive me. He closed his eyes and tried to rest and soon the pull of the Neetanite began to blot out everything else, like a sandstorm blots out the sun. Only one word was left in his head.

Corridor.

22

Gideon wants me to say he forgives you about the chip. DAX! Oh, will you pay attention? What's in your head? There's hardly any space left! What's in your head?

Dax stirred, felt the vibration of the truck's cold window pane against his temple, and then slid away into dreams again.

Corridor. He sent back to Lisa. Was this a dream or was it a real message from her? There were urgent things he needed to ask her, but his mind was filled with Neetanite. All of his thoughts were dragged back to it, like iron filings to a magnet.

You're not making any sense! snapped Lisa. *Oh, Dax—I hope you're OK. We're OK—for now. Mia's still unconscious. So is Darren—but I think he might be starting to come round. Those traitor soldiers shot them with tranquilizer darts. Can you believe it? I hope you're getting this . . . I really do. Because we're moving a long way away, I can tell. And I've never been able to telepath to you across the sea before. We don't know where Spook is. He's not with us. Oh hell. Jennifer is so sick. Alex is too. He's just chucked up all over Jacob . . .*

Dax felt the window judder at his head again and part of him knew something good had been in Lisa's message . . . something about Mia? No . . . it was gone . . . *corridor.*

Anyway, Lisa went on, but she was getting quieter now, so she must be right about moving far away, *we're stuck in a stinky room with no windows, tied to chairs. But Gideon's got a plan. There's a nail in the wall behind him. He's got it behind his head and he's trying to use it to get into his skin and get the chip out. I can't see much but he's whimpering like a kicked puppy so I reckon he's making some progress. Get Owen. Tell him it's a cargo ship—big metal boxes on the deck. OK, Dax? I hope you're getting this. I really do—or it's all down to—*

'Gideon,' said Dax, startling himself out of sleep.

Spook jumped out of his own doze, as the

London trucker drove on, with just a glance across at them. 'I'm not Gideon,' he said. Dax hardly needed reminding. He would give anything to swap the two over. Instead he was stuck with the Cola he cared *least* about and who cared still less about him.

'Your head's messed up,' said Spook, in a low voice. Sleet spattered against the windscreen as the morning rolled towards afternoon and the hills grew into mountains. Dax stared at him and felt the Neetanite move again. The Neetanite was happy. They were going north-west. That was important.

'There's nothing but one word in it,' said Spook. Dax stared at him blankly. 'Want to know how I know that?' murmured Spook, looking smug. 'Your wolf's been in to see me.'

That got through. Dax was able to push the obsession with Neetanite aside just long enough to sit up and blink.

'Wolf boy gave me a message for you. Mia told me about wolf boy once. I didn't believe her but it looks like you *didn't* just make him up to get attention after all. He sat right on you and you didn't wake up, but I saw him. He had to make me see him—you were a waste of time. Said he couldn't get in to you because one word is knocking around in your tiny mind and it's using up all the space. Anyway, he says this: *In the corridor you need an anchor. One will hold you. Or you do not go.* I hope that makes sense to you, because it sounds like a load of cobblers to me.'

'Corridor,' said Dax. The Neetanite moved again and began to pulse against his skin.

'Yes.' Spook narrowed his eyes at him. 'Corridor.' Dax just stared at him, wildly. The word was *drenched* in meaning—made him thrill and catch his breath—but he had absolutely no idea why. 'You're losing it, Jones,' commented Spook.

'STOP!' The word hurtled out of Dax's mouth without passing his brain at all. The trucker braked instinctively.

'You what?' he said.

'STOP! STOP! We have to get out here!' Dax was looking around him wildly, wondering *where* they were supposed to get out. There was nothing out there but winding highland road.

'We're not at Fort William yet, mate,' said the trucker. He glanced uneasily at Spook who shrugged and made a whirly motion with his finger to his head.

'Got to get out NOW! Corridor!'

'What's up with him? He getting travel sick?'

Spook rounded on Dax. 'We're *not* getting out of this truck in the middle of nowhere, you idiot! Get a grip.'

Dax leaned around Spook and stared at the driver, who had slowed and was now coasting at the side of the road, clearly nervous that his cab was about to get spattered with vomit.

The driver looked at him. Dax looked back. He thought falcon but did not shift. He could see his own eyes reflected in the wide, horrified pupils of the driver. They flickered black and yellow, like something from another world, and the driver slammed on the brakes.

'Out!' he said, his voice strangled with fear. 'Both of you. Out—now!'

Spook was protesting but Dax pushed open the cab door and tumbled out onto the road, his heart pounding and the Neetanite pounding with it. Spook slid out after him, helped on his way by a shove from the driver. Dax grabbed his arm and hauled him around the end of the truck and off the road. The truck belched some smoke out of its high exhaust and rolled away at speed.

'What did you want to do *that* for? You total loser!' Spook thumped him hard in the shoulder and then looked around him desperately as the lorry sped around a bend and disappeared and the remote road fell quiet. In the dim winter light of the late morning, the landscape was less than inviting. Mountain peaks rose around them, white at the top and grey, blue, and purple on their slopes. The sleet had stopped but the wiry grass under their feet was crunchy with frost and their breath bloomed around their heads in the cold air. 'You *loser*!' Spook shoved him again and Dax fell over onto his back. 'Now how are we going to get to help? Eh? No phone box here—in case you hadn't noticed! Abso-bloody-lutely *nothing* here!'

Dax took the Neetanite out of his pocket and held it out on his palm, where it spun three times, hovering a millimetre above his skin, and pointed steadily north-west.

'If you wanted to get out and do your freaky thing, you could have left *me* out of it! I didn't ask to come along with you. I'm not Gideon! I don't just blindly do as I'm told! Poor little dipstick had no idea that you were lying to him, did he? About the chip in his skull. He really trusted you. Well, I don't. I know what a loser you are.'

Dax stood up and held out the Neetanite. The pointed end was indicating a path of sorts, winding away from the road and up into the mountains. Dax turned in that direction and began to walk. Spook continued to complain and shout and hiss with fury but after a while the noise died down and Dax realized he was alone on his trip through the heather. He stopped and looked back. Spook was beside the road, waiting for more traffic. He clearly intended to hitch another lift and go on his way. Dax would have let him go—he would get along a lot faster without him—but something in his mind, despite the overwhelming presence of the Neetanite, told him that Spook must come too.

Dax walked back to the roadside, made a momentous effort to order his words and then put his hand on Spook's shoulder.

'Please, Spook,' he said, in a voice which sounded drugged and odd. 'I need you.'

Spook was so shocked his mouth fell open. Then he laughed to himself and shook his head.

'Bet you never thought you'd have to say that, did you?' He looked at his old adversary and seemed about to tell him to go to hell. Then his eyes dropped to his feet and he nodded. 'OK,' he said. 'Wolf boy said this would happen.'

Dax turned back again, the thumping of his heart falling into rhythm with the Neetanite, which now lay in his palm and pulled north-west through every nerve of his body.

'Corridor,' he said again.

'Yeah right,' muttered Spook. 'Corridor. You said.'

23

The sleet picked up again, in a wet icy blast from
the east, as they moved along the path, adjusting
their position every time the Neetanite moved.
Excitement was rushing through Dax like incoming waves. He barely felt the cold or heard Spook
as he stomped along behind him, complaining.
They passed a very steep drop after half an hour
and Spook moaned with fear and edged along it,
anchoring his fingers into the knots of heather
around them. The drop fell away to a black river,
its water shallow across lumps of granite, around
ten metres below.

Dax did not grab any heather or slow down.
He walked steadily.

'It's all right for *you*,' shouted Spook as he got left behind. 'Doesn't matter if *you* fall. Just pop into a budgie and you're OK. I'm risking *my life* here, Jones!' Dax waited on the far side of the drop and as soon as Spook, looking pale, reached him, he walked on again.

'Wait! Will you slow *down*!' Impatiently, Dax stopped and turned back.

'I need a rest! I'm knackered. And I'm starving. Have you got any food?'

Dax shook his head and Spook looked exasperated. As he turned to walk on, Spook grabbed his arm and spun him back round again. The sleet was thickening into snow now, pelting into Spook's angry face.

'I don't know what's happened to you, Jones, and bully for you if you've turned into a mountain climbing robot, but I *haven't*. I need a rest. Half an hour—look—over there!' He pointed away to his left and Dax saw a shelf of granite protruding from the mountain. Some rocks had been placed on either side long enough ago for the wiry grass and heather and lichen to fill the gaps. It was a shelter—half natural and half man-made. It went back two or three metres under the granite roof.

Spook yanked Dax across to it and they crawled under and found they were able to sit up without hitting their heads. Inside was an abandoned empty water flask and nothing else—but it was much warmer out of the biting wind and the snow.

'Can you make a fire?' asked Spook. 'You're always going on about that bush lore stuff. Well, now would be a good time to demonstrate it.'

Dax looked around. It was an immense effort to speak and the Neetanite was pulling him on so hard it was all he could do to sit still, but he realized that without Spook it was all going to be for nothing, and if Spook got too tired and fell off the mountain, it would be all over. *What* would be all over and *why* he needed Spook, he still had no idea. 'No wood,' he said.

Spook scowled and rubbed his arms vigorously, shivering with cold. 'I can't believe I'm on this wild goose chase—with *you* of all people. I—' Then Spook shut up, with pure amazement. Dax had shifted to the fox and was leaning up against him. 'Oi!' protested Spook, but Dax just turned and gave him a look. It was obvious really. Spook needed to get warmer, and fur was needed. Spook muttered under his breath, but he leaned awkwardly up against the fox and after a while his shivering eased off and stopped.

It was the most peculiar situation Dax could imagine. Halfway up a mountain in a cave with *Spook* of all people, keeping him warm. But his mind was Neetanite shaped and the irony of it all didn't really have much impact on him. He would wait until Spook was warm enough to sleep, allow him ten minutes, and then wake him. They had to move on. *Corridor.*

'You're weird, Jones, you know that,' said Spook. 'I mean, you were always barking, but since you went to France last year you're much weirder. They say that Catherine girl crucified you on a windmill—that's why you've got those marks on your arms. Is that true?'

Dax did not attempt an answer. Even memories of Catherine and the splintering of the bones in his arms could not get a foothold in his mind. *Corridor* was all that mattered now.

Spook's breathing became slower and more rhythmic as the animal warmth stole through him. Dax knew that an ordinary fox could not have had this much effect. He knew that the Neetanite was helping in some way—making him focus his energies with ruthless accuracy. His own body was cooler, transferring its warmth one way for maximum effect, but it didn't matter to him. Nothing mattered but following the Neetanite. After exactly ten minutes he shifted abruptly back to boy shape and stood up, leaving Spook blinking, dazedly, in the dim afternoon light that filtered under the granite shelf. Outside the snow had stopped. It was time to move on.

'Got to go,' said Dax. Spook took one look at his face and didn't bother to argue. He just scowled and got to his feet. He plucked a little fox fur from his sleeve.

'If you tell *anybody*, ever, about this, I will kill you. Got that?'

Dax nodded and left the shelter. The icy wind had also abated. He registered that this was good. It made no difference at all to him, but Spook would go faster now.

They climbed the increasingly steep slopes, and sometimes stumbled or slipped on a scree of small rocks. 'Don't tell me we've got to get to the top!' shouted out Spook at one point. 'You've got to be kidding. I'm not doing that.'

'No,' said Dax. The Neetanite was thrumming

loudly now. He knew they were almost there. Below them the Scottish valley shifted from green to violet to blue as the winter sky flowed above them, a patchwork of ever-changing cloud and mist. The road they had jumped onto less than two hours ago was a thin black ribbon, bare of traffic.

'The auction is starting,' said Spook. And something dimly registered in Dax's mind. Something not good was happening far away. Something he had cared about once, immensely, before the Neetanite (*corridor*) took over.

'I said—the auction is starting!' Spook climbed a few more steps and then stood still and shouted after him. 'Doesn't that mean anything to you, dingo? Your mates are being sold to the highest bidder!'

Dax paused and looked back at him and saw that Spook was furious and gritting his teeth—and that his eyes were wet. Some tiny part of what used to be Dax's heart pinged like a weak rubber band. 'I'm sorry,' he managed to get out. 'But . . . '

'Yeah, I know,' said Spook, with a gulp. 'Corridor. Any time soon, do you think? Because I'm going to be dead of exposure in a minute.'

'Now,' said Dax and looked up ahead of

them, where some low thickets of dead-looking shrub clung to the mountain-side, perhaps three or four metres up from the vague path they had been following.

'Yeah? Now what?'

Dax took off his thick gloves and shoved them in his pockets. He was going to need bare fingers to get up. The climb was tricky—quite steep. Spook swore under his breath and removed his own gloves again. Dax hooked his hands into the crumbly ridges of rock and lichen and hoisted himself up. It took three or four minutes, working out the best hand and footholds, with Spook cursing behind him all the way, but then he was at the shrubs, anchoring himself into them and checking on Spook. As Spook caught up with him and grabbed hold of one of the dead looking roots, Dax looked over the top of the grey-green knot of plant matter and saw that the mountainside was smiling at him. A wide, narrow gap in the rock opened out before his eyes, like an eerie grin. A large man would not have been able to get in. But he was small, and even Spook, though tall, was lean and wiry. They would manage it.

Dax hauled himself another metre up and

along and pushed himself, head first, into the cold black mouth. As Spook scrambled in behind him, the Neetanite sang in his pocket; he felt as if a tuning fork had been struck against his head and was singing and singing in a tone so pure it almost hurt.

They were here. This was the corridor.

24

'I can't see a thing!' Spook proved this by hitting his head on the low ceiling of rock. 'Ow! What can you see?' Dax shifted to the fox and saw immediately that they were in a shallow cave which moved back and down into the mountainside, like a funnel. There was no sign of any animal living in it, or of any human adventurer having found it. The sides were surprisingly smooth—perhaps it had once been an underground spring. Dax eased forward on his belly and tried to gauge how steeply the cave moved down. Spook followed him, also on his belly. Ten seconds later both Colas knew exactly how steep it was. There was a shout from Spook and then a slither and he cannoned into Dax, whose fox claws could not keep hold of the smooth cave floor. They both began to slide, faster and faster, down and down, Spook shouting and Dax yelping with fright. There was nothing to grab; nothing to even reach for. They were in a dark, twisting throat of rock and they were being swallowed whole.

Dax shifted back to a boy as he slid and Spook grabbed hold of his leg, and together they shot down and down, twisting and turning as if on a helter-skelter, gathering speed. Dax's hair flew back off his face and the air turned warmer around him. How far down were they going? What would they find when they landed? Would they even survive their landing? Even the hum of the Neetanite was being drowned out by the air rushing past his ears and Spook was now moving too fast to shout any more. And what was really weird was that there was a light source, somewhere, because Dax could make out the curves and ripples in the granite tunnel they were shooting through. How would he be able to see it without some light coming from somewhere?

The fall seemed to last for minutes, although it was probably no more than thirty or forty seconds. Eventually the slope began to ease up slightly, becoming less and less steep until it levelled out and the two boys shot across it like children at a party, coming out of the snake slide onto an inflatable cushion. Only there wasn't an inflatable cushion—just a wall of rock. They cannoned into it at speed and were thrown against its unforgiving surface. The wall cracked at Dax's cheekbone and brow, shoulder and hip. Spook's shout and moan indicated similar injuries. For a few seconds they lay in a tangle, groaning. Dax sat up and looked around them, tenderly checking his face. There was blood on his cheek, but he didn't think his cheekbone was broken. He was too distracted to care, in any case. The pure note of the Neetanite was back in his head, and there *was* light in this cave. Steady, pink, and warm. It came *from* the Neetanite, glowing right through his zipped-up coat pocket. Dax fumbled it open with bleeding fingers and brought out the gift. Its light was dazzling, streaming out in all directions like a dandelion clock made of pink laser beams, and it threw the whole chamber into perfect visibility.

They were in a round punch-bowl of a cave, the shallow throat they had just slid in from high up in the wall behind them. The cave was perhaps six metres in diameter and like the interior of an onion in shape, its ceiling tapering off above them into an inverted peak. The walls gleamed smoothly, like the funnel which they'd shot through. It looked as if it had been *made*—designed for the job of efficiently collecting anything that fell through. Although it could have done with some cushioning, thought Dax, as his hip fizzed with pain.

'You OK?' he asked Spook and the boy staggered to his feet and stared around in amazement.

'What is that thing?' He pointed to the Neetanite, which lay in Dax's palm like a calm pink firework.

'It's a gift from my mum,' said Dax. Now that they were here, the Neetanite seemed to have released its grip on his brain, as if it knew its work was over. There was no way Dax could be diverted by the terrible plight of his best friends now. He and Spook were a captive audience. They weren't going anywhere. 'I call it Neetanite,' he went on, as Spook stared. 'Gideon and I got it from a corner shop in Keswick—you remember?

When we went in with Owen and Mrs Dann that day.'

Spook nodded, his eyes shifting from Dax's palm to his face and back again.

'My dad sent me a letter with a code so I could find it. He said it was something my mum wanted me to have.'

Spook sat down suddenly on the cave floor. 'Cola mothers don't do that,' he said. 'They don't leave anything.'

'Mine did.'

Spook looked up at him for a long time and then a bitter smile wove across his face. 'Yeah, well, yours *would*. Naturally.'

Dax turned away from him and looked all around the chamber. What next? They were here—the Neetanite seemed to be satisfied. So now what?

'All *my* mum left behind was *me*,' said Spook. 'And my dad really wished she hadn't.'

Dax stopped his scanning and glanced back at Spook in surprise. Spook wasn't looking at him, but at his hands, which were also grazed and bleeding across his knuckles. 'He would have been much happier if I'd died too, then he could have a normal life with his new wife and his new kids and stop having to worry about his psycho son.'

Dax sat down about a metre away and stared at Spook. After all the strutting and posing and vanity, this was shocking behaviour. 'I didn't know you had other kids in your family,' he said.

'A brother and a sister. Eight and ten. They're great. Great kids.'

'And your stepmum? Is she OK?'

'Yeah, she's really nice. She made me the cloak things.'

Dax shook his head, trying to get used to the weird gymnastics of his opinions about Spook. A brother and sister—a *nice* stepmum? What had gone wrong, then? Why was Spook such a git?

'Dad hates me,' answered Spook, as if he'd heard Dax's thoughts. 'He doesn't like to look at me. He was really freaked when the glamour stuff happened and then really glad when the government took me away.'

Dax shook his head. 'Why are you telling me this?'

'I have no idea.'

There was a long pause and then Spook

spoke again. 'When I was at home for all those weeks after Tregarren College got swept away, I used to watch him when he didn't know it—with Emma and Oliver—and he was really happy with them. Then, when I came along he would shut up. He would stand up and stop playing and maybe pat my shoulder and ask me how it was going or if I was riding today or something like that—and he never, ever looked at me.'

Dax didn't know what to say. Spook glanced up from his long inspection of his bloody knuckles and Dax just shook his head at him and said: 'I'm sorry.'

'Yeah,' said Spook. 'I expect you are.'

There was another long pause and then Dax turned away, awkwardly. He got up and resumed his checking of the cave walls. There must be something here; something to explain what on earth they were doing here.

'I think you're standing on it,' said Spook and Dax blinked and then peered down at his feet. Around his scuffed, wet trainers was a perfect hexagon cut into the smooth rock floor. He stepped aside with a gasp and dropped to his knees to examine it. Around the inside edge of the hexagon he recognized the same symbols which Clive had tried so hard to read on the Neetanite. And in the centre of the large stone hexagon was a smaller hexagon. A hole, cut into the shape of a hexagonal barrel, the bottom of it tapering off to a point.

'I would say,' commented Spook, at his shoulder, 'that what you have there is a key.'

Dax shivered as he turned the Neetanite over in his hand. Spook was right. The hole in the hexagon was exactly the right shape and size to receive it. He stared across its pink glow at Spook, wide-eyed and gulping. *Corridor* time was here.

With trembling fingers he upended the odd cylinder and dropped it towards the hexagonal hole. He could see that it would fit precisely and smoothly—but as he pushed it towards the hole there was an odd resistance, as if it was being held back by a strong fountain of water. No—it was as if he were pushing two magnets together on the same polarity. They would dodge and weave and push against each other but never meet. Frowning, he turned the Neetanite around—perhaps the pointed end needed to face upwards. He tried again, but still met with the same magnetic thrust, holding him back.

'What?' he said. 'What now? You've dragged us all this way and now what? Have we got to chant or something? Set fire to something? Stand on our heads? What?' He felt anger surge inside him. He *should* be doing everything he could to help Gideon and Lisa and Clive and Mia—and all the other Colas. What on earth was he doing *here*? He tried again, the Neetanite point down this time, and pushed as hard as he could, but it would not go. Would *not* work.

He hurled the useless key against the rocks. It chimed a pure, sharp note as it struck, sending pink beams dancing around the cave walls, and then rolled back towards the hexagon. Spook picked it up. 'You're not really with it, are you, Jones?' he said.

Dax stared at him, panting with anger and frustration. 'Don't you start!'

Spook sighed and shrugged. 'You really should pay attention to your helpful dead wolf mate. *In the corridor you need an anchor. One will hold you. Or you do not go.* Remember that? After all this, I'm so glad to be of some use. So glad that your mum found a way to make me Dax's happy little helper.'

Dax gaped at him, beginning to understand.

'I am your anchor, dog-breath,' said Spook. 'Oh, lucky me.' He held the Neetanite out. 'Go on—take it. Then I guess we're going to have to hold hands. Something else that I will kill you for, if you ever tell anyone.'

Dax was speechless. He took back the Neetanite and then took Spook's hand, which was dry and warm, in spite of the fact that they had slid into the bowels of the earth.

'Thanks,' he said, attempting a smile at Spook. Spook stared at him and his cheek twitched once, but he didn't say anything.

Dax turned back to the Neetanite and upended it once more. He pushed it down and this time it slid neatly into the hexagonal hole, without any resistance. Its pink light turned white and Spook, the granite chamber, and the rest of the world went away.

25

He could see nothing but the white, but felt as if his body was crawling with red ants—every millimetre of skin erupted with stinging and itching. Then he felt incredibly cold and wondered if there had been an avalanche of snow down through the mountain funnel, burying him and Spook. He realized that he was not breathing—his chest felt as if it was encased in concrete. No breathing was possible. He tried but there was no air in his nostrils and his mouth was shut and unable to move.

And yet, he felt Spook's hand move in his, bloody knuckles flexing and fingers pinching tighter, and as soon as he remembered his 'anchor' his vision cleared—the white filled with colour, and warm air slid up through his nose and his chest rose again. The ants departed and the itching and stinging stopped. He felt warm, still, incredibly calm. He was standing in a room, alone. Although he could still feel Spook's hand, he looked down and realized that both of his hands were apparently free, hanging at his sides. Behind him was a wall. An ordinary wall, painted red. In front of him was something which looked a bit like an office—with a desk and a chair, made from pale blue translucent material. Glass? Plastic? Or maybe a kind of crystal. It was beautiful. Beneath his feet were autumn leaves—woven together in a regular pattern. A leaf carpet. He didn't recognize the leaves—they seemed to be spirals in shape and red, gold, and yellow in colour. Nothing he had ever seen before. To his right was another red wall, with a silver square in it. Ahead of him was a door which seemed to be made of the same blue crystal stuff as the desk, with a neat row of shelves to one side, filled with many cubes—about the same size as a Rubik's cube puzzle—but each a single colour. Some of them glowed gently and others seemed to have a mini firework display going on inside them.

To his left was a huge round window, framing a breathtaking view. Dax wandered across the leaf carpet and stared through the round window which didn't appear to have any glass in it but still seemed to hold back any breeze or scent from the outside. Falling away below him was a steep hillside of swirling green and black rock. 'Malachite,' murmured Dax to himself. And maybe it was.

He was looking across a stunning range of mountains—some pale grey, some grey-pink, and some of them formed from what looked exactly like the dramatic green and black ripples of malachite. Snow drifted among them, over the peaks of some, down between rifts in others, and along the valley between them wound a pale gold-green river, lined here and there with green and pink vegetation. The sky above the peaks was golden. Something flew past the window. It looked like a red bat.

Dax drew in a deep breath and tried to find something familiar in the scents in the room. Nothing was. Except, perhaps, the faint stir of a memory. Something . . . almost like cinnamon. He turned to look back into the room and behind him stood a teenage girl. Her brown eyes were large and round. The green robe she wore shook on her slight body as her mouth opened in an 'O' of shock. Then she screamed.

Dax put up his hands and shouted across her terrified shrieks. 'It's all right! It's OK—I'm not—I'm just—'

But she clutched her throat and gasped and let out a torrent of unintelligible words and then shrieked again and ran from the room, her long dark hair whipping out behind her like a flag in high wind. She ran *through* the door, rather than opening it, and Dax realized that the blue translucent stuff had just rippled and let her pass, like some kind of weird jelly. He found he was panting, scared, but also incredibly excited. Where was he? Who was that girl? And why did she look familiar? It was to do with the cinnamon smell—he knew it. He felt as if he had been lightly peeled and dusted in the powdered essence of his surroundings. His body *knew* this place. His mind and his soul *knew* it—but he had never been here before in his life. There was no question of that.

He sat down, cross-legged, on the leaf carpet, and waited for what was to happen next. He didn't wait long. Through the jelly door stepped another person—an older woman. Her dark hair was coiled around her head in an elaborate style and her long robe was a richly embroidered red material. She looked about the same age as Mrs Dann, and carried one of the little cube things in one hand. She, thankfully, wasn't screaming. She stared at him, transfixed, by the doorway for a few seconds, and then stepped across and sank to her knees in front of him. She raised an unsteady hand and touched his cheek, and her eyes widened further. She took a breath and then said, 'Dax.'

Dax giggled. He had no idea why. Then he said the only thing he could think of which might be relevant. 'Corridor . . . ?'

She closed her eyes and gasped and then shook her head. 'Dax. Of course . . . the corridor. I can't believe she did that. No . . . no I *can* believe it. I should have *known* she would!'

'Who? Who are you talking about?'

A smile spread slowly over her face and tears welled up in her brown eyes.

'Your mother, Dax. My sister.'

26

The smell made sense now. That faintly cinnamony smell. It was a family smell, as true and as unmistakable as the scent of his own skin. Goosebumps ran across him like a river.

'You're my aunt?' he whispered and she nodded and beamed at him. 'You knew my mum?'

'Of course. Until she went down for the Quorat. Then I had to let her go, of course.' She sighed and shook her head again. 'You are so, *so* like her. I can't believe it.'

'What do you mean—went down for the Quorat?'

'Oh, Dax—you're not meant to know. You're

really not. She was not meant to give you the cleft-onique. It was forbidden. Trust Anathea!'

'The clef—? That was the key thing, yes?'

'Yes. A cleftonique. A key that works on sound waves and magnetic frequencies. It's a way of going through the corridor between our worlds, but you should not have had it. You were not meant to come here. None of you were. I can't imagine how she managed to smuggle it through in the first place. How long have you had it?'

'About a week and a half,' said Dax, his skin still awash with goosebumps and his heart skittering with excitement.

'Yes . . . sounds right. It would have taken ten days or so to wake up and adjust to your frequencies before it could trigger the beacon. Oh—Anathea! Naughty girl!' She smiled fondly and shook her head.

'Beacon? What beacon?'

'The beacon in the mountain . . . to guide the cleftonique to the corridor. Once it connects with the cleftonique, the holder of the cleftonique will lose all other purpose but to reach the corridor. You were quite incapable of resisting.' She sighed. 'The cleftonique wasn't meant to be taken through at all. Anathea *knew* her trip was one way. I'm amazed the beacon even worked. It's been left there for fifteen years and it was never intended to be used again. Nobody was meant to come back through, least of all you, Dax.'

'So.' Dax struggled to order all the questions that were now tumbling out of his mind. 'Let me get this straight—you're my aunt, and my mum gave me a key to get to you—but you say I shouldn't be here. Why not? Why not, if you're my family?'

She smoothed his hair and looked at him with her head tilted to one side. 'I didn't mean I'm not glad to see you, Dax. This is a miracle. It wasn't meant to happen, but that doesn't mean I'm not glad it has. *Carra! Carra!*' she called over her shoulder. 'Come in here. It's quite safe. Come and meet your cousin!'

The teenage girl who had screamed at him now edged back through the eddying jelly doorway and stared at him in nervous fascination.

'Come on!' urged his aunt. The girl murmured something Dax did not understand.

'Speak English,' chided her mother and the girl nodded.

'Hello,' she said, now kneeling down beside his aunt.

'This is Carra,' said his aunt. 'And I am your Aunt Hessa.'

Dax nodded politely at the girl and then smiled at his aunt. 'Are there many more of you . . . in my family?'

'Yes, there are. But I'm afraid you will not be able to meet them, Dax, as much as they would love to meet you.'

'Why not?' Dax felt a surge of disappointment.

'Because our world is toxic to you. You can last a little while without being harmed, but not for long. That is the sad way of the different worlds, when they are young. It takes millennia to build up resistance and you are *so* young.'

Dax felt crushed. He hadn't even realized until then, how much he had been looking forward to getting out into the valley of malachite and tracing the bank of the river.

'How long have I got?' he asked.

She took his right wrist and showed him his watch, tracing the dial with a slender golden-brown finger. 'From here to—about here,' she said. 'Beyond that, our atmosphere will damage you irreparably.'

There was apology in her voice. It was no more than twenty minutes.

'Great,' muttered Dax, anger prickling through the wonder of his arrival in this strange place. 'Just great.'

'You must want to know about your mother,' stated Aunt Hessa. 'Every Cola wants that.'

'You know about the Colas, then?'

'Oh yes, Dax. We put you there. Well, some of you. The others in the Quorat did the rest.'

'What is this *Quorat* you keep talking about?'

His aunt settled herself down, mirroring his cross-legged position, and clasped her hands. 'It began about fifteen years ago. Fifteen of the years you are familiar with—which is very similar to our time measurements. There are eleven of us in the Quorat.'

'Eleven *what*?' asked Dax, feeling slightly desperate at how slowly she spoke when he knew that time was so short.

'Worlds. Planets. We number eleven and we have been the Quorat for many thousands of years, but we felt that our number was ready to grow. We felt that twelve was coming soon. We surveyed many worlds that could be candidates and all agreed that your world was the one—but that your world needed help.'

Dax blinked and shook his head. 'Wait—hang on. Don't tell me. We're polluting the planet and messing it up with carbon monoxide—or about to blow up all mankind with nuclear bombs or something. And you're trying to stop us before it's too late!'

His aunt laughed.

'Because . . . you know . . . I'm sure I saw that one on *Star Trek* once,' said Dax, unable to keep a little sarcasm out of his voice.

She laughed again. 'No, not at all! I mean, those things *might* happen, I suppose, but it doesn't look that way from the Quorat's survey. From our reports it looks a bit better than that. As a race, the people of your world are actually doing quite well. Not top of the universe, certainly—not even the galaxy. But not too badly at all. You show great promise, in fact. There's a strong seam of decency through your people.'

Dax rubbed his hands through his hair. 'OK—so, you all decided we were doing jolly well and then what? What did you do? Put us in an inter-galactic booster group?'

'All eleven worlds in the Quorat were allowed to send some of their people to the planet, to seed it,' said his aunt. 'There has always been some small ability on your world—a little psychic and dowsing power and some low-grade healers and glamourists—but nothing like what you will all become. We wanted to gradually introduce the Earth to some of the talents of other worlds in the Quorat, so that when we make proper contact in the future there is less alarm and mistrust. We needed children to be our ambassadors. Each planet sent females to find a good Earth male to marry—through the corridor to the mountain chamber you've just found, in fact. Women were chosen because they were better able to cope and would last longer. It was a huge, huge honour to be selected as a seeder. Your mother was so excited. It meant—*you* meant—everything to her.'

Dax's mind was stretching and twisting, trying to get all this staggering new knowledge inside, but it still managed to hook one specific thing out of Aunt Hessa's words. 'Last longer?' asked Dax. 'What do you mean—they would *last longer*?'

'As I said before,' smiled Aunt Hessa, 'it takes millennia to build up resistance to the many natural viruses and diseases of other worlds. You cannot last here—even with your mother's blood line. If you were a normal child of your world, you would be dead by now. However, the women from the Quorat were strong and highly developed and could remain on Earth for years. But once they fell pregnant, the physiological changes would trigger a breakdown in their immune system. They knew this. They would not be able to last four years after pregnancy . . . if that. This is why no Cola has a living blood mother. Your father's immunity would be passed to you and you would be safe, but your mother could only last so long. It was her choice, Dax. It was incredibly hard for her, knowing she would not see you grow up—but she still made that choice willingly.'

Dax shivered. She knew then. All along. She knew what he would become—had *made* it happen. 'Was she a shapeshifter, too?' he asked.

'Yes—as am I—see . . . ' Aunt Hessa flickered and a red creature, with wings like a bat but a head like an eagle descended onto the edge of the blue crystal chair. Its eyes glittered silver. Another flicker and his aunt was back, smiling, and sitting down with him again.

'We all have different forms we can shift to—up to three. That's my prime form. We were relieved that your shapeshifting was to native species. Your fox and falcon are wonderful.'

But Dax was doing some calculation now. 'Wait a minute,' he said. 'If you sent all these women, how come there aren't any other shapeshifting Colas? There were only two, weren't there? Me and wolf boy, who died.'

'Oh, our world isn't just of shapeshifters. We also have glamourists—and more of them. Most of our seeders were glamourists,' said Aunt Hessa. 'Your friend Spook—his mother was from this planet. You are distantly related, in fact.' Dax gasped. 'Most of the Quorat planets have a good mix of talents now—but only our planet produces shapeshifters and we are quite rare even here. Only two shapeshifting seeders went to Earth. And yes, sadly, the boy in Scotland did not survive. But some of the seeders were exceptionally strong and managed to have more than one child. The Quorat was pleased. It went very well.'

'Did it?' said Dax. 'What about Catherine?'

His aunt opened her mouth to speak and then closed it again, dropping her eyes to her hands

313

for a moment. At length she looked up at him again. 'Catherine,' she said, 'was a mistake.'

'You're not kidding!'

'A Quorat member planet—Ayot—decided to activate another Cola, as you call yourselves, without consulting with the rest of us. The kind of child we had decided not to seed. Luke and Gideon's mother was tricked in a way that's difficult to explain. Catherine shared the same womb as Gideon and Luke but she is actually not a true triplet. Luke and Gideon were twins. Catherine was—a sort of passenger. It had all gone so well until then. Ayot has apologized unreservedly to the Quorat. It was an error of judgement.' She sighed.

'Parasites,' said his cousin, speaking up for the first time since saying hello. Dax nodded. 'They exist on Ayot and they cause trouble and imbalance wherever they go. Some are just a nuisance, but others are worse even than Catherine.'

Dax looked at his watch. The minutes were ticking away too fast. 'How do you know all these things about the Colas? Are you watching us or something?'

His aunt held out the cube in her left hand. It was red and a tiny firework display inside it was yellow and gold. 'ViewCube,' said Carra, over her shoulder, as if it was the latest games console on the market. 'We have them for the people we love. And we managed to make them work even across the galaxies. Look. Hold it with both hands to make the connection.'

Dax cupped the ViewCube in his hands and peered at it. Immediately the slightly opaque surface became clear and he could see Spook, wearily sitting on the floor of the cave, still holding on to Dax's estranged hand and looking rather stressed.

'Your friend is a good anchor,' said his aunt. 'If he let go of you, you'd be lost.'

Dax nodded. 'He is a good anchor,' he agreed. Part of him could, bizarrely, still feel Spook's hand in his, even though he was nowhere to be seen in this room.

'You see, we can watch, but we're not allowed to interfere in any way,' said his aunt. 'We don't spy on everything you do—we do have our own lives to lead! We normally dip in every few days . . . see how you're getting along. When the ViewCubes get bright and sparkly we know there's something up, so we watch more. Most of the cubes are just dim lights now, of course, since Catherine . . . '

she sighed again, ' . . . since she sucked the power out of the others. Only eleven of them look like this—and all eleven are like thunderstorms at the moment. Dax, this is the worst trouble you've all been in. I'm really worried about you all.'

'Well, can't you do anything to *help*?' said Dax. 'You *put* us there! Don't you have a responsibility? And what *about* Catherine? Where is she? Show me *her* ViewCube.'

'We don't have one. She is not loved by anyone. And ViewCubes don't tend to work on parasites even if they are loved. We've seen her though, through the ViewCubes of other Colas.'

Dax's mind was freewheeling again—faster and faster, aware that time was running away. 'Did my dad know? About Mum and about me?'

'We're not sure,' said Hessa. 'We don't watch intimacy. ViewCubes don't allow that—it wouldn't be right. In intimate moments your mother—any of the mothers—might have told their husbands something about the Quorat and the seeders and senders. They weren't meant to, of course, but it could have happened. We're senders. We're not controllers.'

Senders . . . Dax felt his hairs prickle along

his arms as he had a sudden flare of memory. An image of Mia's father, alone and desolate in their poor little high rise flat, rose in his mind—just after he had told Dax, Lisa, and Gideon to take his daughter away with them. Mia had been healing his alcoholic hangovers and making herself sick. Dax had last seen the man listening to Elvis and talking to himself about his dead wife. What had he said? Dax couldn't remember. But he always remembered the vinyl disc crackling on the turntable. 'Return To Sender'. 'I think some of them knew something,' he said.

'It's certainly possible. They were chosen for their intelligence.'

Dax stared back down at his watch and felt desperation rise in him. So much to ask and nowhere near enough time. 'What about the weather?' They blinked. 'You know—the weird weather when I was born; when all the Colas were born. There were hurricane-force winds followed by a major heatwave on the day I was born. Others had snow in high summer or freak tornadoes or—'

'Oh—that!' said his aunt. 'Yes, we heard about that. Just a cleftonique aftershock. Sending causes a huge power surge which tends to affect the elements immediately around you. It happened when your mothers arrived and it also happened again when each of you was born, much to our surprise—we called it cleftonique aftershock. It will almost certainly happen again, shortly after you go back, so take care. Oh, Dax, I'm so sorry, but you do have to go back *soon*. We're running out of time. You must get back to Spook and go on with your lives. Please take our love and best hopes for you all back with you.'

'Is that *it*?' gasped Dax. 'Just hello, nice to see you, goodbye? Is that what all this has been for?'

His aunt and cousin looked at each other and back at him, uncomfortably.

'You mean to tell me that I have wasted hours and hours on *this*, climbing through mountains and sliding into potholes, when I should have been trying to save my friends? Just to meet an *aunt*? That's not enough! That's nowhere near good enough!' Dax felt he might combust with rage. 'You've got to help me! Help us!'

'No, I told you,' said Hessa. 'We have to stand back now. Seeding was allowed, but further inter-ference is forbidden. It's not the Quorat way.

We're only senders! And maybe it's meant to be like this. We chose Britain to seed you all because it was an island inhabited by some of the most tolerant people on the planet. We felt you had the best chance there. But really, you do need to spread out across the planet and seed your own Cola children one day. Maybe this is the way.'

'Being *sold* to the highest bidder? Like slaves?' Dax slammed the ViewCube back into Aunt Hessa's palm. 'Get me Gideon's!' he demanded.

The woman and her daughter exchanged glances and then Carra got to her feet and ran to the shelving by the door. She pulled a pale green ViewCube out and Dax could see sparkling silver lights arcing backwards and forwards inside it. He grabbed it from her and peered down into it as the view cleared. In dim light he could see Gideon, grimacing, with blood in his fair hair and on his neck and shoulder. But as Dax stared, gulping with horror, knowing that his best friend was trying to dig out the chip he had failed to warn him about, with a blunt nail in the wall behind him, Gideon's face transformed. His eyes opened wide and Dax saw him say, clearly, through gritted teeth, *Yessss!* Now a coolness slipped over his features and the hint of a smile.

'Yesss!' echoed Dax, aloud. 'He's got free of it! Now he can free the others!'

Aunt Hessa and Carra leaned on his shoulders and watched with him now, as Gideon's bindings began to explode into frayed clumps of rope. All around him the other Colas were being similarly freed. Now Lisa was in view, helping Clive to his feet and talking across his head to Gideon. 'Luke!' she was saying. 'You need Luke next. You've got to get together! Now!'

Dax felt goosebumps tearing across his skin once more. He looked at his watch. 'I've got two more minutes. What happens then?'

'We'll send you back, with another cleftonique,' said Aunt Hessa. 'It's not a problem.'

'No! You're not sending me back there!'

Aunt Hessa blinked. 'But you have to go—I told you! You'll get sick if you stay any longer. You'll die.'

'Not there! Not into that mountain!'

'It's quite safe, Dax—you can climb back out again; so can Spook. We'll boost your energy levels at the same time, through the cleftonique.'

'No,' insisted Dax. 'I'm not going. Not there. If you send me back anywhere, send me back to the ship—where the other Colas are.'

The look that passed between Hessa and her daughter was not a look that told him this couldn't be done—but that it *shouldn't* be done. He was heartened. 'Both of us. Me *and* Spook! On that cargo ship. Or I'm going to shapeshift and fly out of that window, now, even if it *does* kill me. I'm not going to let my friends get sold. Send me to them. I know you can do it.'

'We can do it,' said Hessa. 'But it's interference. It's not allowed.'

'I don't *care* if it's allowed!' shouted Dax. 'The rules have already been broken once, haven't they? When my mum left me the cleftonique. What's the difference? I'm here in your world and that's not allowed either, is it? Do this one thing for me! Get me and Spook to the ship. I'll keep your secret if you want me to. I won't say a word about seeders or senders. Your Quorat will never have to know I was even here.'

Hessa and Carra looked at each other again, and this time they were working out not *what* to do, but *how* to do it. 'It's fair enough,' said Carra.

'He didn't ask for this, did he? And we have to put him back anyway. Nobody will notice a bit of a change of co-ordinates, will they?'

Hessa nodded. 'Get another cleftonique. And hurry. He's only got fifty-four seconds.'

27

A wall of water smashed into his face and he heard Spook scream. Torrents of grey sea pounded them both backwards and it was several seconds before they could even try to breathe. As they slid along the metal deck amid foaming salt water, Dax grabbed Spook's flailing leg and anchored them both to some metal rails.

'What? What?' spluttered Spook, as the deck plunged back down again and the sea rolled back off it. He might well splutter, thought Dax. Ten seconds ago he had been sitting in a warm, pink cave, hanging on to Dax's disembodied hand—now he was being thrown across the deck of a cargo ship in a violent North Sea storm.

Dax saw lights from the bridge and began to gauge the size and shape of their landing place. The long deck was stacked with metal containers and he could see that there were small lanes between them—places to shelter and get out of sight. He scrambled to his feet before another big wave could hit, and hauled Spook along after him.

Between the containers, which were stacked two high, Spook stared at him in fury and fear. 'What the hell have you done?'

'I made them send us here,' he shouted over the roar of another incoming wave and the groan and whine of the metal containers and the miles of steel cable holding them in place.

'What?'

'The senders! They weren't allowed to but I made them. This is where the others are. We're here to rescue them!'

Spook's appalled face was swiped by a spray of sea water, buffeting down between the containers as the next big wave made the ship wallow and groan. 'Are you *insane*?' he shrieked, as soon as he could. 'What happened to getting to Owen? There are *trained professionals* who can save them!'

'Oh, sorry, Spook!' Dax thwacked him hard on both his sopping wet shoulders. 'Is this all a bit too much for you? You scared?' Spook glared at him. 'Right,' said Dax. 'We need to find the others. I'll try to make contact with Lisa.' But the raging sea around them and the whining and groaning metal made it impossible to get his head focused. They had to get inside. Dax waited for the ship to roll down and the water to recede and then poked his head out from between the straining containers. Further up the deck was a covered walkway, which must lead to the interior of the ship. He withdrew and waited for the next wave to hit and subside and then shouted to Spook. 'Now! Follow me!'

They both ran up the slippery metal deck, grabbing hand to hand along the steel ropes which pinned the containers down, and managed to make it to the walkway before the next wave hit. A few feet further on there was an oval metal door with a wheel lock. Dax gripped it hard and turned it, with some effort, as Spook stared out, aghast, at the churning grey sea. His borrowed trawler clothes were drenched.

'Yes—come on!' They clambered in through

the oval opening and rammed the door shut before the next wave came in, screwing the handle around again and sinking to the floor with relief.

For a minute they just sat there, dripping and gasping. They were at the bottom of a stairwell; steep metal steps rising above them and pale yellow lights set into the metal walls. 'Now what?' muttered Spook.

Dax shifted to the fox, steadying himself as best he could, but sliding as the floor pitched beneath his claws. He needed to listen. Spook grabbed the thick fur at the back of his neck, while anchoring himself to the stair rail with his other free arm, and helped the fox stay steady. Dax was surprised, but accepted the help without a glance at his distant cousin. First he had to listen. The engine machinery of the ship hummed and throbbed and clanked through the high wind, and above that was a layer of crackling electrical traffic—the ship's radio and navigation systems; individual mobile phones; assorted gadgets up on the bridge. He could hear people too. Men. Three or four on the bridge—maybe five others in the living quarters. And of course, there were the Colas—all nine, plus Clive—somewhere here in this network of narrow alleys and cabins. He could faintly smell them, but not hear them.

He shifted back to say: 'I'm going up. You'd better wait here.'

'Oh no! You're not leaving me out now! Not after everything I've been through!' Spook got up.

'No—I won't. I'm going to need you. But I have to listen in first, as a fox, and it'll be quicker and safer on my own. I'll be back in five minutes!'

'All right,' said Spook. 'But you'd better be. I'm not staying here all day!'

'Five minutes,' repeated Dax and went quietly up the stairs in boy form, ready to shift again as soon as he could, without being knocked off his paws. After a turn in the steps, out of view of Spook, he arrived at the first landing and saw corridors going off in two directions, with metals doors at intervals. They were dimly lit and he could detect no sound or human scent here. He went on up and then froze as he reached the next turn in the stairwell. Light, warmth, and noise shafted down from above and he realized this was the bridge. A dark alcove with a fire extinguisher in it provided the perfect cover, just by the doorway to the bridge. He shifted to the fox and slid in easily behind the red canister, supported by the snug fit of the alcove, so he didn't slide and give himself away with his scrabbling claws.

The most distinctive smell was Mr Eades: familiar, and now repulsive. He was enjoying a glass of whisky with the captain of the ship. Two other men were there too. Dax did not recognize their voices or their scent, but one of them was French, judging by his accent. He was on the phone, talking rapidly in his own language and letting out the occasional harsh bark of a laugh. He snapped his mobile shut and walked over to Mr Eades.

'They insist it is their final offer,' he said. 'What do you think?'

Mr Eades let out his dry chuckle. 'Tell them their neighbours have made a better one. Are they still talking in millions? What do they think this is? Bargain basement day? Tell them we are dealing in *billions*, and if they cannot afford it, they can withdraw at any time. Who is it they're bidding for?'

'Reader and Hardman,' said the Frenchman. 'They want the second boy too, but we make more if we sell them separately.'

'Both are equally able,' said Mr Eades. 'I have

328

tested them often enough. Gideon has caught up with Luke since Luke was comatosed by their delightful sister. How is she, by the way?'

'Charming little snake,' said the Frenchman. 'Where would we be without her?'

'When does she get here?'

'As soon as the storm drops, which should be any time in the next hour if the World Service forecast is accurate.'

Dax gasped, in his tight alcove. Catherine was being brought here? What for?

'And the buyers? Are they still on schedule— after our little mishap last night?'

'The buyers will be arriving later. Most of them are anchored within five miles of us and waiting to send aircraft or launches. Syria has dropped out. They only wanted the shapeshifter.'

Dax heard Mr Eades click his teeth with frustration. 'That boy has been a thorn in my side for years. I should have left him to drown in the lake.'

'But it is not only the Syrians who are aggrieved, *monsieur*. We had an agreement, too, remember. Catherine will not be pleased. It was her deepest wish to have the shapeshifter for an hour before he was collected by his purchaser. One hour. The illusionist was a disappointing loss too. But we have another, even if he is weaker. Only one shapeshifter, however. I cannot believe you lost him.'

Dax shuddered. He could well imagine what Catherine would do in an hour. She would leech every drop of Cola power out of him; something she had been longing to do since she had first met him, but had never yet managed. He guessed the auctioneers would have prevented her from totally draining him, if he had also been promised to Syria.

'We'll find him again,' said Mr Eades, sounding a great deal more confident than he smelt. 'He'll go back to Hind. The boy's very attached to him. We'll watch Hind and sooner or later we'll get Dax Jones. Until then your little parasite can feast on all the others. She should be happy enough with that. Just don't let her kill anyone, or I will be most put out.'

'She will behave. We have an agreement. She doesn't want to end up back in the tender embrace of the French government again. With their protective suits and plastic screens.'

'You don't mean to say that *you* let her touch you? Are you insane?'

'No—I keep my distance. We all do. But we don't lock her up in one room. And we let her have pets. They don't last long, of course. Three cats, two dogs, and six guinea pigs so far. She loves them to death. She gets through them faster and faster. We think she'll stabilize once she's had her fill of the other Colas. And she'll make them nice and compliant for you, too, when they're collected by their owners. They'll be too wiped out to struggle.'

'Good, good. Well, nothing ever goes perfectly. We lost two—but we still have *nine*. It was an exceptional operation—right under the noses of the Ministry of Defence. They really were amazingly complacent; always keeping so careful a watch for attack from the *out*side.'

'Don't get too complacent yourself, *monsieur*. You say the first illusionist is drowned in the dock but with the shapeshifter still loose . . . what if Hind already knows? They could be searching the North Sea already.'

'Hind is a minor nuisance, that's all. His unit have no idea where we are. It's a big sea and we can evade most of their radar and sonar trackers, thanks to my late scientist friends.'

'But the telepaths? You say the shapeshifter is a receiver? What if they make contact?'

Mr Eades laughed. 'Have you forgotten *this*?' Dax knew he was waving the little black remote control. 'This, my friend, is the whole reason we are here. Without my talented scientists' special project we could never have done it! Shame I had to kill them all. Terrible way to go . . . burning alive. Still—couldn't leave the evidence behind, could we?'

'But how reliable are your chips? The shape-shifter's chip failed. He attacked as a falcon.'

'He was always the riskiest. That morphing business—it interferes with the connection. It must have detached somehow, before we activated the blocker again after he fell into the lake. The others are still intact—and they have all worked perfectly in every test. The Colas can't do *anything* until I press this button. I will give individual controllers to all of their new owners—but—and this is where, if I say it myself, I *am* a genius—I keep the master controller. And if our customers become in any way *unruly*—I will switch off their new toys. For good. The chips are also small explosives, you see. Bang, bang. Dead Cola.'

There was an awed silence, during which Dax felt sicker than ever before. He could not have imagined how the chip could have been worse than simply blocking off their powers— but an explosive buried inside them? His stomach clenched. He checked through what he knew— Mia and Lisa were safe and so was Gideon and probably Luke by now. However clever Eades thought he was, he clearly had not detected that any trackers had been removed. But how many more chips had they managed to get out since he had seen them—perhaps fifteen minutes ago— in the ViewCube? Barry, Jennifer, Jacob, Alex, and Darren—how long would it take to free them when they had nothing but a blunt nail from the wall? He had to find them now, and put his beak and talons to work. They were in terrible danger.

But before he could go, he heard the French-man speak again, and the man's words rooted him to the spot.

'What about the little nerdy boy? That—*Clive*? What use is he?'

'Ah—well, we thought he might be useful in controlling the others. In case they weren't certain about how serious we were. Teach them a lesson—that they're never too valuable to die— if we think it's necessary. He's a bright boy, but he has no powers, so he's of no value. But they're fond of him, so slitting his throat will be useful, if Catherine doesn't subdue them enough.'

'Ah. I see. You have thought of everything.'

'I do my best. Any more of that single malt, captain?'

The captain grunted a reply and Dax, through his horror for Clive, picked up two things in the captain's scent—anxiety and confusion.

'What is it?' said Mr Eades and Dax could hear him get to his feet and cross the bridge towards the captain.

'Something's not right here. We should be travelling north-east.'

'And aren't we?'

'No. We're going north. And I haven't altered our course.'

'The storm. You've been blown off-course.'

'This is a North Sea-going vessel, Mr Eades. It is well used to storms. Something else is wrong.'

There was a noise of instruments being punched and turned.

'Are we back on course *now*, Captain Durrance?' said Mr Eades. 'After all, I am paying you a considerable amount of money to steer this godforsaken hulk of metal. I would think the least you could do is manage to keep it on course for another two or three hours.'

'It'll be fine,' said the captain, curtly. But Dax knew better. The captain's scent had curdled from anxiety and confusion to absolute fear. The ship was still not doing as it should, but he had decided that his paymaster didn't need to know. Dax let a foxy grin spread across his snout. He knew what was happening now . . .

28

He slipped out of the alcove and shifted silently back to boy form before creeping around into the corridor that led away from the bridge. He would follow his nose now, and make straight for the other Colas. Their familiar scent pulsed lightly along the narrow walkway and he could pick it up easily, even in boy form. After thirteen or so metres the walkway turned a sharp left and Dax paused there, listening hard. He imagined there would be some kind of guard outside the room where the Colas were being kept and he was right. Both of the guards were unconscious. Dax saw that they were slumped on the floor, their rifles askew. He saw vivid red welts on their foreheads and realized that Gideon and Luke must somehow have taken possession of their weapons and made them crack into the guard's foreheads, rendering them senseless. But the door behind them was still shut. Dax couldn't understand why.

Now he leaned against the wall, noticing that the ship was not pitching and rolling as much as it had been—the calmer weather was arriving as forecast. This meant Catherine would be landing soon. Why were his friends still behind that locked door? *Lisa!* he sent. *Lisa! I'm here. Outside the door. What's happening?*

In response he heard Lisa shout out to the others and then heard them all begin to talk excitedly. *Dax?* she sent back. *How on earth did you get here? Is Owen with you?*

No, he responded. *It's just me and Spook.*

Spook? We all thought he was dead! How did . . . oh, never mind. Thank God you're here. Get the door open.

Can't Gideon and Luke do it? asked Dax, as he stepped across and grasped the handle of the door.

Not at the moment—they're too busy on the rudder. If they let it go for a second it reverts to its proper course. And we can't let it.

Not even for a few seconds?

No. Dax felt cold fear filter through with Lisa's words. *It's her again, Dax. Catherine. She's coming. We're steering away from her. We've got to keep her away. She's bringing death.*

Dax wrestled some more with the door, chills running through him, and then spotted a key on the belt of one of the senseless guards. He unhooked it and drove it into the keyhole below the handle and could hardly believe it when it fitted and turned smoothly.

As he opened the door the Colas fell silent in their windowless room and stared at him as if he had arrived from another world. Which, in fact, he had. Darren and Mia were now both awake, but looked groggy and pale. Lisa stumbled across to him and hugged him. 'Sylv says we must go north—that it's our best chance. Dax . . . ' she stared at him again, biting her lip, and he *knew* what she wanted to say, even though she was now trying to stop her mind broadcasting it directly into his.

'I know—it's OK,' he said. '*Death is not the end.*'

Behind Lisa, Gideon tried to give him a smile

but he and Luke were gripping each other's shoulders and concentrating so hard on holding the rudder that sweat was dripping off them. Barry and Jennifer were sitting close together; he had his arm around her shoulders. Jacob, Alex, and Clive were standing, rubbing their wrists which were red and sore from the ropes.

'There's no point in going off anywhere before we get further north,' explained Lisa. 'We may as well sit tight for a bit longer, rather than risk bumping into any of the crew.'

'So why did you knock out the guards? Why not just leave them alone?'

Lisa shrugged. 'Sylv's advice. Before Luke and Gideon started on the rudder. I guess she knew you were coming. Where have you been? What's happening with Owen?'

Dax told them all, quickly, about his brief telephone contact with Owen and then about what he'd just heard on the bridge—some of it. He left out the bit about his trip into the mountains with Spook, it was too big to explain. He also left out what Mr Eades had planned for Clive and held off before telling them about the explosive in the chips.

'So Owen will be searching for us. I know he will. He knew about us being by the docks and in the container, so I'm sure he'll work it out. He'll be here. I know he will.'

Lisa nodded. 'I think he will be,' she said, although she didn't sound very sure. 'I tried to dowse for him but it was no good. My head's all messed up.'

'Who still has a chip in?' said Dax, now filled with urgency. 'There's something else about them you don't know. Let me get them out first.'

As he had thought, Barry, Jennifer, Darren, Jacob, and Alex still hadn't had theirs removed. It was not surprising. Digging them out with one blunt nail was a horrible task—although clearly Luke had also withstood it to join Gideon. Mia, pale but steady, stood alongside as Dax shifted to the falcon and performed vicious surgery on each of his friends. When they were all healed and regaining their composure, he held all of the chips in the palm of his hand and told them about Mr Eades's final betrayal. They looked horrified.

'Stamp on them!' choked Barry, but Dax just flung them into the corner of the room.

'They might notice if they all go dead,' he said. 'Although they haven't noticed anything yet. I think—' Dax froze and cocked his head as a familiar rhythm caught his ears. 'Uh-oh,' he said and Lisa's eyes widened.

'I think she's here,' said Dax. The sound of a helicopter above them was unmistakable.

'She is,' agreed Lisa, her face growing pale.

'That means they'll be coming for us,' said Dax. 'We need to get out of here.'

'Where to, though? There's nowhere to run?' She bit her lip. 'We're in the middle of the North Sea! There's nothing out here!'

Dax felt a tingle run across his neck. 'Yes there is,' he said. 'Lisa—can I have a word with Sylv?'

'You what?'

'I need to find out why she's sending us north. I think—'

'Oh!' Lisa blinked. 'She says you're right. We're nearly there. She says . . . it's been a long time coming. Does that mean anything to you?' She shook her head and shrugged. 'It doesn't make any sense to me.'

'Well, it does to me,' said Dax and a strange gurgle of laughter followed his words. 'Mountain comes to Muhammed,' he added. He dashed back into the walkway, past the comatose guards, and found a small porthole. The grey sea had calmed and darkened as the afternoon light faded and there was no land in sight—but on the northern horizon, far out into the ocean, was something that made him catch his breath.

It was a flare of fire.

'Can you make this ship go faster?' Gideon and Luke stared at him, straining to keep their mind power on the heavy cargo ship rudder, which was probably four or five times their size and trying to resist them with incredible strength.

'I know—I know,' said Dax. 'But if you *can* do it, now would be a good time!'

Jacob walked up and placed his hand on Gideon's shoulder. 'Come on,' he said. 'I know it's not our thing—but we might be able to send in some extra energy or something.'

'Yes,' said Mia. 'Yes—you can do that! We all can. Everyone connect up and send energy in— just *think* it. It's like heat, you can send it over.' The Colas crowded around the telekinetics, putting hands on their shoulders and backs and Dax believed he could feel the heat pulsing from them across to Gideon and Luke. He also felt the ship speed up, although he could barely believe that.

He went to add his own hand and energy but some instinct told him not to. That he had to keep himself apart. He glanced back through the door. How much time, before Catherine emerged along the walkway? Maybe he could stop her coming in. 'Keep going!' he said to the others. 'I'll try to distract her or something, if she comes this way.' He shifted to the fox and ventured back into the corridor, listening hard, lifting his nose. Through the porthole the flame on the horizon loomed much larger and higher. They were definitely speeding up.

He reached the top of the stairwell and suddenly remembered Spook. He had said he would return in five minutes, but he'd completely forgotten. He needed to warn him. Dax shifted again and ran down the steps but something stopped him dead on the next landing down, just before he could turn the corner and see Spook below. A scent. One he had last breathed in moments before he nearly died, many months ago. It made his throat close and gag and instinctively he flickered into the falcon and rose up, finding a talon-hold on a metal strut across the sloped ceiling above him.

Up the stairs came Spook. His face was impassive, and he moved as if he were sleepwalking. Holding his hand was Catherine.

29

She was thinner than he remembered her. Her hair had grown back into a short dark bob and her skin was tanned across prominent cheek-bones. Her green eyes glittered hungrily as she drew Cola power into herself for the first time in months.

'Oh that's *good*, Spook. You always were one of my favourites,' she sighed, her Californian accent heavy with satisfaction.

Behind her were two men, one of whom Dax recognized, by his scent, as the Frenchman from the bridge. They wore thick leather gloves and jackets and stayed a few steps behind Catherine, holding black rifles across their chests.

'Is it working? Like you said?' demanded the Frenchman. 'Show me.'

Catherine glanced back at him with a smirk and he froze, his eyes flying open with shock as the air around them wavered. Catherine had clearly just thrown a very effective illusion.

'How's that?' she asked. He nodded, growing pale.

'Make it stop now,' he said and apparently she did, because he and his colleague let out sighs of relief a second later.

'Now—it's time to collect the rest of the set,' said Catherine as they reached the turn in the stairwell.

The Frenchman looked uneasy. 'Not *all*, I am afraid. We lost one. We thought we had lost *two*. This idiot boy must have stowed away. Not very clever, eh? Imbecile!' And he poked Spook in the back with his rifle, and Spook's eyes rolled a little but he made no sound.

Catherine let go of Spook, who slumped down on the first landing, unconscious. She spun round angrily. 'What? You promised me *all* of them! ALL! Don't you dare go back on it! We had a deal.'

'It can't be helped,' said the Frenchman. 'And

346

don't lecture me, *mademoiselle*. Yes—we had a deal! A deal for me to get you out of that government zoo. And all you have to do is be yourself. In every way I ask. *When* I ask!'

Catherine, who was dressed in a dark blue jersey and jeans, put her hands on her hips and glared at him. 'Who? *Who* did you lose?'

The Frenchman looked bitter. He began to say 'The sha—' but her wail of frustration cut him short.

'No! No! No! Don't say the shapeshifter! Don't say it!'

He shut his mouth and glared back at her.

He stepped away down the stairs, backwards, as Catherine moved towards him. 'I—wanted—the *shapeshifter*—the MOST!' She jabbed out at him with a skinny finger, on which the nail had been filed to a point. He flipped his rifle and drove her back with the butt of it.

'Get away from me! You have all the others. Now go! The buyers will be here in less than an hour. We are already late. If you want the others, we go now!'

Catherine turned back and viciously kicked Spook's ribs with a black leather boot. 'I've got enough from *him*,' she said. 'Don't worry. He won't get up again until tomorrow.'

She stormed on up the stairs and Dax clung to the metal strut and wondered what on earth he could do to stop her reaching the others. As his frantic brain raced at bird-speed and his heart kept pace with it, he realized how weak he was—how useless his rescue attempt had been. Spook was out for the count and Dax knew Catherine and her armed back-up would squash him if he tried to attack her. She'd nearly killed him last time.

He sent a message to Lisa: *She's coming! With men with guns! You have to run! She's coming!* But what came back was odd. Lisa's telepathic voice sounded steady.

Dax! she sent. *Brace yourself!*

And before he could even try to work out what she meant there was a deafening crash and the ship lurched so hard he was flung forward into the angle of the upper stair. The metal ceiling above him buckled and twisted, and had he not been a small bird, he would have buckled and twisted with it.

He heard himself scream—a high, peregrine shriek, and then felt a blast of cold air hit him. Below, Spook slid down the steps, still dead to the world, but the lower stairwell was intact and he didn't look hurt. Dax lifted his falcon eyes up and saw something that filled him with amazement. How had they done it? How had they got here so fast? He shot through the ruptured wall of the ship, weaving up between thick metal girders and out into the dying afternoon light. Heat was rising around him and he rode it, climbing higher and higher until he could look down upon the cargo ship which was twisting slowly in the sea, recoiling from the shock of its collision. The small helicopter on the foredeck was lying on its side, rotor snapped.

As he rose higher he could look down even upon the vast flare, blooming from a stack which angled out from the structure, seventy metres above the sea, like an enormous Olympic torch. The metal edifice it rose from was ugly and wonderful and amazingly familiar to Dax. He had seen it in photos—many times.

He scanned the deck and saw several figures running to the rails, staring down in amazement at the ship turning agitatedly at the thigh of an enormous leg which planted its foot into the ocean floor. Many wore hard hats, but not all. And even if he had, the man the peregrine sought would never have escaped his view. A familiar head of hair, light brown and turning grey, leaned out of a cabin door, scanning the running men and shouting for information. Before he could join the others peering over the rails, Dax dropped as fast as gravity would allow. His talons struck the man's thick workcoat without piercing skin, but at such speed that the man cried out in shock. A second later Dax was standing as a boy, on the platform of Guillemot B.

The man gasped and put both hands to his face.

'Hi, Dad,' said Dax. 'I need your help.'

30

He didn't have time for his father to be shocked. He needed him now.

'Dad!' Dax reached up and grabbed his father's shoulders. 'We need to get through to Owen Hind. You need to send a Mayday out and get him here. NOW!'

'Dax,' murmured Robert Jones, still staring at his son as if he were dreaming.

'Dad! Stop it! Wake up! I am *here* and I need you to help me! Can you help me? My friends are in terrible danger on that ship down there.' Now he dragged the man across the busy platform and pointed over the rail. The other rig workers were too distracted to even notice a teenage boy on the platform with them. Below, the container ship still turned slowly against the huge iron and concrete leg of the rig.

'My friends are there and they're in big trouble! Dad! Please! Send an emergency signal out to all shipping—all aircraft—whatever it is you do when there's a big, big emergency!'

At last Robert Jones seemed to wake up. 'Right!' he said. 'Come with me!' He grabbed Dax's hand and hauled him along the metal mesh surface of the platform, up some steep iron steps and into a cabin. Inside there were communication panels and receivers and a stunned looking colleague. 'Phil—meet my son, Dax,' said Robert Jones. 'He just dropped in.' The younger man stared from the father to son but didn't get a chance to speak. 'We need to put out a Mayday and an alert to all sea and air traffic.'

'About what? The collision of that cargo ship? It was only minor,' said his colleague. 'I mean—yeah—they need help but it's not a multi-agency job.'

'Tell them it's COLA project—code 47,' said Robert, surprising Dax greatly.

'You what?' His workmate screwed up his face.

'TELL them,' insisted Robert Jones. 'COLA project. Code 47. That, Comms Officer Stevens, is all you need to know.'

The man stood up and nodded and then turned to his instruments, pulling up a receiver, flicking switches, and then issuing a series of watchwords and commands before concluding, somewhat uncertainly, that this was a Cola project, code 47.

'What's a code 47?' asked Dax, astonished.

Robert touched his son's head, as if to check he was really there. 'It's a code all the Cola fathers were given, right at the start, in case of emergency with their kids. Code 47 has priority.'

'Over what?'

'Everything.'

There were squawks and chatters of response now coming in from the communications console and the comms officer was now issuing co-ordinates and other information about the ship strike. Now he turned to Robert and Dax Jones and raised his eyebrows. 'Royal Navy choppers and an aircraft carrier already within a five mile radius,' he said. 'That's got to be a record.'

'No,' said Dax, a thrill of pride coursing through him. 'They were already out there, looking for us. We just needed to attract their attention. Send up a flare.'

'Well, you've got the biggest flare in the northern oil fields,' said his father, opening the comms room door to a draught of cold, oily air. 'Come and have a hot drink. You must be exhausted. You can tell me all about it.'

'I can't,' said Dax. 'Sorry, Dad. Something came up.' He didn't mean to be sarcastic but his father's face crumpled. Dax had no time for it—not now. The comms officer's back was turned so he shifted immediately and was gone in less than two seconds.

He could see the bright lights of the military helicopters—four of them—growing larger in the western sky, but he couldn't wait for them to arrive. He had to get back onto the ship to help his friends.

He dropped down and flew back through ripped metal into the stairwell. Spook was still at the bottom of the stairs and he dropped onto the step beside him and shifted back to boy, so he could check that the boy was still breathing. Spook felt cool and still, but there was a pulse in his throat and his eyes moved behind closed lids. 'You'll be all right,' whispered Dax. 'Help is coming.' A wave of exhaustion hit him. The air around him seemed to waver and suddenly he fell back against the steps, gripped with horror. He couldn't see her yet, but he knew she was there. With a long sigh of delight, Catherine rippled out of her vanish into full view, and wrapped her arms around him.

As his energy began to pour out of him and into her, she giggled and told him stories. 'It's been amazing, these last few months, Dax. You wouldn't believe how *important* I am to the French. They treat me like a princess! Well—mostly. And of course, once they knew there were others—more Colas—they wanted them all! But then I told them they didn't *need* you all. They only needed me. Everything you could do, *I* could do, just as soon as we'd got you all rounded up together. At first they were quite happy for me to get all your powers and finish you all off, so there'd be no more worrying about anyone else. But then I got taken away from the holding cells and put in a nice house in the country and they got me a new dad! He's here with me today! He's clever. He said we need money, so we decided I wouldn't kill you all—that we'd sell you all off once you were empty. You're worth a lot of money, you know. And then, of course, you'll all go out like light bulbs when the button gets pressed. Pop. Cola pop! Oh, did you hear that? I made a funny. Cola pops! And you're all non-refundable.'

Dax wanted to shift to the fox and sink his fangs into her throat, but he didn't have enough energy. He realized she must already have got to the others—certainly she must have got to Barry or Jennifer, to be able to do the vanish.

'You can't get away,' he said and his words were beginning to slur. 'Your helicopter's broken.'

'Won't need it in a minute,' she replied cheerfully. 'Oh, wait—I want you to be a falcon first. Go on. Shift.'

'No.'

'Shift,' she repeated, squeezing his throat. 'Or I'll kill you now.'

Dax shuddered into falcon form and her hands were tight around him before he could stretch out one wing.

'Good. Nice and light. I want you to come with me. I'm a shapeshifter now and I've waited so long for this! So you can share the moment. I'm going to be an eagle.'

Dax wanted to say that you didn't get to choose. You shifted to whatever you shifted to. But now her hands were talons and she was indeed a huge bird of prey, although she didn't look like an eagle. She looked more like a giant crow with a curved beak and ugly mustard-yellow eyes. There was no questioning the talons which drove into his feathers and pierced his skin. Catherine's avian eyes glittered much like her human ones and she lifted her wings in triumph. Two seconds later they were both airborne as she launched back out through the tear in the ship wall, with her prey clasped firmly beneath her.

You were too late, Dax, she sent him, telepathically and he realized with a further plummeting heart that she must have fed upon Lisa—and Jacob and Alex too, probably. *Even if your precious Owen gets here and rescues them in time, you're too late. It's over. I got Spook first and that was really handy. My illusion was excellent. You'll never guess! I sent 'Owen' in ahead of me and my men. Oh—you should have heard your little friends cry out in relief! They thought they were saved! And then I just marched in and got Luke and Gideon, before they even knew it. And then I did Darren, Barry, and poor snivelling Jenny and then those Teller boys. I got Lisa next. I was going to take my time but I had to do it real fast in case the ship was sinking. I was just going to have sweet, sleepy little Mia for dessert and then I thought I'd try a dowse for you first—just in case—and hey! There you were, down the stairs! Neat, huh? I've been looking forward to getting you for such a long time. I didn't want to rush it, but I had to—and now you're nearly all used up. It's kind of sad how quickly you all empty out.*

Dax, hanging and buffeted by the wind, could make out the golden glow of the oil rig gas flare beneath them, blooming out of the crane-like stack. He could feel the heat from it although they must be thirty metres above it.

Feeling cold, Dax? Catherine's cruel grip loosened on him slightly. *I know a great way to warm you up . . .* Then she retracted her talons from his weak body and dropped him into the flame.

31

It would be quick. He would be vaporized in a second. There was no hope of trying to fly; his wings were like bits of rag. Dax plummeted towards the golden flare and had only enough time to feel rather sad for his dad. They never did get to talk.

Just as he felt the feathers around his eyes begin to singe he was belted violently sideways by a shocking, cold force of . . . of . . . what? Dax whirled and tumbled, in great surprise—huge, *dumbfounded* surprise. He was being borne along on a twisting, churning stack of . . . water!

There were crackles of electricity dancing to and fro in the funnel of dark grey sea which had abruptly thrown itself up into the sky. Buffeted and thrown but somehow remaining on *top* of the waterspout, Dax had that feeling, once more, of being bitten by hoards of angry red ants. He'd last had it in the mountain 'corridor'. *Cleftonique aftershock!* his mind shouted out in amazement and delight. *You've been saved by your own cleftonique aftershock!* As his aunt had warned, a localized weather phenomenon had struck just after sending—a freak waterspout. And it had saved him!

Now it seemed to be filling him up with energy, and he wondered if Hessa and Carra were watching through the ViewCube and had broken the rules just once more, to save him. The biting red ants feeling intensified but with it came a throb of electrical power and his limp falcon wings began to beat. A few seconds later Dax, fully recharged, soared above the waterspout, which was already beginning to warp and tumble back into the ocean, sending the cargo ship into a frenzy of tilting and rolling. Below him, two military helicopters hung in the air, one had landed on the oil rig helipad, and another had set down on the flat surface of the containers on the deck of the ship and now it rose quickly from the pitching deck.

The main platform area of the rig was now empty—its men were being held back by dark military figures—but two people remained in the centre of it. Mia stood still, her hair whipping around in the downdraught from the helicopters. Next to her stood Owen Hind. They were both gazing up into the sky, but not at Dax. They probably couldn't even see him. What they were seeing, though, was the huge black bird of prey which swooped some seven metres above their heads. Owen, clad in the same black combat gear as his military team, raised his rifle. He had shot Catherine dead once before. He had promised Dax that he would not miss the opportunity to do it again. Now though, he was wrestling with the rifle, which was turning inwards, towards his own head. Behind him, his men also began to struggle with their guns, shouting out in aston-ishment and dismay.

Dax landed next to Owen and the man, still wrestling against his possessed weapon, glanced sideways and yelled, 'Dax! Get behind me!' But Dax stood alongside him and stared up at the dark ragged shape in the sky. When the shape saw him it flexed convulsively in the air and then alighted on the rail at the edge of the platform. As she shifted back into a girl, sitting on the rail and smiling sweetly, Owen's gun stopped twisting against him. But before he could regain it, it flew high into the air and exploded. As did all the guns of the military around them, in a violent firework display which sent shards of gun casing raining down around them.

'Hold still!' yelled Owen, and the men did.

Catherine smiled. It was a charming smile. A smile filled with sparkle and fun. A smile which had cost several people their lives.

'Want to kill me again, Mr Hind?' she cooed. 'I bet you do!'

Dax stepped forward, ready to shift. 'If he doesn't, I will.' Mia stood still behind Owen and said nothing. Dax guessed Owen had found her on the ship, the only one still conscious, and brought her up to the rig on the helicopter, keeping her with him for safety.

'Hey, you are one hell of a comeback kid, Dax Jones! Didn't I just barbecue you?'

'You tried.'

'But you got away! It was that weird water-spout thing. Maybe Luke's been doing his sea water thing again . . . Although I thought I left him pretty much dead—like old times!'

'Cleftonique aftershock,' said Dax. 'You wouldn't understand.'

'Well, y'know, guys, I'd love to sit here chatting all day, but I have one more Cola to collect and then I have to fly. So be good—hand over Little Miss Feelgood and I can wind this up.'

'You know that's not going to happen, Catherine,' said Owen. His face was like stone.

There was a metallic grating noise and several of the cabins which made up the strange oil rig village began to judder in their housings.

'You don't really want me to kill an entire oil rig crew, now do you?' said Catherine. There were shouts of alarm from the men being held back by the military unit, as one of the cabins teetered above their heads. Suddenly one man burst past the disarmed soldiers and ran towards Dax.

'Son! Son! Are you all right?' Robert Jones grabbed hold of him fiercely and Owen cursed. Dax immediately knew why. The amused stare of the girl on the rail swept from Owen to Robert Jones and a giggle escaped her lips. Catherine had found a new entertainment.

'Oh my! A family reunion! Dax's daddy! Why, Dax—I'm quite glad I didn't cook you now. I wouldn't have missed this—for—the—*world*! Here you are! Seeing your dad at last. Now . . . c'mon, Mr Jones . . . let me in!' Dax realized, with revulsion, that she was using her stolen telepathy to forage around in his father's head. 'Oh yeah, I get it now! Oh, you feel so *bad*, Mr Jones. Or can I call you Rob? Yeah, I'll call you Rob. You feel so bad, Rob, because you miss his mom so much you can hardly bear to look at him.'

'Shut up!' shouted Robert Jones, hoarsely. 'You don't know what you're talking about.'

'Oh yeah, I do,' went on Catherine. She was lit up with fun. 'When his mom died, you were angry. You knew why she had to go, didn't you? You knew! And you didn't think it was fair. Not a fair trade. One little boy for the love of your life.'

'That's not true!' yelled Robert, but the grief in his voice was too clear. 'He's my son!'

'Yeah, and you *do* love him—kinda.' Catherine shrugged and wore an expression of grotesque sympathy. 'It's just that every day he looks more like her. It's the eyes—and the skin and the hair.

364

And you just can't forget and that hurts. You must have been so glad when he turned Cola and the government took him away. Don't worry though—I'll take him away for you. For good!'

Robert went to rush at her, but Owen grabbed him with both hands. 'No!' He yanked the burly rig worker back. 'You can't touch her!'

Dax felt his mind whirl. This was *not* the time. *Not* the time at all. And yet he knew that every word that Catherine had said was true. His dad could *not* bear to look at him. Just like Spook's dad. He just couldn't cope with being reminded. Dax's heart wrenched with sorrow. He understood.

'It's all right, Dad,' he said. 'It's OK.'

But it was far from OK. Before he could draw breath to say another word, there was a sudden updraught of heat and then Dax and Mia were staring at each other, an empty space between them.

'Oops!' said Catherine, still perched on the rail. 'Where *did* the big brave men go?'

She lifted her face and gazed up, up, up. Dax followed her sightline with horror. Way out on the angle of the stack, sixty metres above the cold

North Sea, two figures were dangling, hanging from the metal struts by their hands alone.

There was a movement among Owen's men and Catherine said, 'Oh no! Behave!' They fell back like tin soldiers as if they'd been hit by a wave. 'Well, Dax,' she prompted. 'What are you waiting for? Fly to the rescue!'

He shifted and shot up, reaching the criss-cross girders of the stack in seconds and looking down at the strained and desperate faces of Owen and his father. The men were hanging on to the metal struts only with the grip of their hands. Both looked up at him grimly. Owen grunted out, 'Dax! Go! Get away! Don't let her do this to you.'

Dax shifted to a boy, clinging to the struts above them. 'Climb up! Climb up! Owen, you're strong! You can do this!'

'Can't,' he gasped. 'She's wiped me out. We'll fall when she wants us to fall.'

'Do as he says, Dax. Fly off! Please, son!' His dad's eyes were wet and his face a mask of misery. 'Tell Alice I love her. And I love you too, boy.'

'I know, Dad—I know. But you've got to try! Don't give up!' Dax pressed his chest and head against the struts around him and reached down with both hands. He *could* reach them both. He grasped his fingers over their knuckles, but he couldn't possibly get a grip with just one hand.

'Oh, Dax. What a thing! Who to choose?'

Catherine was just behind him now, perched casually on the angled strut above.

'You know, I'm impressed. You've done so well. So I'll tell you what—you get to keep one of them. Just one. Just grab the one you want and I'll help you get him up. You can let the other one go.'

Dax cried out then. It was a long, torn, wretched cry. He was to choose between Owen and his father? Right here. Right now. And whoever he did not choose would fall to his death. He heard himself begging. Begging and crying. His falling tears were whipped away by the wind.

Owen shouted at him. 'No! Not by her rules, Dax! Not this time. You're not choosing! You're NOT! Remember this, Dax . . . it was *not your choice.*'

Owen tried to reassure his boy with one last smile, even as he disengaged his fingers.

He made no noise as he fell.

32

Dax grabbed his father with both hands and something of the remaining cleftonique energy rose in him; enough to pull the man up onto the main girders where he clung, gasping and shocked silent. Or maybe Catherine did help. She still sat behind him, beaming with delight.

'That was really quite moving, wasn't it?' she asked. 'That guy really loved you.'

Dax shifted and flew for her eyes. Instantly she was the black bird of prey and they were swiping and tumbling through the air, talons clawing for each other's eyes and throats. She was stronger but he was much faster. They swooped low towards the platform, where scores of shocked faces peered up at them; the rig workers and the military, all unable to move.

Catherine landed and shifted and then raised her arms. Dax was belted backwards by her stolen telekinetic power and struck the unforgiving corner of the comms cabin before tumbling several feet to the deck. She danced like a cheerleader and shouted, 'Yay! You go, girl! You go, girl!'

Dax lay crumpled, his back broken. He had shifted back to a boy and could see Mia standing, still, upon the platform, watching Catherine. He wished he could have died *before* he saw Catherine feed upon the last Cola left.

Catherine was still doing her victory dance, waving imaginary pom-poms at the sky. 'You go, girl! You go, girl!' she continued.

'OK,' said Mia.

'Oh!' Catherine turned and gasped theatrically at Mia. 'I almost forgot! My little pamper package. My goodie bag. The lovely, lovely Mia!'

She had not bothered to immobilize Mia. Mia the healer was no threat.

'Don't try anything, Mia, honey!' Catherine sighed and put her hands on her hips and her head to one side, as if she were talking to a toddler

369

who was inclined to run out into the road. 'I'm pretty tired after all the excitement, so let's just be pals, uhuh? Give me your hand.'

'Sure,' said Mia. 'I'll give you everything you need.' Mia walked to the platform's edge, lowered her eyes, her hair billowing out behind her in the sea breeze, and held out her ungloved hand. Catherine smirked and skipped across to her.

'See? It's so much better than fighting, don't you think? You always were my favourite, y'know.' She took Mia's hand in her own and let out a long, delighted sigh as the healing power began to pulse across from one girl to the other.

'Hmmm. Feels warm! That's good,' murmured Catherine, closing her eyes. 'Ooh. That *is* warm.'

'Is it?' said Mia.

'Hey—maybe you should turn it down a bit, honey.'

'Should I?' said Mia. Her free arm hooked around the rail at the platform's edge.

Catherine's green eyes sprang open in shock. 'Stop it! Stop it now!'

'Can't,' said Mia. 'I'm giving you what you need.'

There was a smell. It made Dax think of summer barbecues. Catherine began to scream and desperately try to wrestle her hand away from Mia's but Mia would not let go. Catherine screamed harder. First the fire moved up her arm quite slowly, flames curling and flickering delicately as the girl screamed and screamed and her skin curled and blackened. 'No! No! This doesn't happen to *ME*!' shrieked Catherine. But now the fire had reached her shoulder and it suddenly whooshed out like a torch and engulfed her upper body with a roar. Catherine bellowed and tried to run as her hair went up, but Mia, her teeth gritted and her eyes black, anchored herself to the rail and would not release the girl's hand.

'Getting what you need?' she enquired. Catherine's blackening face was a mask of fury and confusion as the sea wind whipped the flames into a spinning cone around her head. *'Not ME!'* were her last intelligible words.

The screams were almost drowned out by the spitting and crackling of the fierce blaze which turned blue and green at its centre. Catherine shifted into the black bird of prey and Mia finally let go as the flaming wings rose up into the air, whirling and pitching in a clumsy circle. The bird opened its smoking beak and screamed in a higher pitch than the girl had. And then it erupted into a ball of flame and exploded about fifteen metres above the platform.

As charred feathers fell around them Mia walked across to Dax. She sat down next to him and laid her warm hand over his broken spine.

'That showed her,' she said.

33

Owen's funeral took place on a bright day in late February. He was given full military honours and a high ranking government minister read out a long eulogy for him in the small London church.

'Owen Simon Hind,' he read, 'was one of this country's finest men. He died to protect his country and I can think of no better calling.'

The words went on. Other men in suits rose and spoke and the words pitter-pattered down from the pulpit like the rain which nature should have provided for the occasion. Words like 'loyal' and 'courageous' and 'outstanding' and 'sadly missed' and none of them even began to touch the essence of what Owen really was, so they might as well have not bothered. In fact, silence, absolute silence, was the only thing approaching how it should be, thought Dax. Silence. No surprises. No drama. Just nothing.

He raised his chin from his chest—a huge effort—and allowed his eyes to take in the row of men in dark suits. Chambers, Owen's colleague who had allowed the chipping to take place, he recognized, grave and staring at the coffin. Then there was the high ranking government minister and three others he didn't know at all. Government men. Telling everyone about Owen. They didn't speak for any of the Colas, lined up together three rows back, some with fathers sitting behind them. Their red, white, and blue piles of flowers were for *their* Owen—the small wreath of knotted twigs and bark and berries from the wood at Fenton Lodge was for the Colas' Owen. Robert Jones touched Dax's shoulder and Dax wearily worked the little levers inside his head which made his body turn and his face conjure up something like a smile. Then he turned back again and looked at the representatives of the government once more.

The government was so much part of this

whole disaster. It was the government that had funded the scientists to tinker with the Colas' brains. And Owen was the only one who had tried to stop them. And now he was dead.

'I'll dowse for him!' Lisa had promised, through streams and streams of tears. 'We'll be able to talk to him again! He'll come through to me—I know he will.'

But Lisa hadn't been able to. She was much too weak. All the Colas, except Mia, were still shattered. Even Clive had been wiped out by Catherine. She had decided, on a whim, that his scientific talents might be useful, so she had even included him when she had attacked them so fast on the ship. They had been found unconscious and immediately transported to the military helicopters while Owen, keeping Mia at his side, had taken six of his men with him and tracked down the crew, the captain, Catherine's French accomplice (a former French Direction de la Surveillance du Territoire agent who had cheated his own people for money, it turned out) and, of course, Britain's own traitor, Mr Eades.

Mr Eades had held them off for a while, with his remote control and threats to explode the

Colas' heads—but then Mia had explained that all of the chips were now removed. Mr Eades detonated them as he was seized and a chair in their windowless cell got slightly charred. Mia told them later that Owen had held Eades by the throat and nearly snapped the man's neck. For a few seconds his own men had needed to restrain him.

The Frenchman had immediately begun to bargain with Owen, promising to give up all the information he had on Eades and Catherine and the whole auction plan. The international buyers scattered back across the globe without their purchases.

Owen had helicoptered up to the rig with Mia, because Catherine was nowhere to be found on the ship. And there, of course, he had found her. What happened to Owen afterwards was scored into Dax's memory and hung before his eyes every second of every waking moment. Playing and replaying. A smile. Fingers letting go. End of story.

'Maybe he's not dead,' Gideon had said, pale and shocked, from the stretcher at the military hospital they had been flown to. 'Maybe . . . '

'He's dead,' said Dax. And he should know.

As soon as Mia had mended his spine he had run to the far corner of the rig, beneath the angled stack where his father was already being helped down, and jumped over the edge. He heard Mia scream after him for a second before the air rushing past him whipped away all sound. He did not shift into a falcon although, in a vague copy of it, he pointed his arms and legs and made an arrow shape. Something was going to happen. Something was happening *now*. When Dax struck the water it seemed to allow him in, without too much protest, although the sheer impact should have cracked his bones. His clawed hands carved through the surface and soon he was deep down in it, flexing his streamlined body with precision and confidence, as if he had been an otter for life, instead of just a few seconds. The glory of such a moment—a brand new shapeshift—was obliterated by his desperate, desperate search for Owen, somewhere here, somewhere in the murky waters between Guillemot B's three vast feet.

He had swum and swum, nose down against the sea bed, sending up plumes of silt and tiny sea creatures, his mind refusing to admit that if he *did* find Owen, the man he knew and loved would be long gone. When he at last made out the shape of a body it was, oddly, above him. Through searchlights from the military craft which were now descending in all forms on and around the rig and the ship, he made out the base of a small inflatable. A man-shaped shadow was being dragged towards it. Dax had used his formidable otter limbs to shoot himself up through the seawater and to the surface within seconds. He launched himself out of the waves and onto the grey curved sides of the inflatable in time to see Tyrone, looking grey and grim, pulling Owen aboard with help from another man. Tyrone glanced across at the otter with vague astonishment, but was too occupied with his task to do more than shake his head, as if he were seeing things. He and the other man worked on the body, trying to push the cold North Sea out of it and some life back into it. At length Tyrone put his head in his hands and then asked the other man to get the body bag. The man turned away and Tyrone stared for a long time at Owen's face, although Dax could only see the soaked mat of dark hair on the back of Owen's head. Tyrone leaned down and seemed to be touching Owen's face and saying something into the dead man's ear. Goodbye, probably. It wasn't until his mate had returned with the bag and they had begun to zip it up that they noticed the otter again. Otters cry noisily.

After the funeral there was the wake. The bleak party where everyone stands around and learns to laugh again. In some cases. No laughter was heard at the little hall to one side of the church, just muted talking and clinking of cutlery and glasses as people filed along the buffet table. The Colas huddled together, quiet and slow. They were recovering well physically, and those whose fathers had come seemed to feel a bit better. Robert Jones kept his arm around Dax but could find little to say.

The fathers had been taken to Fenton Lodge two days after the events at Guillemot B and fully briefed on what had happened. Robert told Dax later what had been said. Apparently, Mr Eades had been planning the abduction of the Colas for many months and had one scientist working with him on the plan—and later he had bought out the loyalty of three of the soldiers on the regular

Cola Project rota. These soldiers, with more hired help, had disabled their unwary colleagues on the night of the kidnapping. The DST agent—Jacques Bellancourt—had made contact with Eades not long after Catherine was taken by the French, proposing the auction, and they had been working closely together. Bellancourt had 'released' Catherine from detention and taken her to a safe house. As soon as she had fed off the others and the others had been sold, he had planned to sell her right back to the DST. Foolishly, he had believed he could control her.

Of course, none of it could have happened if the Cola Project had not allowed the chips to be inserted. The fathers were livid. There was almost a stampede to get to their children and take them home there and then. Mrs Sartre had managed to calm them enough to explain the risks, if they did this. Nowhere in the world was better equipped than Fenton Lodge to protect their children from further abduction attempts. Nowhere.

The Cola Project also gave a written statement promising that no further such 'experiments' would ever happen. Within all reasonable, non-emergency circumstances. It would have a Cola Fathers' committee meeting once a month for updating and consultation. The luxury cottage up on the fells was booked solidly with Cola fathers intent on spending much more time keeping an eye on what went on at Cola Project. The Project announced its intention to build six more cottages and to have Cola fathers present all year round if necessary.

'I'll be spending a lot more time with you, Dax,' his dad had told him. Dax looked up into his grey eyes and after a few seconds, Robert Jones looked away.

'Spend more time with Gina and Alice,' said Dax.

'Is it too late for you and me, son?' His father gulped.

'I don't know,' said Dax. 'I don't know anything any more.'

'I owe it to your mum, you know, to try harder to deal with this. That's why I sent you that thing she wanted you to have. I knew I had to do it for ages, and I finally, finally made myself do it. I didn't want to let it go, you see. I was selfish. It was something of hers. What was it?'

'A sort of key,' said Dax. 'I'm afraid I haven't got it any more.'

'Oh. OK.'

He guessed his dad deserved more, but he had promised the Senders that he'd tell nobody. Hey! Once again, a promise to lie. His promises had a nasty way of backfiring on him.

A woman was approaching him. She was wearing a pale green dress and had wavy dark hair and bright blue eyes, which were puffy with crying. 'Um . . . are you Dax Jones?' she asked and he nodded, disturbed by the familiarity of her.

'I'm Rebecca—Owen's sister.'

His breath caught in his throat. He'd had no idea Owen had a sister. Or any family at all. He'd never thought about Owen's life outside Cola Club.

'He . . . he thought a lot of you.' She smiled and sniffed. 'Said you were the most courageous boy he'd ever met. I know he'd want you to have this.' She pressed an envelope into his hand. 'Maybe not now,' she said, quietly, leaning in towards him. He slid it into the pocket of his stiff grey suit. 'When you're alone.'

34

In the end, Dax didn't have to keep his promise to the Senders. In the coach on the way back from the funeral, Spook stood up and told everyone about their strange collaboration. Everything he knew. Which turned out to be quite a lot more than Dax had realized.

'While Dax was in the corridor or wherever it was he went to, I was still in the cave, holding his hand,' he said, without a hint of embarrassment. They'd all been through too much together for that. 'I couldn't see anything, but I could hear it all. Every word.'

Spook then related, in detail, the conversation Dax had had with his aunt and cousin, even the bit about himself and Dax being related. He spoke of the cleftonique and the ViewCubes, of the story of the Seeders and the Senders and why their mothers—the Seeders—could never live long enough to explain. Some of the Colas cried yet more tears, but most nodded and smiled as if it made perfect sense. Mrs Dann and Mrs Sartre wept unreservedly and Mr Tucker handed around tissues and cleared his throat a lot.

Spook was coming to the end of his story. He paused and gave Dax an appraising look, and Dax wondered if he would rebuke him for keeping this secret. He wouldn't blame him—or any of them. He had kept too many secrets.

'Dax wasn't going to tell you any of this,' said Spook. 'He had to promise not to tell what happened, so that he could get put back onto the ship to rescue you. We would've been OK, both of us. We were quite safe and we can both look after ourselves these days. But he wouldn't let them send him back to the mountain. He said . . . ' Spook paused and looked at Dax as if he couldn't quite believe his own words. 'He said he would stay there and die if they didn't send us both back to the ship.' There was a pause as everyone looked from Spook to Dax and back to Spook again. 'I'm telling you this,' went on Spook, 'in case any of you still think he let you down. Over the chip business. He wasn't to blame. Owen stopped him talking, and whatever any of you might say, you know that if Owen had made *you* promise, you would have done the same as Dax.'

There was another amazed pause and then Gideon stood up.

'I can't believe I am saying this out loud,' he croaked, a tissue knotted between his fingers, 'but you've said it all exactly right. Exactly. Thanks. Mate.'

If this was a film, thought Dax, *the weepy music would be swelling up right now and we'd all be hugging and saying everything will be OK.*

As it wasn't a film, everyone settled back into their seats. The waistband of Dax's funeral suit rubbed uncomfortably on his thin stomach. He couldn't wait to take it off and never look at it again.

Things became normal quickly. Not quickly

enough for some. Too quickly—much, much too quickly—for Dax.

Lessons with Mrs Sartre and Mrs Dann and Mr Tucker were resumed. With Owen and Tyrone gone (Tyrone had taken extended sick leave, apparently) all Development classes were suspended. In any case, the Colas needed to recover their strength and spirit. Dax wondered, idly, if the remaining teachers really *knew* about Mia. The only witnesses to Catherine's death appeared to be himself and Mia. The paralysed military and oil rig workers had been unable to remember much at all. It seemed that even Catherine had not known about Mia's firestarting talent, despite the fact that Mia had set her hair alight last year. Back then, there had been several Colas and other people around, but there was also a damaged helicopter with a leaking fuel tank and perhaps she had really believed that the spontaneous combustion of her hair had been down to that. It was probably to Mia's greatest advantage that people simply *refused* to believe she could ever harm anyone. Dax knew different.

Mia was a wonderful, warm, caring girl. She was also a killer, if it was necessary. In de-briefing sessions with Chambers Dax had said his back was broken and he couldn't see clearly. It wasn't exactly a lie. Nobody knew for sure what had happened to Catherine, because only remnants of charred feathers and bird bones had been found. What Mia said Dax never found out, but the general agreement was that Catherine had probably flown too close to the rig's flare. Another confirmation that she really was dead was that some of the other hundred Colas whose powers had been wiped out by her, many months before, were apparently showing signs of recovering. Fenton Lodge might have to be extended for more students.

It was hard to concentrate in class. The lessons were very quiet and it was all the teachers could do to get the Colas to even answer their questions. But as the days passed Lisa began to get a bit bolshy again. Jacob and Alex Teller started mucking around. Clive began to do his odd experiments in the lab. Barry vanished from time to time and got told off by Mrs Dann. And the more normal it got, the more Dax wanted to stand up and scream, 'NO! Stop it! You can't just GO ON like this! What are you DOING? Don't you remember about Owen? Don't you know Owen's not coming back? Don't you *know* that?'

He never did, of course, but sometimes he just got up and went out, even in the middle of class, and the teacher never tried to stop him. He was moving and talking and eating and sleeping as if he was normal too, but each night sleep sank down on him like a shroud and every morning, confusion woke him with the promise of something better until his memory returned like a polluted tide. Owen was dead. This time two weeks ago he was alive. This time seventeen days ago he was alive. This time twenty-one days ago he was alive. Was alive. There was life. And it seemed impossible that he couldn't reach back through time and grab that last day of Owen's life and *stop* it from ending. There was too much life force there for it to stop like that, with no warning, no words, no chance to say, 'I *don't* hate you! I *never* hated you! I didn't mean it. And I forgive you.'

He traded, all the time, in his head. *I'll stop being able to shift, if you'll come back. I'll give up living at Fenton Lodge if you come back. I'll go blind if you come back. I'll go deaf if you come back. I'll be anything, anything, anything I have to be. I'll stop being anything*

I have to stop being. If you come back. And then Owen would say again the last words he ever spoke. 'Remember this, Dax . . . It was *not your choice.*' And there would be the smile. The loosening fingers.

Gideon followed him upstairs on the twenty-third day after Owen's death. Mrs Dann had said, 'Yes, go on, Gideon—go after him.'

He sat down on his bed and looked across at Dax. Dax's palms lay folded in his lap and his breathing was even and shallow, as if he was asleep. 'You can't go on like this, mate,' said Gideon. 'You're a wreck. When did you last shift? I haven't seen you fly since . . . '

Dax looked at Gideon and felt a stab of compassion. Gideon looked so worried about him. 'I can still shift,' he said. 'I just . . . it just hasn't . . . '

'We—we're all really cut up about Owen,' said Gideon. 'You know that, don't you?'

Dax nodded.

'But if Owen taught us anything about life, it was that we have to live it—*here, now*! While we've got it. I mean, yeah, there's other stuff we go on to, unless Lisa's just a big, big con, but you can't just wait around for that stuff. Here and now—that's what's important. You've still got us, mate. You've still got me.'

'I know,' said Dax. 'I'll get over it . . . sooner or later. It's just that it's so . . . there's so much . . . just nothing left. How can there be nothing left?'

Gideon shrugged and sighed. 'That's how it is, eh, for Colas? We don't get messages left behind—apart from your Neetanite. We don't get letters explaining anything, we don't—what?!'

Dax suddenly shot bolt upright and stared wildly around him. 'My funeral suit!' he gasped. 'My funeral suit! Where is it?'

Gideon looked even more concerned now. 'Look—you've got to move on . . . '

Dax grabbed him by the shoulders. 'I need to know. What did we do with our funeral suits?'

Gideon shook his head and then frowned. 'Well, we were *supposed* to put them in a pile in the laundry room, but to be honest, I think I just scrunched mine up under the bed.'

'And mine? Did I do that too? Did I?' Dax was hopping from one foot to the other with agitation.

'Um . . . no . . . you were out of it, mate. You

just left yours on the floor. But I sorted it out for you.'

'You mean you took it down to the laundry room?' demanded Dax.

'Nah—I scrunched it up under *your* bed! Have a look.'

Dax threw himself onto the floor and hauled out the stuff from under his bed. Among the boxes and pencil collections, wildlife books and half-eaten biscuits he found some crumpled grey material. His suit. He clutched the suit to him and let out shuddering sighs of relief.

Gideon was backing towards the door. 'I'm going to get someone,' he said. 'I'll be right back.'

Dax pulled out the squashed envelope that Owen's sister had given to him. He ripped it open and inside was a slip of paper which said: 'Death is not the end. Go where your cousins sleep.'

The hairs on his neck and arms prickled and he felt as if the planets were slowing down. Something . . . something *other* was happening here. A second later a peregrine falcon shot out of the window and across meadows of daffodils nodding in the late afternoon sun. He reached the wood and flew as deep into it as he dared before shifting to a fox, which hit the ground running. He found the sett within a minute, sniffed once to see if anyone was in—they were—and then entered anyway. The badgers looked mildly affronted at his speed as he scrambled down the earthy passageway and looked wildly about him. At first, in his excitement, he could make out nothing but a blur of brown and white and black and a warning scent from the chief boar, who was none too impressed. He eased back up the passageway slowly, catching his breath and scanning the walls and floor for a clue—anything! There—a glint of glass above him. He stared up and saw a pale green glass bottle, wedged firmly in among the network of roots, just two feet in from the entrance to the sett. It had not been here before. Or maybe it had. He wasn't sure. He scrabbled at it with his paws and it fell down at length, with a thunk. He collected it awkwardly in his teeth, and trotted back outside the sett.

In the wood only faint birdsong and rustle of spring leaves disturbed the peace. He set down the bottle and shifted back to a boy, his trembling hands snatching up the bottle at once. It had a cork stopper and there was a note inside. Tipping the note out took an agonizingly long time, but at last he pulled it through the bottle neck and unrolled it. He shouted out when he found it was a typed message.

Dear Dax
Death is not the end.
8 March, 9p.m., St Christopher's Church, Derwent; 10 March, 8p.m., the clock tower in Keswick; or 15 March, 6p.m., the ferry terminal on Lake Windermere (east).
Be careful.

It was unsigned, but his heart soared. What if? What *if*?

But wait! Wait! The dates! He'd had this letter scrunched up under his bed for *weeks*! Dax grabbed at his watch and scrutinized the date counter window. It was the 15th! March the 15th! Now! And it was already nearing 5p.m. He had little over an hour to get to Lake Windermere.

He flew back to his room to find Gideon sitting disconsolately on his bed. 'What?' said his best friend, as soon as Dax arrived.

Dax shifted and bounced down next to him, beaming from ear to ear. 'It was a message!' he gasped. 'It *was* a message! Look! This is it! It was left for me in the badger sett!'

Gideon stared at Dax as if he thought his friend was losing it, big time, but now he read the message.

'You don't think it's . . . ?'

'It *could* be! Couldn't it?' Dax felt his pounding heart go unsteady.

'But you said he was definitely dead.'

Dax saw again the lifeless body; Tyrone saying his goodbyes. Heard the zip of the body bag.

'Whatever! What are you waiting for?' said Gideon. 'Go! Go! Or you'll be too late to find out!'

'But I don't know where Lake Windermere *is*!'

'It's directly south of us. South! And it's a huge lake—really big. With a ferry crossing. Should take you about an hour to get there. GO! I won't tell anyone! Oh, blimey!' Gideon bit his lip and began to grin but Dax was already gone.

Flying in the early evening air was bumpy, but he was faster than ever before. He crossed range after range of Cumbrian fells, many still topped with snow, but lush and green in their valleys as

394

spring advanced. Many lakes, or tarns as they were known locally, winked up at him under the pale blue evening sky, but they were too small. It was a big, long lake he was looking for, he reminded himself, near a small town, with a ferry crossing halfway down. The east side—he needed to go to the east side.

It was more than an hour before he found it. Dax felt sick by now. What if all this was for nothing? He alighted in a tree on the edge of the lake, not far from the small ferry crossing point. He dropped down and shifted quickly. It was ten past six. Despair assailed him. What if he was too late?

For what? a stern voice chided him. *Do you really think Owen is coming back from the dead?*

He walked slowly across to the wooden ferry house, which was quiet. No cars were waiting for the crossing. He could see nobody who looked like Owen. But then, Owen would not be waiting around in full view, would he? Even if he *had* come back from the dead.

Dax reached the ferry house and nodded at a man in the ticket booth who barely nodded back. Nothing. Nobody here. He sat down on a bench under a shelter, by a tourist information sign, and felt the elation seep out of him as steadily as the sun set behind the fells.

'Not much to do around here at this time of year, is there?' A young man, a student maybe, with a rucksack and a floppy woollen hat, sat down next to him. 'I like to go abroad some- times. Spain is good. Some great hideaways.'

Dax gasped: 'Ty—' The student elbowed him hard in the ribs.

'Like I say, certain parts of Spain. Great places to get lost in, when you want to. I tend to *want* to get lost when I find that people I trusted have stuck things in my head.' Dax blinked. Of *course*. Tyrone had got the cold too, and he and Gideon had seen Janey give him the sleeping draught. Owen must have realized Ty had been chipped along with the Colas and warned him. It looked as if Tyrone had decided to leave the Cola Project because of it. Dax couldn't blame him.

'It's not always easy to get away from the kind of people who would do something like that,' went on Tyrone, still not looking at Dax. 'I was only a freelancer and I didn't know too much, so it was easier for me to sign off. It's harder when you're staff. They don't give you a gold watch and best wishes. Sometimes the only way out is death. Sometimes you need a good friend to help you to die—and stay dead. Do you know what I mean?'

'I think so,' murmured Dax, still hardly daring to believe.

'If you know how, you can look really dead, even to the expert eye. Especially if you've just been dropped into the North Sea and your friend is there when you get fished out, barely alive, and realizes what a great chance this is. What a gift.'

Dax began to laugh, silently shaking, his heart filling up and up with joy.

'The hard bit is leaving everyone behind, especially the people you care about.'

Dax couldn't stay quiet. 'Is he really OK?' he whispered. 'Really?'

'Yeah,' said Tyrone, smiling under his hat. 'Apart from worrying about *you*, of course. We'd just begun to give up on you ever making it to meet us!'

'How did you do it? There was a funeral!'

'He had another good friend at the government mortuary who swapped him for a real corpse. They wrote his death certificate together over a glass of brandy, along with his sister who'd come in to identify him.'

Dax closed his eyes and leaned back against the wooden shelter behind him. He couldn't keep the smile off his face. He even dug his nails into his palms to check that he was really awake.

'Anyway—we're off to Spain. There's a good place there in the mountains where we can start building.'

'Building? Building what?'

'Oh, I dunno—call it a retreat, if you like. A retreat for any Cola that might ever need to get away. Do you think you might like to get away?'

Dax thought about Gideon and Lisa and Mia and how miserable he had been in the past three weeks. How Gideon and Lisa and Mia had never stopped talking to him—even though he'd said almost nothing back to them. How Clive, only yesterday, had self-consciously tried to give him half a hug, his big grey eyes full of compassion behind his spectacles.

'Sometimes I think I want to get away,' he said. 'But not right now. One day . . . yes, certainly one day I will want to get lost—maybe in Spain. Definitely in Spain. I might bring a friend.'

'I went to the pencil museum at Keswick, you know,' said Ty. 'They did these amazing pencils with maps in—all rolled up inside the barrel, with little compasses under the pencil rubber on top. Brilliant. Airmen used them in the war. Shame you can't get that kind of thing today. Unless you're very well connected.' He handed Dax a pencil, with a pink pencil rubber on the top. 'Don't lose that,' he said. 'Me and your old friend will be off to Spain then. Tell Gideon and Luke that I'll miss them—and say I said *"Restraint!"* And . . . well . . . ' Ty gulped and sniffed sharply. 'Drop by when you need us. We'll be waiting. Cheerio then.' Tyrone pulled his hat down round his head, hitched up his backpack and began to move away; he looked back, smiling up under the brim of the ridiculous woolly hat.

'Wait!' Dax stood up, and Ty looked back, smiling up under the brim.

'I need—I mean—where is he now?' said Dax, wretchedly. The door of the ticket booth opened and a well-built man with shaggy dark hair stepped out. Dax stood, transfixed, still barely able to believe it. A car was approaching and Dax would have upended it if he had been a telekinetic.

The man stepped across and gave him a rough hug. He smelt exactly of Owen. 'When you need us—when *any* of you need us—you'll know where to find us, OK? You're never going to be alone in this world—do you understand?' he said.

Dax nodded, his throat too full to speak. Owen's blue eyes blinked twice. 'Don't lose your pencil, shapeshifter,' he said. With a grin he added: 'Have a dip in the lake while you're here, otter boy. I wasn't ever so dead I didn't see *that*!'

And then he turned the corner of the booth and he and Tyrone were gone.

35

Gideon was waiting by the window, gnawing at his fingers. 'Did you see him? Was it true?'

'Yes!' Dax stood still on their bedroom floor and felt a new calm wash over him. His world felt right again; waterfalls of happiness poured all over him. 'He and Tyrone faked his death. I still don't know exactly how.'

'Are you—you know—going to him?'

Dax sat down and grinned at his best friend. 'No,' he said. 'Not now. But when we need him, I know where to find him. And Tyrone too. Is that good enough?'

'Yeah,' Gideon stretched out on his bed and sighed with relief. 'That's good enough for me.'

Ali Sparkes is a journalist and BBC broadcaster who regularly exploits her sons as an in-house focus group for her children's novels. She reckons it's a fair trade for being used as a walking food and drink vending machine.

Ali was a local newspaper reporter and columnist before joining BBC Radio Solent as a producer and presenter and then chucked in the safe job to be dangerously freelance and write scripts and manuscripts. Her first venture was as a comedy columnist on *Women's Hour* and later on *Home Truths*.

She grew up adoring adventure stories about kids who mess about in the woods and still likes to mess about in the woods herself whenever possible. Ali lives with her husband and two sons in Southampton.

Also in this series

ISBN 978 0 19 275465 3

Dax Jones didn't ever want to become a fox . . . it's
not how he expected his day to go but, backed into a
corner and frightened, he finds himself changing . . .

And his change attracts attention. A government agent
is suddenly waiting to whisk Dax away to a secret school,
a haven for others of his kind.

But danger follows Dax. Someone else has noticed him
too and will do anything to track him down. As he
fights to keep the school's
secret safe, Dax starts to wonder what is really going on.
All at once his fox senses are on high alert . . .

The first book in this must-read series.

ISBN 978 0 19 275466 0

Falling out with his best mate wasn't exactly the start
to the new term that Dax Jones wanted, but when
Gideon's life changes, it seems that he's leaving
Dax behind.

And as if that's not bad enough, everyone at school has
started acting weirdly. Is Dax really the only one who
can see their strange behaviour? Gideon thinks Dax is
being paranoid, so what's the point of telling the
staff—especially as it could be *their* experiments that are
putting Dax and his friends in danger . . .

Dax's fox instincts have never let him down before—he
has to trust them. But before he can help Gideon and
the others, he must first overcome his own rising panic
and learn more about his shapeshifting powers . . .

The second book in this exciting series.

ISBN 978 0 19 275467 7

When Dax Jones receives an urgent call, he knows he
has to drop everything and race to the aid of his
friends. But that's not as easy as it sounds.

Strange events are happening—unbelievable
occurrences that seem to be following Dax and his
friends wherever they go.

And that's not all that's after them ... Government
agents are stalking their every move—tracking them
down. The very people who are supposed to be
protecting them seem to be the biggest threat. Who
can they trust? Where should they run?

Each of the friends must call upon their special powers
to try to outwit their pursuers—but will these abilities
spell the end for them all?

Book three in the fantastic The Shapeshifter *series.*

ISBN 978 0 19 275468 4

Dax Jones didn't plan for Gina to find out about his shapeshifting powers this way, but she was going on and on at him and it was the only way to make her shut up. Then the screaming started . . .

On top of that, he and his friends have been asked to take part in some kind of weird ritual to try and track down Luke and Catherine—Gideon's dead brother and sister. But when they do finally receive a message, it doesn't give them the reassurance they're after.

Dax must take to the air and use his falcon power to fly to France. Could Luke still be alive? And if he is, evil Catherine must be too—and the person she's out to get above all others is Dax Jones . . .

The fourth book in the must-read series.